AN EDNA HEATHCOTT MYSTERY

THE CHOCOLATE BOX

Leslie Watts

General
—PAPERBACKS—
Toronto, Canada

Published in Canada in 1991 by
General Paperbacks
30 Lesmill Road
Toronto, Canada
M3B 2T6

Canadian Cataloguing in Publication Data

Watts, Leslie Elizabeth, 1961-
The chocolate box

ISBN 0-7736-7303-2

I. Title.

PS8595.A8756C56 1991   jC813'.54
C90-095898-7
PZ7.W37Ch 1991

Cover Design: David Montle
Cover Illustration: Ken Suzana
Concept: Leslie Watts

Typesetting: Tony Gordon Ltd.

The characters and situations in this book are imaginary
and bear no relation to any real person
or actual happening.

Printed and bound in the United States of America

For Greg, who took no prisoners,
and Pam, for her courage

acknowledgements

While I was writing this book I asked for and received good advice from several people. I would like to thank Furio Brighenti, Sylvia Priestley-Brown, Harriston Chief of Police Ron Faulkner, my parents, Joan and David, and especially my wonderful husband, Tony Luciani.

one

HEINZ GROBBELAAR'S TWISTED body lay halfway down the stairs that led from his apartment to his shop. The venetian blind in the window was closed, but two of the slats were sticking together, and a rectangle of morning light lit a prickly halo on the back of his fat red neck. One arm was caught under his enormous body; down the other, flung out in front of him, blood had run and dripped in a diminishing series of blackened puddles on the steps below. His legs were splayed at an angle that would have been terrifically uncomfortable, had he been alive.

I had seen plenty of dead people before, laid out in good shoes and dress suits at funeral homes, even grey and naked in the basement of the medical building at the university where I had once drawn cadaver studies in carbon pencil. But this was the first time I had ever seen a body freshly killed. I screamed and slammed the door at the bottom of the stairs.

The vibration must have been too much for the precariously balanced corpse. For a split second I heard nothing. Then, from behind the door, came a sound like heavy books sliding off a tilted table. And a dull thump.

I'm going to be sick, I thought, and was, right in front of the door. I was hazily aware that I should have made at least an attempt to clean it up, but all I could think of was getting away. I stumbled through the shop, past the revolting candy counter, and out the front door to Hazelton Avenue where I leaned for a moment against the wrought-iron railing, taking in great gulps of Toronto-flavoured air. Then I turned, lurched up the three steps into the Fineberg Gallery, and somehow made it to the desk where Gerald Fineberg was sitting with a small slide viewer wedged into his right eye socket.

"Well, what'd the old skinflint say?" he asked, looking at me with his left eye.

"Nothing," I whispered, wiping my lips with a Kleenex and trying to keep my knees from knocking together by pressing them against the front of the desk.

"Good," said Gerald. "I knew you could talk some sense into him." He pulled a slide out of the viewer and dropped it onto the desk. "You should have been out in the sun yesterday, Edna. You look a little pale."

"Mr. Grobbelaar is dead," I said.

Gerald was smirking. His left eye was focused off in space, and he was popping another slide into the viewer. "Crap," he said. "Why is it always the ones who talk the most who can't paint worth a crap?" He put the viewer down in front of him. "What do you mean, he's dead?"

"I mean, he's dead. His body's on the stairs. I think he's been killed. You'd better call the police. I'm going downstairs to finish throwing up."

The washroom under the Fineberg Gallery was wedged in between the storage area — where Gerald kept his filing cabinet, computer, and any unsold paintings — and a safe large enough to contain a few particularly pricey works. I knelt on the linoleum in front of the toilet, bent my head over the bowl, and waited for the return of the rest of my breakfast. The last thing I remember was seeing a rust ring under the rim and thinking that Mrs. Cipollone would have to be more careful when she was cleaning, or else get one of those blue things for the tank.

"YOU'RE LUCKY YOU DIDN'T DROWN!" my mother shrieked over the phone a couple of hours later.

"No one drowns in a toilet," I replied and moved the receiver slightly away from my ear.

"It only takes two inches of water to drown if you're unconscious," said my mother, unearthing a little gem I remembered from my childhood.

"I wasn't unconscious," I sighed. "I passed out for a few seconds."

"Isn't it the same thing? Imagine! Fainting in a basement toilet! I hope you had a good wash when you got home."

I realized that I probably should have let her read about my discovery of the body in tomorrow's paper. Then at least she could have had the pleasure of swooning at the variety store counter in full view of at least a dozen interested observers. As we talked, I could picture her perched on the edge of the kitchen table, her feet on the chrome chair padded in chipped marble-print vinyl, her head ducked so that she could see out the window in case the neighbours across the driveway had left their curtains open. I knew what she was going to say next.

"I just wish you weren't all by yourself in the city. It's far too dangerous for a girl alone these days. Why don't you come home to Elegance? There's a Help Wanted sign in the craft store. It would be almost like working in an art gallery, but without all the risks. And you'd be close to your family. You know I don't sleep well at night."

That was probably true. But it was also probable that her insomnia was more a result of my father's snoring than it was of my living in the city. After all, she'd had nearly ten years to get used to my absence. My father's snoring, on the other hand, had only begun to attain significant levels of sonority within the past five.

"Oh, Mother," I said, hoping to reassure her. "Do you know what the policeman who drove me home told me?"

She sniffed. "Probably that you're lucky to be alive."

"No," I said, "that I'm living in one of the safest areas of the city."

"That may well be true. But I can't help thinking that it could have been you lying there with your throat slit instead of that man."

I tried to laugh. "Why would anyone want to kill me? Listen, Mom, I'd better go now. I just wanted to tell you that I'm all right, in case you heard anything on the news."

"All right then, Edna. But for heaven's sake be careful. Keep your door locked and make sure your curtains are closed. Anyone can look right into that apartment of yours."

"Right, Mom."

I hung up the phone and, thinking that I should probably have some lunch, took the cream-cheese-and-jam sandwich that I had made for work that morning out of its plastic bag. I put it on a plate and carried it into the living room. But as I sat on the couch looking at it, all I could see was the ghastly vision of Grobbelaar's body.

It was possible, I tried to reassure myself, that Grobbelaar hadn't even felt the pain. It might have been one of those injuries that take a few seconds to describe itself to the nervous system, like a stubbed toe. I wondered if there had been enough time for pictures of his boyhood to flash by his eyes. I couldn't imagine what sort of life he had led before he became grey and bloated.

On the surface, it seemed that it must have been perfectly quiet and uneventful, the kind that news reports of victims were always describing. But the truth was that if anyone had asked me whether I was surprised that Heinz Grobbelaar had been murdered, I would have had to say no. It wasn't that anyone with a likely motive immediately leaped to mind. It was just that the look on his face had always suggested a poisonous temper kept carefully under control, and I had often suspected that the flat, dull expression in his eyes was really just a sign that he was suppressing unpleasant memories and ugly thoughts. It was easy to imagine that he might have crossed at least one person's threshold of tolerance.

But whose? From what I had heard, Grobbelaar had been a friendless recluse. He had lived by himself in the second-floor flat of the building he owned on Hazelton Avenue. Below him were the Lillian Allford Gallery, the Fineberg Gallery, and his own store, The Chocolate Box, which was really just a glorified sex shop for members of the upper class in need of a chic little boost.

Grobbelaar had achieved notoriety selling every imaginable body part, perfectly moulded in chocolate: white, milk, or semi-sweet. But I figured that most of his income had come from renting videotapes and camera equipment to the home entertainment set. Next to the exhibition openings at the commercial art galleries, The Chocolate Box was the busiest shop in Yorkville on Saturday afternoons. Yet, in spite of that fact, Grobbelaar had always worked alone.

I had always found him to be a tasteless and unlikable man, but I wouldn't have imagined that he was obsessed with weird bodily pursuits. If anything, I had thought of him as an apparently sexless old man with a tighter than normal grasp on the concept of making money. I had never known him to say much more than "I don't give credit to anyvun."

He must have been over seventy, although he looked considerably younger. Perhaps the fat under his skin had puffed out the wrinkles. Or, for all I knew, he could have had plastic surgery. I felt a little sorry now that I had never had the opportunity while he was still alive to do a quick, close-range search for telltale scar tissue at his hairline.

I was also sorry that I had let the police talk me into coming home. It would have been far better to stick around the gallery and hear what they had to say about tracking down the murderer than to spend the afternoon cringing in my apartment.

I gave up on the sandwich and stuck it in the fridge. I decided to have a cup of tea.

One advantage to living in a basement apartment on the street side of a building was that I had a clear view of people leaving and arriving. One disadvantage was that I could only see them from the waist down. I was just filling the kettle when, through the window above the sink, I saw a pair of male legs clad in the unmistakable polyester-cotton blend of Metro's finest, travelling in shiny black shoes at a fast clip up the walk towards my apartment door. I let an extra cup of water run into the kettle.

I had a buzzer, not a bell. That meant that I could tell before I answered whether the person calling me to the door was someone I knew or a stranger. All my friends had been warned to go lightly with the buzzer finger. People anticipating defeat — particularly carpet cleaners and Jehovah's Witnesses — liked to nail their digits to the button or use a continuous ten second hold-release pattern until I opened the door. But this man tapped the button three times quickly, and from the amount of starch and polish on his lower section I imagined that he was probably clicking his heels together at the same time.

I had to open two doors to reach him: one at the bottom of the seven stairs that came down to my apartment and one that led outside. I admired his patience. He managed to hold off buzzing again before I reached him.

"Edna Heathcott?" he said, and I got the feeling that this was more of an exclamation than a question. Perhaps he was surprised to see that I wasn't grey and shrunken. People who have never met me generally assume that there are no Ednas left under thirty years of age.

He flashed his ID in my face. Beside the shiny metal badge there was a bluish-coloured photograph of him, looking earnestly towards the camera. His ears stuck out a shade too far, and his nose seemed slightly out of focus, as if it had been too close to the lens.

He stared at me for a moment before he said, "I'm Detective Owl."

I couldn't resist. "Who?" I said, opening my eyes wide and blinking once, slowly.

He didn't flinch. "I'm with Fifty-two Division, and I have some questions regarding the murder of Heinz Grobbelaar. May I come in?"

"Certainly." I held the door open wide, wondering why he sounded so grim. "I'm just making some black currant tea. Would you like a cup?"

"All right, thank you." He followed me down the steps and ducked into my living room. "I hope you're feeling better now."

I looked at him out of the corner of my eye, realizing with dismay that he must have seen the mess I had left in front of Grobbelaar's back door.

"Almost fully recovered, thank you," I murmured. "Please sit down. I'll be with you in a minute."

He hitched up his trouser legs and sat on the couch, and from the kitchen I watched him examine the small room as though he were looking for clues to some crime. His eyes roamed over the rosewood coffee table and rested briefly on the bookcase containing my university textbooks, my small video library, which consisted mainly of old classics filched from late-night television, and a couple of hundred exhibition catalogues. Then they moved past the old music cabinet where my television was perched, around the tarnished brass floor lamp and the stack of paperbacks on the carpet beside it, across the set of rose-coloured wing chairs that had once belonged to my great-grandmother, and up the wall to a small framed drawing on cream-coloured paper. There they stopped.

"That's an original Spencer you've got there," he said after a moment.

"It is," I agreed.

"That must have cost you."

I poured boiling water into the teapot and put five shortbread cookies on a plate. "It comes out of my paycheque every week. How come you know so much?"

"I have a photographic memory."

"That must come in handy," I said as I brought the tea and cookies into the living room and set them on the coffee table. I sat on the wing chair nearest the couch and took a better look at him. I decided that his expression was far from friendly. His mouth was turned down in a tight little line, and he didn't even seem glad to see the tea. I set the cups on their saucers. "Hope you don't take milk. I was supposed to go shopping on my way home from work this evening."

"It's fine without," he said brusquely. He pulled out

his notebook and glanced through the first few pages. "Now, I know that you already answered a hundred questions this morning, Ms. Heathcott, but in light of some further discoveries we've made, I do have a few more."

"Further discoveries?" I leaned forward as if to pour the tea and tried to read what was written in the notebook.

Detective Owl flipped to a blank page. "Do you live alone?" he asked.

"What's that got to do with the price of eggs?"

"Plenty." He looked up at me. His eyes were blue. "Some of these questions may seem completely irrelevant to you, but I'd like you to answer them to the best of your ability, please. Your responses may provide us with a great deal of valuable information."

"I see," I said, picking up the plate of shortbreads and extending it towards him. "And what sort of valuable information are we looking for?"

"Thank you." He took a shortbread. "But I meant we, the police. Would you please just answer the question?" He stuck the entire cookie into his mouth and chewed it impatiently, as if he weren't even tasting it. He probably had another interview to rush off to, with another plate of cookies and another cup of tea.

"I'm divorced," I said. "I live alone."

"Fine." He made a quick note.

"Aren't you too young to be a detective?" I asked, noticing the freckles on the backs of his hands.

"Aren't you too young to be divorced?" he replied instantly.

"I should have been younger." I smiled slightly. "One lump or two?"

"None," he said. "How long have you worked for Gerald Fineberg?"

"Three years and a bit. How come you're asking these questions about me? I thought you'd want a detailed description of the body."

"We have photographers to look after that. I'm more interested in your relationship with Mr. Fineberg, actually. How long have you known him?"

"As long as I've been working for him, I guess. I mean, I'd met him in the gallery several years before that, but I didn't actually know him then." From the way Detective Owl was asking the questions, I was beginning to suspect that I didn't actually know Gerald now. There was a decidedly ominous tone to this interrogation.

He looked at me and asked, "How would you characterize your relationship with Mr. Fineberg?"

"We're on good terms, if that's what you mean."

"Would you say that your relationship goes beyond one of employer and employee?"

"What?"

He seemed embarrassed. His eyebrows rose and fluttered. "Did he ever . . . take you out?"

I tried not to laugh. "Mr. Fineberg," I said, "wears clear nail polish and cologne. And a toupee. He's not exactly my type."

He nodded seriously and, I thought, with relief. His eyebrows resumed a more conventional position. "Has he ever asked you to do anything that might be illegal?"

"Illegal? Like what?"

"Holding or selling stolen property, for instance?"

I snorted. "You're joking! Do I look like a fence to you?"

He responded by writing something in his book and underlining it twice. "Were you ever aware of any feelings of antagonism between your employer and Mr. Grobbelaar?" he asked, watching me carefully.

"I can't imagine Gerald slitting Mr. Grobbelaar's throat, if that's what you want to know," I said mildly.

"You'd be surprised at who does what in the heat of the moment," he said with a sigh.

I stared at him. "Gerald? In a heat? That's a laugh."

Detective Owl took a quick slurp from his black currant tea and studied his notebook. "I should tell you, Ms. Heathcott, that after you were taken home this morning Gerald Fineberg left the gallery, and we haven't been able to find him. Do you have any idea where he might be?"

"You're kidding!" I exclaimed. "You mean he's disappeared?"

Detective Owl looked at me sternly. "I'm afraid you're not taking this situation very seriously, Ms. Heathcott. Now, I understand that you've experienced a certain degree of shock, but I'd hoped that you'd at least try to co-operate with our investigation." He began to raise his voice, as if he thought my attention was lagging and he wanted to get it back. "A man has been murdered. May I remind you that we are seeking your assistance in good faith?"

"I'm sorry," I said. "It's just that I've had such a terrible morning, and this is the last thing I expected to hear."

"So you're telling me, then," he said loudly, "that you weren't aware of any motive that Mr. Fineberg might have had for killing Mr. Grobbelaar?"

"Not really," I replied with equal volume.

"Not really?" he repeated.

Any minute now, I thought, he'll be taking out his flashlight and shining it in my face. "Well," I said, "I sometimes heard them discussing late rental payments." "Discussing" was not exactly the word for it, but I didn't think that a slight modification of the truth would make much of a difference in the long run. I looked down at the carpet and tried to remember the last time I had vacuumed.

Detective Owl contemplated my original Spencer for

a moment, then asked, "Did Mr. Fineberg owe Mr. Grobbelaar money?" His voice had become quiet again, almost soothing.

I swallowed a mouthful of cookie. "Just a few months' rent."

He looked at me. "And approximately how much money would that have been?"

"Approximately," I said, "twenty-four thousand, five hundred dollars."

Detective Owl wrote something in his notebook and then turned it over and balanced it on his knee while he bit into another shortbread.

"I guess that's a motive," I said, wondering how much hot tea I would have to spill down his leg in order to get the notebook to land right side up on the floor.

He frowned. "I hope you're not playing dumb, Ms. Heathcott. I hope that you're being forthright and honest with me."

I picked up my teacup. "Are you originally from Toronto?" I asked, crossing my legs in what my mother would have called a ladylike fashion.

"Ms. Heathcott!" he said with a scowl.

"It's just that you don't hear too many people around here using words like 'forthright,'" I explained. "I thought maybe you came from somewhere else."

Detective Owl closed his eyes. It appeared that he was employing some kind of relaxation technique. There was a tiny crumb of shortbread stuck to the corner of his mouth.

I watched him for a moment before I said, "Detective Owl?"

"Yes, Ms. Heathcott?"

"Am I correct in assuming that you believe Gerald killed Heinz Grobbelaar?"

He opened his eyes. He looked as though he had been up all night. "If a man with a motive disappears right after a murder has been committed, then that makes me think he might be a suspect. So, yes, I'm afraid that's exactly what your Mr. Fineberg has become."

"He's not *my* Mr. Fineberg," I told him indignantly. "And surely you don't really think he killed Heinz Grobbelaar over twenty-five thousand dollars? That's nothing to him."

"Maybe." He shrugged noncommittally. "Now, there's one more thing I want to know. Were you aware that Mr. Grobbelaar had a rather extensive collection of fifteenth-century Italian religious artifacts?"

"He did?"

"And you never heard him discussing this collection with Mr. Fineberg?"

"Never," I said. "I never heard anything about a collection. In fact, I'm surprised to hear about it."

"Why is that?" He gazed at me intently.

"Well," I replied, feeling slightly uncomfortable, "I never thought that Mr. Grobbelaar was inclined that way . . . towards having a collection of anything special, I mean." I looked at him. "Does this have anything to do with the murder?"

"It might." He snapped his notebook closed and stood up. "Well, I guess that's it, then. Thanks for your help." I couldn't fail to hear the irony in his voice.

"Wait!" I said, following him to the door. "What's going to happen now? Am I supposed to go back to the gallery tomorrow as if this never happened? Isn't anyone going to tell me what's going on?"

Detective Owl looked at me oddly. "I'm sorry," he said. "Of course you wouldn't know. The Fineberg Gallery went into receivership just before noon. I'm afraid you don't have a job to go back to."

two

IT WOULD BE TRUTHFUL TO SAY THAT I had never before felt as personally disaster-struck as I did when Detective Owl dropped the tidings of my new situation into my astonished lap and left me gaping at my apartment door. I didn't have a clue what to do. So, even though it was only two o'clock in the afternoon, I went to bed. Thankfully, I almost immediately fell into a deep sleep that lasted until six the next morning.

When I opened my eyes again I was amazed to find that I actually felt a little better. Even the memory of finding Heinz Grobbelaar's body didn't seem quite as horrible as it had the day before. As close to refreshed as I could be under the circumstances, I got up, had a quick bath, and even managed to choke down a small breakfast before I went out.

Wondering guiltily whether I was on the verge of becoming a sluggard and a wastrel, I headed first for the unemployment office to fill out an application for my insurance cheques. I informed the eager young clerk, who had great and immediate ambitions for me, that I had a full two and a half weeks' vacation and sick leave coming to me and that I'd be darned if I was going to spend it serving cheeseburgers.

Actually, my real plan was to try to figure out why I hadn't realized that Gerald must have been cooking the books behind my back for more than a few months. By the time I got back on the subway, the only reason I could come up with was sheer, unerring stupidity. And when that thought only made my condition seem gloomier, I decided that it might be a good idea to learn why he had disappeared before the police had had a chance to question him about Grobbelaar's murder.

I got out at Bloor and walked over to Hazelton. There was a Day-Glo orange sign in the glass door of The Chocolate Box, stating cheerfully, Sorry, We're Closed, and above that, attached with transparent tape on the inside, a notice warning of the maximum penalty that could be imposed by law on any unauthorized persons entering therein. There were no lights on, and as far as I could tell there was no one in the shop.

At the Fineberg Gallery there was a bankruptcy notice in the front window and three disagreeable-looking people sitting around the desk with polystyrene coffee cups and a stack of manila files between them. The door was locked. When I thumped on it, the woman said something to one of the men, and he rose to open it.

"Hello," I said, smiling brilliantly. "I'm Edna Heathcott, Mr. Fineberg's assistant, and I've come to retrieve a few personal belongings."

The man threw back his shoulders and puffed out his chest until he looked like a fat starling guarding a suet-and-seed ball. "That's absolutely out of the question," he said in a voice unmistakably lowered several tones below its normal pitch. "This gallery has been closed for an audit, and all property has been seized. Nothing may be removed from the premises." He folded his arms across his chest and glared at me, spreading his legs a little, as if to brace himself against any sudden moves that I might make.

I fixed him with a stare and thought quickly and desperately. I wasn't much good at non-verbal show-downs. But as I looked into his eyes, I suddenly realized that I had encountered men like this before and that I might actually know something about him. His wife would be tiny, cute and blonde, his preferred meal an extra rare twenty-four-ounce sirloin with baked potato, and his favourite TV show Monday night football.

"You mean you even want my Maxithins?" I asked.

That threw him. He stepped back a little, just enough to let me shoulder my way past him.

"Your what?" he shrilled in a clear treble, which I took to be his real voice.

"Thinner than a maxi, more than just a panty liner." I smiled, striding into the gallery. "Don't tell me that the bank's going to auction off my feminine protection to raise money to cover a defaulted loan."

I stood at the desk. The woman was drinking her coffee and looking at me through narrowed, heavily mascaraed eyes. She plainly despised my cheap tactics.

"I must warn you, Miss Heath-whatever-your-name-is," she said in a voice reminiscent of ungreased hinges, "that we are here under the authority of the Payco Loans Company, and that if you attempt to interfere with our business we won't hesitate to call the police."

"I have no intention of interfering with your business," I told her. "I just want to get my coffee mug and my spare pair of shoes. They're in the storage room downstairs. It won't take me long to find them."

She took a drink from her cup, perhaps hoping to reinforce her steely resolve, which by now, I felt, should have been showing at least some signs of erosion under my caustic stare. "I'm afraid there's absolutely no way," she said firmly.

"Oh, *please*," I begged. "That mug has more sentimental value than the bank could ever hope to recoup in dollars."

She said something under her breath that sounded remarkably like "Nosy bitch," and then added more audibly, "you'll have to sign for them."

"I'd be happy to."

"Very well," she sighed, and pointed her index finger with its red, pistachio-shaped nail towards the basement door.

I flicked on the light and descended, heading straight for the storage room and Gerald's computer. The desk was locked. Apparently the auditors hadn't had the foresight to bring a crowbar with them. I took my keyring out of my purse. It took three seconds to open the drawer, lift up a pile of correspondence, and discover to my delight that the cardboard diskette organizer was still underneath. Swiftly I pulled my shirt out of the back of my pants, stuck the diskette organizer snugly into my waistband, then tucked my shirt back in.

I had always kept an emergency pair of flat Chinese slippers in the basement, in case I broke a heel or lost my shoes on the way to work. I took the shoebox from its shelf and climbed the stairs with my cracked, handleless coffee mug balanced on top of the box.

"Would you like to inspect my shoes to make sure I'm not leaving with any valuable miniatures wedged into the toes?" I inquired.

The female auditor rolled her eyes and engaged the sirloin-and-potato auditor in an incomprehensible dialogue concerning balance sheets and forward averaging. The third auditor, who was a pale, serious-looking man with a beige droplet of coffee clinging tremulously to his lower lip, lifted the lid of my shoebox, glanced briefly inside, clucked sympathetically at my mug, and had me sign a brief statement in which I declared that I was removing articles of a purely personal nature from the gallery.

I left Fineberg's with the shoebox under my arm and a warm sense of accomplishment in my heart.

Bypassing The Chocolate Box, I opened the smoked

glass doors of the Lillian Allford Gallery. The air inside was pleasantly scented by the flowering oleanders in pots by the desk. Between the plants, in a large, green leather chair, was Ellen Mitchell-Spence, sometime poet, dancer, photographer, and now business partner of Lillian Allford. She was dressed in an Armani suit with a blouse that was exactly the turquoise of her eyes. She was talking on the phone. She had the kind of voice that could have made her famous if she had gone into over-dubbing for cartoon mice instead of selling art. It was high and wispy and floated on the air like milkweed seed. I have a voice that is inclined to boom at times, and I've always held a vague sense of awe for women who can speak in sighs and sound as if they mean it.

Ellen raised her arm straight up and fluttered her thin pink fingers at me. She began to lead the conversation to a breezy finish. When she had hung up the phone, she stood up, swept past the oleanders, and wrapped her arms around me.

"Oh, Edna!" she cried. "I'm so glad you're here. How are you? You must have been absolutely ill. I can't imagine it, you poor, poor thing!"

"Thank you, Ellen," I said quietly, "but I'm feeling much better now." I took a closer look at her. I would never have mentioned it, but she looked a lot more like someone who had recently discovered a body than I did. When she tilted her head at a certain angle I noticed a thick sheen of concealer cream under her eyes.

She shuddered. "It must have been horrible."

"It was," I agreed. "I'd rather not talk about it."

"I can imagine how you must feel." She shook her head sorrowfully. "Was he covered in blood?"

"Ellen, please."

"I'm sorry, Edna. But it's just like a horror movie. You know how what you imagine is always a thousand times worse than what you ever see on the screen? Well, I just can't help thinking that if I *really* knew what he looked like, I wouldn't keep having these awful, gory images in my mind." She fluffed her hennaed hair. "And what's going to happen to you now?"

That was a good question, one that I had been repeatedly asking myself. Unfortunately, I couldn't seem to come up with a good answer. However, the last thing I wanted was to present myself as confused and discouraged to Ellen, the epitome of punctilious self-direction. I smiled thinly. "Actually," I said, "that's part of the reason I'm here." I looked towards Lillian Allford's office. "Where's the big cheese?"

"Out for coffee with a client. Did you want to talk to her?"

"No," I said. "I have to ask you for a favour. Can I use the computer in her office?"

"What do you need that for?"

"I need to get a printout of Gerald's books. I have the disk with me. I want to try to figure out what was going on."

Ellen sniffed. "I can tell you that in ten seconds, Edna."

"I'm sure you can," I said evenly. "And I'd like to get your opinion, too. But right now I really want to have it in print. I'll pay for the paper, if you like."

"Don't be silly," she said. She turned towards the office. "How come you have the disk? Don't those auditors need it now?"

"Probably." I looked up at the ceiling. "I sort of took it without anyone noticing."

"Ahh." She nodded and shrugged. "Well, as far as I'm concerned you're entitled to whatever you can get from that bum. Come on. Do you know how to work this thing?" She turned on the computer and printer.

"I think I can figure it out."

"Okay," she said. "Then I'll leave you to it."

I looked around the office. Like Gerald's, the walls were made of sound-proof glass so that Lillian would have a clear view of most of the gallery. The only furniture was a maple desk, three chairs, and an antique washstand where the computer sat. There was a four-foot cactus in a tub beside the window. Above the desk was a large Jack Bush, and above the washstand, a small Kurelek.

I took the disk organizer out of my waistband. It was a small, grey, booklet-shaped folder. I was surprised to find two disks inside. Gerald had frequently asked me to add names to his client file, and there had never been more than one disk to work with. Great, I thought. He finally took my advice and made a duplicate. Too bad he had to wait until the business collapsed.

I removed one of the disks and put it in the A drive. After I had typed instructions to print the entire disk, I left the office and found Ellen sitting at her desk reading a copy of *Art in Canada*.

"Do you actually understand that stuff?" I asked curiously.

She put the magazine down on the desk. "Oh, I never read the articles," she said, giggling. "I only look at the pictures."

I picked it up and flipped through the pages, but I kept my eyes on her face. "Been getting enough sleep lately?" I asked casually.

She looked startled. "What do you mean by that, Edna?"

"Nothing much. I thought you looked a little tired, that's all."

"I am," she said after a moment. "We're going through a very busy time, you know, with this retrospective coming up, and," she lowered her voice, "Lillian's been a real crank."

I wondered if she might be having trouble at home. She opened her desk drawer as if to look for something.

I pretended to concentrate on an ad for an upcoming print-and-drawing exhibition as I said, "Now, I have to ask you a few questions. I want to find out as much as I can about Gerald and what he's been up to."

"So you think he did it, too?" Ellen said, slamming the desk drawer shut.

"Gerald?" I snorted. "A murderer? You've got to be kidding!" I sat down in a chair in front of the desk and crossed my legs.

"No, I'm not," Ellen said defensively. "I never trusted Gerald for half an instant. But the strange thing is, I could never have seen him cutting anyone's throat. Even Fat Heinz's. I would have thought he'd be a gun man, if anything. He'd hide it inside his raccoon coat and then, blam! One, two shots at the most, and then he'd walk away."

"And show up for work the next day?" I asked, shaking my head. "Aren't you forgetting about that?"

She considered this before she spoke again. "Well, you know he needed money. If you'd only listen to a little gossip now and then, you'd learn all kinds of interesting things."

I leaned forward. "Like what?"

"Like the fact that Gerald's been sticking it to most of his stable for the past couple of years."

I set the *Art in Canada* on the desk and picked up a copy of *Slate*.

"Don't tell me you didn't see it happening!" Ellen waved her right hand accusingly. "Everyone knew."

"Everyone did not," I said firmly. "You're just guessing, now that you know the gallery's gone under."

"No, I'm not. One of Gerald's artists — now I'm not saying who — came in to see Lillian a few weeks ago. He was planning to leave Fineberg, and he wanted to know if we'd represent him. Anyway, he said he hadn't been feeling good about Gerald for some time. He'd tried to get some paintings back that hadn't sold after his last show, and Gerald kept putting him off. Now he thinks Gerald might've sold them without telling him."

"No way," I said, plunking the *Slate* down on the desk. "I would have known."

"Right," said Ellen. "*If* he had actually sold them. But I don't think he did. I think he used them to pay back the sharks who loaned him money."

"Oh, for God's sake, Ellen! Loan sharks? Why would Gerald take money from loan sharks?" It was a ridiculous question. I knew the answer perfectly well.

"Because," said Ellen, who was happy to tell me anyway, "he was up to his yellow eyeballs in debt to everyone else."

I thought that she seemed rather smug. She smiled as she looked at me. I realized that she was probably glad that Fineberg's had folded. I wondered if she and Lillian were already discussing plans to pick up the artists and clients that Gerald had lost with the gallery. She reached over and patted my hand.

"Brighten up, Edna. There are worse things than losing your job."

"Name one."

She blinked. "Never mind. Just be thankful that the the police didn't find the murder weapon in your gallery. Then you might have quite a lot of explaining to do."

"What?" I yelped.

"Edna," she said. "Everyone knows that you and Gerald had a long-standing battle with Fat Heinz. Imagine how this whole thing looks from the outside."

"Gerald and *I*?" I said. "Gerald and *I*? I'd appreciate it if you'd leave me out of it. You know I never felt anything for Heinz Grobbelaar but indifference. It was Gerald who didn't get along with him."

"He'll probably be asked to leave the dealers' association," she said, as if that would be the worst of his troubles.

I stared at her for a moment. "You actually think he killed Grobbelaar, don't you?"

"What am I supposed to think? You find Fat Heinz's body on the back stairs. The next thing you know, the police arrive to talk to you, and Gerald takes off like a shot. It sure looks like he did it."

I shook my head. "It may look that way, but there has to be some other explanation. I just can't believe that Gerald could kill anyone. I can't believe I'm so dumb that I wouldn't recognize blood-lust in the man I work for."

"Well," she said quietly, "you *did* miss the business with the loan sharks."

"Thanks," I said coolly. "That makes me feel better."

"Oh, Edna," she said. "You'll get another job. In a few months this will all be behind you. Now, cheer up. Did I tell you that Walter's buying me a new car? Sheba tore the back seat out of my Volvo."

Sheba was Ellen's Bouvier. Sheba had outlasted Ellen's three previous marriages, the first to a motorcycle mechanic who had supported her during her poet-dancer stage, the second to a photo artist who had taught her all there was to know about f-stops and museum mounting before she divorced him and sued him for the business, and the third to the soft sculptor who had introduced her to Lillian Allford. Walter Spence was president of an investment dealer and fast approaching retirement. His well-padded stock-and-bond portfolio was the reason that Ellen had been able to move from her position as Lillian's assistant to buying out almost half the business.

I listened as she told me about the planned renovations to her home in Forest Hill, her ski chalet in Collingwood, and her cottage in Muskoka. Then I stood up and said, "Well, that printout must be done by now. Can I pay you for the paper?"

"Don't be silly, Edna. You'll have to watch your pennies for a while. Until you get another job, I mean."

I went back into the office and detached the paper from the printer. There weren't as many pages as I had been expecting. Without bothering to take the time to look at them, I rolled them up and put them in the shoebox. Then I turned off the computer and removed the disk.

"Thanks a lot, Ellen," I said on my way out.

"Not at all. I hope you find out what you need and sue the pants off that guy. Have you considered that?"

"Goodbye, Ellen," I said, and laughed, because if what Ellen had told me was true, then Gerald might not have any pants left.

I GOT HOME with my shoebox shortly after one. I put it on the kitchen counter while I made a sandwich. Just as I was about to sit down and eat, the telephone rang. I picked it up and said emphatically, "If this is Gerald Fineberg calling to apologize, Edna is not here to listen to your lame excuses."

There was a slight pause. "Ms. Heathcott? This is Detective Owl. I'm wondering if you could answer a couple of questions for me."

"Oh, Detective Owl," I said, recovering neatly. "What did you forget to ask me?"

"It occurred to me this morning," he said slowly, "that it might be worthwhile taking a look at Mr. Fineberg's books."

"Oh?" I kept my voice finely modulated, projecting

what I hoped to be a sort of guileless charm across the line.

He didn't sound particularly charmed. "I assumed," he said in a sombre tone, "that since he has a computer he might have his ledger on disk. Was I correct?"

"Yes," I replied calmly, although I could feel my heart beginning to pound. "It should be in the desk drawer below his computer — in the basement of the gallery."

"It should be. That's where I looked first."

"And it wasn't there?"

"Ms. Heathcott, why do I have the impression that you are playing games with me?"

"I have no idea, Detective Owl. Perhaps the auditors have seized the disk."

"No, Ms. Heathcott, the auditors have not seized it. They did, however, tell me that you were in for a visit this morning."

"To get my coffee mug and my slippers," I said quickly.

"And your panty liners."

"And my panty liners. But I changed my mind about those. I thought I'd leave them for that lovely woman."

For a moment he said nothing. I could hear his well-controlled breathing over the sound of a type-writer in the background. I could also hear the sound of my own blood banging in my ears. Then he said, "Ms. Heathcott, I'd like to suggest that you have a package ready for the police officer who will be at your door in a few minutes. Do you understand what I'm saying?"

"Isn't this called . . . intimidation?" I said faintly.

I heard a snort at the other end of the line. "It's called quietly recovering stolen property without pressing charges. You should be thanking me."

Realizing to my chagrin that I was whining, I said, "I didn't steal it, anyway. My own work is on that disk, in case you didn't realize. That means that I hold part of the copyright."

"Copyright?" He chortled. "On a ledger?"

I hung up the phone feeling miserable. The door buzzer sounded.

"Shit," I said, and shouted, "hang on!" as loudly as I could, hoping that my voice would be heard through the open kitchen window.

I took the disk organizer out of the shoebox, removed one of the disks, and slid it under the couch. The organizer with the remaining disk inside went into a plastic shopping bag. Then I left my apartment, dashed up the steps, opened the outer door just a crack, and thrust the bag out.

"Thank you, ma'am," said a low voice.

I peered through the opening and saw a uniformed police officer looking back at me. "Will that be all?" I asked with as much finesse as I could manage, considering that my face seemed on fire.

"Yes, ma'am. Thank you." He turned and walked away.

I sat on the top step for a few minutes before I went back downstairs. I had never actually broken the law before, and although I wasn't absolutely certain that I had just committed theft, I realized that Detective Owl could have given me a lot more trouble than he had. I didn't know whether to be grateful or humiliated. At least, I thought guiltily, I still have the second disk and the printout.

I went back into my kitchen and unfolded the first two pages onto the table. I bent over them and frowned. What I had expected to see was an inventory list, a record of all the paintings that were in the gallery, whether they were hanging on the walls or stored in the basement. Instead, I saw a list of people's names, most of which I knew, with an address and telephone number for each.

I swore. He's erased the inventory, I thought in dismay. No wonder the file seemed so thin! All that was left was the client list.

But as I read through it, I knew right away that something else was wrong. These weren't Gerald's clients. There were only a dozen names listed, and Gerald's own was among them. I turned to the third page and blinked. The printout wasn't even in English. It was all in German, and there was an entire page of print for each name on the list. I swore again. I had the wrong damned file!

Then suddenly I had to sit down. I felt dizzy. Gerald Fineberg was fourth-generation Canadian. He didn't even speak German. The only German I knew was dead.

Was this Heinz Grobbelaar's disk?

three

MY FATHER'S DENTAL OFFICE IN Elegance, Ontario, was on the east side of our house, in what had once been a closed-in veranda. One of my earliest memories is of standing on the piano stool in the front hall and looking through a gauze-covered window into a yellow room, where I could make out the faint, greyish images of people with various lumps, aches, chips, and holes sitting on repainted kitchen chairs, waiting for my father to minister to them. Many of them were of German descent, and as I listened to their low-pitched German murmurs, which were often accompanied by great moans and clutchings of faces, I somehow came to associate the German language itself with tooth pain. So naturally when I got to high school and was given the choice of studying German or Latin, I took Latin. I never once imagined the frustration that this would cause me fifteen years later.

I sat up in bed with the light on, feeling the weight of my callow decision resting solidly on my shoulders. On my lap was the printout of what I was sure were Heinz Grobbelaar's personal files, and I knew that if I could only understand it, I might learn why he had been murdered.

I flicked off the light and got under the covers. There was something else even more disturbing than my linguistic deficiency: if the disk was Grobbelaar's, then what had Gerald been doing with it? Was Detective Owl right after all? Had Gerald murdered Grobbelaar in order to get the disk? What could possibly be on it that would be worth killing for? I stared into the darkness of my bedroom and tried to come up with a less alarming scenario. The problem was that even if Gerald hadn't killed Grobbelaar, then one of the other eleven people might have. And since I knew or had met most of them, that meant there was still a chance that someone I knew was the murderer.

I realized, of course, that I might be wrong about the disk. There could have been any number of explanations why someone would have wanted to keep a file on Gerald Fineberg or Lillian Allford, or even Ellen Mitchell-Spence. Not that I could come up with many offhand.

There was only one thing to do. Tomorrow morning I'd wrap up the disk and mail it to Detective Owl who, with a wealth of investigative experience under his black leather gun belt, would no doubt glance over the file and tell me that the disk had nothing to do with Grobbelaar's murder.

I fell asleep, comforted by the thought of a two-week vacation, free from the burden of responsibilty that came along with possessing the mysterious disk.

But then I woke up again at three-twenty, convinced that the disk must have been Grobbelaar's and consumed by the desire to find out what he had written about Gerald and Lillian and Ellen. I turned the light back on and went into the living room. Yesterday's paper was still lying unread on the coffee table. I picked it up and turned to the Metro News page. The headline read, "Sweet-Shop Slaying." There was a blurred picture of a corpulent Heinz from some years back with an article underneath:

Controversial landlord and candy-shop proprietor Heinz Grobbelaar, 73, was found Wednesday morning by an unnamed person in the stairwell leading to his apartment. His throat had been slashed. Police spokesperson Mary Beth Bone said it appeared that Grobbelaar had been killed between seven and nine o'clock the previous evening.

Grobbelaar's store, The Chocolate Box, which specializes in erotic candies, is located on Hazelton Avenue in Toronto's posh Yorkville district. Most area shops and galleries close before six o'clock, and police say it is unlikely that there were any witnesses.

Gerald Benjamin Fineberg, 54, of Coldstream Avenue, is being sought for questioning. Fineberg, a tenant in Grobbelaar's building, disappeared yesterday, shortly after police arrived at the murder scene. Detective Bone was unable to comment on whether a warrant for Fineberg's arrest will be issued.

Lillian Allford, whose fine art gallery is situated next to Grobbelaar's shop, said, "We are shocked and saddened by this news. Mr. Grobbelaar was a very private person."

Grobbelaar made headlines several years ago when he lost a battle against a court injunction forcing him to bar admittance to his shop to persons under eighteen years of age.

He had no living relatives.

I put the newspaper down and my feet up on the coffee table. So, I thought glumly, I am an unnamed person. There couldn't be anything much worse than that. Nevertheless, I tried to keep a detached perspective on the article. The important thing was that I had learned when the murder was supposed to have taken place.

I went into the kitchen and got a notebook out of

my junk drawer. Then I began to copy the names and addresses from Grobbelaar's list, one to a page.

"HELLO. MAY I SPEAK TO MRS. CUNDERLIK, please?" I was calling first thing in the morning, so I spoke as gently as I could in case I was waking her up.

"This is she."

Dottie Cunderlik, member of the Toronto Symphony Orchestra Women's Committee, representative for the Shelter for the Homeless Project, booster for the Metro Food Bank, adviser to the Council against Family Abuse, wife of Dr. Harold Cunderlik, optometrist and collector of contemporary fine art, sounded surprisingly bright, as though she'd been up since five and around the block several times. I imagined her in a neatly pressed jogging suit, enjoying a healthful breakfast of whole-grain toast and rose-hip tea.

I cleared my throat and said, "Mrs. Cunderlik, this is Julie at the paper, and we have a photograph that we'd like to put in our society column. I'm sorry to bother you about this, since it really is our fault, but we wouldn't want to miss a photo opportunity, so to speak."

Dottie said, "Of course not," and I continued.

"This is really rather embarrassing, to say the least. Anyway, we can't tell if this is you or not, and our photographer has lost his notes. Were you and Dr. Cunderlik at the save-the-whales gala on Tuesday last?"

"Oh, no," said Mrs. Cunderlik. "I was at the Mauve Ball on Tuesday. That can't be me in your photo, I'm afraid."

"Oh, drat," I sighed. "I'm sorry to have troubled you."

"No trouble at all," she said, and hung up.

I've noticed that rich people tend to hang up the phone without saying goodbye. I had experienced this frequently while working for Gerald. I guess they didn't want any conversation with a plebeian to sound more social than it actually was. In any case, they left me feeling that my proper place was at the bottom of some titanic, muck-filled pit. I said goodbye to the dial tone and made a small note in my book: Mauve Ball. Confirm.

Now, what about Dr. Harold? Dottie had said that *she* was at the ball, but she hadn't said where her husband was on Tuesday night. When I talked to him I'd find out if he'd been there, too, and confirm Dottie's alibi.

Alibi. I was beginning to think the way I imagined Detective Owl must think. Alibi. Motive. Opportunity. That's what it was all about. Whenever I heard real-life detectives interviewed on the radio or television they were always saying things like, "It's not as glamorous as most people think. It's mostly paperwork." But I could always tell that they were only saying it because the job was actually utterly compelling and they didn't want crowds of people showing up and applying for it. Besides, what was paperwork but writing down everything you knew about something? That could be pretty glamorous if what you knew was every raw detail of someone's private life. And detectives knew how to get to that stuff.

I dialled again.

"Dr. Cunderlik's office." The voice belonged to a young woman who was obviously bored but trying to make the best of it. She had probably said "Dr. Cunderlik's office" ten thousand times in the past year and wasn't looking forward to doing it again over the next twenty. "May I help you?" she asked.

I could hear typing as she spoke. She must have had one of those shoulder attachments that held the phone so that you could keep your hands busy while you talked. An inspirational gift for obscene callers.

"My name is Edna Heathcott. I'd like to make an appointment as soon as possible."

"Have you seen Dr. Cunderlik before?" She had an unusual twang in her voice. She probably listened to country music when Dr. Cunderlik was out of the office.

"Not as a patient," I said. "Actually, it's kind of an emergency. I lost my glasses, and my regular optometrist is on vacation, so I was kind of hoping — "

"Mm-hmm. I understayand." The typing stopped. I could hear pages turning. "Monday? At nine-forty-five? I have a cancellation."

"Oh, perfect. That's wonderful."

There were several other names on Grobbelaar's list that I knew: besides Lillian Allford, there was her husband, Allan, a big-time lawyer who had his right hand in the federal political scene and was rumoured to be a contender in the next Conservative leadership race. Then there was John Henderson, the respected but abstruse critic for *Art in Canada*, whose own collection of twentieth-century paintings and drawings was legendary; Giovanni Pasqualino, a middle-aged painter of decayed and fossilized animal matter, who had begun to attract a large and eager following in recent years; Gwen Tattersall, a radical feminist sculptor who was made notorious by her refusal to show in any group exhibitions that featured work by male artists; and finally, Gerald and Ellen.

There was an obvious pattern there, but what I couldn't figure out was why Heinz Grobbelaar would have had his nose in the business of the biggest artsy-fartsies in Toronto. Fat Heinz, who had seemed as interested in fine art as I was in crotchless panties and phosphorescent body paint: not much. But then there was that collection of fifteenth-century religious relics. How could that be explained? Knowing Heinz, I surmised that the artifacts probably had nothing to do with anything except money. Maybe he had bought them on speculation, figuring that he could unload them someday and make a killing. Unfortunately for Heinz, someone else had done the killing.

There were two people on the list whose names I didn't know — Arthur Birch and Anna Dellarosa — and one — Zylie Wedge — whose name was familiar, but I couldn't for the life of me remember why. I decided that I'd better start phoning. It was obvious that I had nothing to gain by sitting back and thinking about it.

But I couldn't just call up someone on the list and say, Hey, how are ya? Tell me where you were between seven and nine on Tuesday evening. Heard you might have had something to do with that Grobbelaar killing. For one thing, he'd never tell the truth. For another, it would be foolhardy. A murderer was not a person to toy with. What if he somehow found out who was calling and came after me? There had to be another way.

Then the phone rang. I felt a flash of anxiety, imagining that it must be Detective Owl again. I considered not answering, but my curiosity got the best of me. If it really was the detective, I could always pretend to be the hired help.

"Hello?"

"Edna?"

I could tell immediately who it was. I knew only one person with a voice like Minnie Mouse. But today she sounded as though Mickey had just left home for good with the car and all the cheese. "Hi, Ellen," I said.

"Oh, Edna, I'm so glad you're there. I just have to talk to you."

"What's up?" I asked.

I thought that I could hear her discreetly blowing her nose. Then she said, "Are you busy right now? I need to talk to you."

"I'm not busy. What is it?"

"No, I mean in person. I don't want . . . I'm at the gallery. Could I possibly come over?"

"You want to come here?" I had known Ellen for three years, and she had never once expressed an interest in seeing where I lived.

"Will you be home? I could be there in half an hour."

"I'm not planning to go anywhere. Would you like to have lunch here?"

"I don't think I can manage it, actually," she whispered. "I just want your opinion on something."

"All right," I said. I gave her the directions to my apartment, and after she hung up I spent a few minutes racing around breathlessly, opening curtains, making the bed, and hiding all traces of my armchair investigation.

Ellen looked ghastly. She had washed off her makeup, and her face was puffy and pink, as though some mad plastic surgeon had gone wild with the silicone needle. She did manage to glance around and murmur, "Nice place," as I led her to the living room. That, I thought as she sat down and looked at her hands, was a good indication of her state of mind. Under normal circumstances Ellen would have found my comfortable but well-worn furnishings less than appealing and would probably have said so. I realized that she was waiting for me to say something.

"So," I said, wondering why I felt the urge to giggle nervously, "what seems to be the problem?"

"I've come to you because I can't discuss this with any of my friends," she answered softly.

"Oh," I said.

She looked up at me with her bloodshot eyes. "Oh, Edna, you know what I mean. Of course, you're my friend. I should have said any of *Walter's* and my mutual friends."

"That's all right, Ellen. I can see you're upset."

She bowed her head again. "I thought maybe you'd

know what to do without going into histrionics and telling everyone that you know."

I was beginning to squirm. "Are you sure you should be telling me this?" I had a sudden and ominous vision of her confessing to Grobbelaar's murder and asking me to help her to go into hiding. And all that I had to offer was the cupboard under the kitchen sink.

"I found out the police came to see you," she said.

"Yes, they did," I said cautiously.

She grabbed my hand suddenly. "Did they tell you anything? About me, I mean?"

"Ellen, I saw you the next day. I would have told you if they'd mentioned you. What are you talking about?"

She let go of my hand and covered her face. "I did something really stupid back in the seventies."

I looked at her curiously. This was something new, to see her in a confessional mode. "Yes?" I prompted. "What did you do?"

"You know I've been married before," she said.

"I think you've mentioned that, yes."

"Three times, in fact."

"I think I knew that, too."

"Well, after my first marriage ended, I was very poor, believe it or not. I needed money to pay the rent. So I did some modelling." She looked at me, waiting for a reaction.

I looked back in surprise. "You're embarrassed about that?"

Ellen sighed loudly. "It was for some advertising posters."

I stared at her. "For what? Cigarettes?"

"No," she murmured. "For a bookstore and cinema on Yonge Street."

"Oh. I see." Although I still did not.

I must have given her a blank look, because she said impatiently, "Think, Edna. Yonge Street? Seventies?"

"I only moved here nine years ago," I said with a shrug. "I was raised in Elegance." I liked to get that phrase in whenever possible, and in this case it gave me an excuse to grin at Ellen, who looked as far from grinning as anyone could get.

"Edna, please be serious. Do you know what Heinz Grobbelaar did before he owned The Chocolate Box?"

"Don't tell me," I said, and sighed. "He was a publishing magnate and a movie mogul?"

"No. Well, yes. In a sense. He owned a skin shop on the strip."

"I'm beginning to see where this is leading," I said wearily.

"I had rent to pay. I wanted to eat."

"Couldn't your parents have fed you?" Somehow I had always imagined that Ellen's parents would be the kind who felt that all was right in the world as long as Ellen had a second helping of turkey and dressing at Christmas dinner. Somewhat like my own.

"They didn't want to have anything to do with me after I married Herk," Ellen sniffled.

"Herk?" I yelped.

"My first husband. He was quite muscular."

I pictured Ellen on the back of a Harley-Davidson, clinging to the black-leather torso of a tattooed hulk in bell-bottom jeans and a red bandanna. The image was well co-ordinated with everything else I knew of her. But this blotch-faced weakling falling to pieces on my couch was not.

"So you did publicity shots for Heinz Grobbelaar," I said. "So what? Do you think anyone remembers? You wouldn't believe how much *I've* changed in fifteen years. Are you worried that someone will recognize you? Forget it! And even if Heinz did know you," I added, thinking about the file that he had kept on Ellen, "he's dead."

"That's just it," sobbed Ellen.

"I hope you're not going to tell me you killed him."

"No, no," Ellen cried. "But Grobbelaar did recognize me. He'd even kept some of the posters. And he told me that he was going to show them to Walter if I didn't . . . pay him."

"And you did?"

Ellen closed her eyes and wailed, "What could I do?"

"Blackmail," I said, and thought, So I was right! "How much did you pay him?"

"Fifteen thousand dollars."

I gasped. "All at once?"

"I figured it was worth it. If Walter ever found out, it would shatter him. He idolizes me."

"But he knows about Herk, I presume."

"Oh, he knows. Of course he knows. But to him it's just another indication of my girlish naiveté, that I could have eloped with a great big mechanic who could lift me with one hand."

"But he'd never go for this story."

Ellen shook her head. "Not a chance," she whispered. "If you ever saw the posters, you'd understand why."

"Are they really that bad?" I wondered how many things you could print on paper that Walter might not have imagined before.

Ellen sobbed loudly.

"Well, you don't have to worry any more," I told her. "Fat Heinz is dead, and I certainly won't tell Walter."

"You still don't understand, do you?" Ellen said. "The police have searched Grobbelaar's apartment. I saw them coming out with boxes and boxes of things. They must have found the posters. And if they did, they'll recognize them for sure. They interviewed me, too, you know."

"Oh, Ellen, stop it! Do you think they care what you

did way back then? The police have more important things to worry about."

"I know that, Edna. But they will care that I had a motive for killing Grobbelaar. You know, at first I was so relieved to hear that he was dead. I couldn't believe it was over. And then when Gerald disappeared I thought, well, at least they've got a suspect. But then, this morning, a policewoman came by to ask Lillian some more questions, and I thought, my God! What if they start investigating me? How could Walter not find out? What am I going to do?"

"Well, if it makes you feel any better," I told her gently, "I don't think you're the only one."

"What? You mean other people have come to you?"

"Oh, sure," I said, laughing. "What do you think I am? A consultant to extortion victims?"

"Then what makes you think that there are others?"

"I don't think I can tell you that. Just trust me. I'm quite sure about it."

"The police told you."

"No, they didn't."

"Then how?" asked Ellen. Her face had dried, but her eyes were still puffy, and her lips were red and blubbery looking. I felt sorry for her, but I also felt a little irritated. She obviously thought I was such a dull quiet person that I could never be a candidate for blackmail myself.

"I really can't tell you, Ellen," I said. "I'm sorry. Now, I think you'd better go to the police and tell them what you just told me."

"I couldn't!"

"Look. Do you want to keep on being racked with guilt and anxiety, or do you want to go home tonight and be able to look Walter straight in the eye?" I had met Walter once, and I couldn't see why she'd want to look at him anywhere else.

"Oh, God!" said Ellen. "Oh, God!" She ran her hands

through her hair until it was an even wilder mess than it had been before.

"You have to find out if you're being investigated. Now, for heaven's sake, pull yourself together! This is not the worst thing that can happen to you."

"Then what is?"

I reflected for a moment. "The person who killed Fat Heinz could have found the posters himself."

"Oh, my God!" shrieked Ellen. "I never even thought of that!"

"Well," I lied, wishing I hadn't answered her, "chances are it's no one who knows you, anyway. Now, my bathroom is right over there. Get yourself cleaned up, and then you can go talk to the police. You will, won't you?"

"I guess so," she mumbled.

I led her to the bathroom and gave her a clean facecloth. I wanted to get her out the door as quickly as possible, because all of a sudden I had figured out a way of getting to the other names on the list.

four

AMONG THE FINEBERG GALLERY'S
clients had been a Mrs. Gladys Roach, who had at one
time had a laryngectomy. Lacking the ability to use her
voice in the normal way, she had perfected a loud
whisper with such resonance that it instantly caused
everyone within earshot to stop what they were doing
and give her their undivided and obsequious attention.
My plan was to use this technique when I made my calls
from a phone booth on the corner near my apartment.

A woman answered after two rings. "Haylew?"

"Arthur Birch, please," I whispered in my huskiest
Gladys Roach imitation.

"I'm sorry, he's still at school. He should be home by
five. May I take a message?"

Several possibilities crossed my mind: Arthur Birch
was a ten-year-old boy, and this was his mother; Arthur
Birch was a teacher, and this was his wife; Arthur Birch
was an aging janitor and this was his daughter. In any
case, I didn't want my message to reach him second-
hand.

"No, thank you. I'll call back later."

"All right. I hope you're feeling better by then.
Goodbye."

So much for husky and dangerous, I thought with
disgust.

I looked at my notebook. The next name on my list
was Anna Dellarosa. No answer there. Chances were

that she worked. I put my quarter back in the phone, thinking that it would probably be smarter if I worked too. I dialled Zylie Wedge's number.

I still couldn't remember where I had heard that name. Was it a man or a woman? I certainly couldn't tell from the voice that answered.

"Zylie Wedge?" I rasped.

"Yes. That's me."

"I want to talk to you about a murder."

There was a sound of breath being sucked in, a faint rattle, and then a high-pitched whistle so excruciatingly loud that I actually dropped the phone and leaped backwards. I held my ear with one hand and grabbed with my other for the receiver, which was twisting wildly at the end of its grey metal cord. But by the time I replaced it warily against my ear, Zylie Wedge had hung up.

I opened my notebook and wrote furiously, "Highly suspect. Paranoid. *Find out more.*" I felt like a real professional, temporarily deafened in the line of duty, but still undaunted. I checked Zylie Wedge's address and stuck the notebook in my purse. It was only two-thirty. My call to Gwen Tattersall could wait. I put on my sunglasses and headed for the subway.

I CAN'T SAY it didn't cross my mind that I probably had no business doing what I was doing. As I stood looking at my swaying reflection in the darkened windows of the subway car, I realized that I was hardly cut out for undercover work. For one thing, I didn't look mean enough. Private investigators were supposed to be hard-boiled. I would have been thrilled to be even half a stage past coddled. In spite of having lived in the city for almost ten years, I had to admit that I still looked as though I had just hopped off the potato truck. Not that I didn't dress in a fashion appropriate to urban life. As a matter of fact, I wasn't too bad at keeping myself informed of the latest trends. It was the look on my face that wasn't big city. "Fresh" was the only word to describe it — people were always assuming that I was younger than my years. That was fine for grandmothers, or teenagers who wanted to sneak into theatres for half price. But for me a pair of heavy eyelids or a few permanent frown lines would have come in handy at times like this. Times when I wanted to project an air of knowing confidence.

Like now. Because, regardless of the fact that my only experience in investigation was finding out what art collectors took in their coffee, I suddenly knew that I had to get to the bottom of the Grobbelaar murder. If I passed up this this chance to do something unusual for a change, I might as well pack my bags and go straight back to Elegance.

As I climbed the stairs to get out of Bathurst Station, I let the only four words I had heard Zylie Wedge speak ebb and flow over my inner ear. "Hello. Yes. That's me."

What kind of person would blow a whistle over the phone? It sounded like something my mother would advise to ward off national consumer surveys or crank calls from giggling adolescents. If Zylie Wedge had been able to react that quickly, he (she?) must have been expecting to receive calls he didn't want to contend with.

Once I got onto Bloor I walked east to Brunswick and turned left at the Lick'n Chicken. My intention was to take a quick look at Zylie's house just to get a feeling about the person I was dealing with. I felt quite safe in doing this. Zylie wouldn't know who I was, so even if he happened to step out to water his grass, I could probably walk right up to him and tell him what a fine-looking patch of fescue he had.

There were two small red-haired children in front of

the house, trying to tie a green plastic skipping rope around a cat's neck. I squatted on the curb to pat the cat and warn the children about the perils of strangulation. As I spoke, I glanced quickly and subtly at the house. The first-floor curtains were open, and I could see right through to the leaded-glass windows in the back.

"Why are you staring at that house?" asked one of the children, letting go of the cat and gaping at me.

"I'm not staring," I replied, swiftly jamming my index finger into my right eye. "I'm adjusting my lens."

"My mother wears lenses," said the other child. "My father wears glasses. I'm going to get blinder when I grow up."

"How upsetting for you," I said, hoping that I hadn't done permanent damage to my cornea. I stood up and peered with my remaining eye at the second-storey window. All I could see was a reflection of the locust tree growing on the front lawn. I couldn't see any deranged killer skulking in the shadows with an unsheathed straight razor gleaming in his hand.

I gave the listless tabby a farewell stroke and continued walking, turning back after a few paces to wave goodbye to the children and to catch a glimpse of Zylie's house from another angle.

I didn't hear the car door open behind me, so when I turned around again I nearly slammed into it.

"Get in," said a man.

My horrified reaction was My God, it's Zylie, the Butcher of Brunswick. He'd been watching me the whole time, and now he was going to drive me to behind some industrial park in Mississauga and slash me from ear to ear. I wanted to run, but his hand reached out and grabbed my wrist so tightly that I thought my fingernails would pop out.

His freckled hand.

"Detective Owl!"

"Get in," he said through his teeth. "And hurry up."

I sat down in the passenger seat, which was covered with a navy plaid wool blanket. Detective Owl was dressed in green shorts and a T-shirt with a purple-and-green fish on it, and the words Gulf Shores in turquoise.

"Nice car," I said, running my hand over the synthetic velour covering the door. There was an empty potato chip bag on the floor at my feet, and two apple juice tins were nestled cosily in the rubber waste basket. I checked the straws for lipstick. None.

"Would you mind telling me what the hell you think you're doing?" His eyes were narrowed in what he probably thought was an intimidating expression, but he reminded me of my brother at age seven when I took his favourite Hot Wheels car.

"What the hell do you think *you're* doing?" I asked coldly. "I take a walk down a quiet street, and next thing I know I'm being forcibly confined in an unmarked cruiser."

"Don't play stupid. I don't know why you do that."

"Did you ever consider," I said, "that I might really *be* stupid, and that you could be seriously hurting my feelings with a comment like that?"

"Jesus Christ," he said. He started the car and pulled into the street. "Just tell me what you're trying to do."

"I'm putting on my seat belt. I wouldn't want to get a fine. I'm living on unemployment now, you know, and I can't afford frivolities."

"Well, neither can I!" he yelled, shifting ferociously into third gear. "Now, how the hell did you find out about Ms. Wedge?"

"*Ms.* Wedge? Ms. Zylie Wedge?"

"Who else would I be talking about? Do you know any other Wedges?"

"That's it!" I cried. "I knew I'd heard that name

before. She's the feminist writer who's involved with Gwen Tattersall. She's a suspect, isn't she? I knew it!" I grinned broadly.

He didn't grin back. He turned the corner and parked the car. "Now listen, Ms. Heathcott. I'm going to ask you again. How did you know about Zylie Wedge?"

"I'd rather not say."

"I'd rather you did."

"I think I'll go now." I undid my seat belt.

"All right," Detective Owl sighed. "You're under arrest."

"You're kidding. For what?"

"Obstructing justice. Possession of stolen property. Probably theft under a thousand dollars. I'm sure there's more." He turned his face towards me again, making another attempt at the narrow-eyed look, but ending up with something more like a myopic squint. I noticed that his hairline was beginning to recede.

"Okay," I said, holding out my arms. "Clamp on the cuffs. At least you can't get me for resisting arrest."

He blinked. "You think you're pretty smart, don't you?"

"Now I'm smart? Two minutes ago I was stupid."

"Ms. Heathcott!" he shouted. "All I want to know is why you are so *goddamned* interested in this case. It seems that no matter what turns up, you have somehow gotten your nose into it already. What's with you?"

"Mystery," I said with what I hoped was a bewitching smile. "Intrigue. I love a good thriller, don't you?"

He turned to me and said in an admirably well-restrained voice, "Do you realize how common, how usual, how predictable you are being? This is a disgusting, violent act that we are talking about, not a goddamned Agatha Christie novel. And you're acting exactly like a hundred and seventy-nine other people I've met, who, for some reason that escapes me, feel their lives are so empty and "dull" that they have to go out and be junior detectives. Isn't there a movie you could see? A book you could read? Why don't you do volunteer work? Be a Big Sister. Coach a baseball team. Don't you have a boyfriend?"

That, I thought, was hitting below the belt. Although I would never have classified my existence as empty, I knew that I hadn't exactly been living a life of high romance. In fact, the word "dull" wasn't entirely inappropriate. Nevertheless, I didn't feel that it was up to Detective Owl to point this out to me.

"I'm no good at sports," I said calmly. "But I'm reasonably adept at reading, and I love movies, although I don't particularly want to see one right at the moment. And no, I don't have a boyfriend, but thank you for your concern. As far as Ms. Wedge is concerned, all I know is that Heinz was probably blackmailing her. I have no idea for what. But I don't think that really matters. The point is, she had a motive, and that makes her exceedingly interesting, don't you think?"

He gazed at me for several seconds. I thought I could see his jaw clenching and unclenching. Then he said, "Put on your seat belt."

I did. He started the car again and drove down to Bloor where he made a fast and illegal left turn. Rush hour was in full swing. The car immediately slowed to five kilometres an hour.

"Why don't you put your siren on?" I suggested. "Wouldn't it be a lot quicker?"

"I don't have a siren in this car. This is my own private car. I have no handcuffs with me, either, so don't get your hopes up. I won't be dragging you shrieking into the station."

"I never shriek," I said.

"No, that's right," he replied. "You just throw up and faint."

I looked out the window. "Where are we going?"

"I'm taking you home."

"Stop!" I shouted. "Let me save you the trouble. I'll take the subway."

"Then what? You'll mail me the disk? Oh, come on! I know you have it. Did you get this one out of Fineberg's basement, too? I'd like to know what you think you're trying to prove."

I didn't respond.

He made an impatient sound in his throat. "There's only one way you could have known what you just told me. And do you know how I know?"

"No. How *do* you know how I know what I know?"

He made a face that was supposed to look like a smirk, but I was certain that he was trying to hide a smile. He stopped at a red light and looked at me again. Great forehead, I thought.

"You're the one who's so smart," he said. "You tell me."

I closed my eyes and pondered. "Grobbelaar left a printout in his apartment," I said finally.

"Good. And?"

"And? What do you mean, and?"

"I mean, what else?"

"Oh. You speak German."

"No, but I know someone who does."

I looked at the apple juice tins. "Your wife."

"No," he said, stepping on the gas just before the light turned green. "Another detective. The fingerprint guy."

"So you know what she did, then?"

"Who?"

"Zylie."

"Yes."

"Good. And?"

"I thought you said it didn't matter."

"You're right," I said. "Forget I asked. I guess this means that Gerald isn't the only suspect after all, eh? So I may not be wasting my time checking out Anna Dellarosa and Arthur Birch."

"What?"

"Anna Dellarosa and Arthur — "

"I heard what you said!" he bellowed. "And I can't believe it."

"Oh, come on, Detective. Do you think you squelched me with your little speech back there? Well, you didn't. I won't give up that easily." Actually, I might well have given up that easily if it hadn't been for the unmistakably challenging glint I could see now in his eyes. I felt the way I imagined Hillary must have felt when he first gazed at Everest. "What if you worked next door to a guy for three and a half years," I went on, "a guy who seemed to have no personal contacts with anyone other than to sell them things to enhance their sex lives? Then one day you go over to tell him that your boss can't pay the rent again, and you find him lying dead on the back stairs. Wouldn't you want to know who did it?"

"No. I'd want to leave that to the police."

"Oh, get real!" I laughed. "Don't be so virtuous. What made you decide to be a detective, anyway? The money? I doubt it. I'll bet you anything you spent your tender years with your snotty nose stuck in the Hardy Boys books and you think it's just as fantastic as I do."

"It's hardly fantastic. It's mostly — "

"Paperwork. Right. And after you drop me off you're going back to your office to type up a boring report on how you spent your afternoon looking in Zylie Wedge's living room window."

Detective Owl kept his eyes on the road and whatever thoughts he was having to himself.

"You're at an advantage, you know," I continued. "If

I knew someone who spoke German I'd be way ahead of you. Don't forget I already know most of the people on the list."

He snorted. "That's a prime example of what I was saying before. You seem to think that all you have to do is draw up a list of suspects and figure out who has the most compelling motive. I don't think you realize how subjective you're being. What about *objective* evidence? Direction and depth of laceration? Fingerprints? Footprints?"

"Hairs, cigarette ashes, dried skin flakes. I know, I know. So, tell me. What have you found?"

"That's absolutely confidential."

"Why?"

"That's the way it is."

"And you don't even give out hints? What is this, a competition? Do you get a promotion if you crack it before anyone else?"

He shook his head. "I don't know where you get these absurd ideas. If you knew anything about police procedure — "

"I wouldn't be wasting my time asking stupid questions."

"And you wouldn't be wasting *my* time, either," he said loudly.

He turned the car into the driveway to my building. I snapped open the door and leaped out.

"I'm not fooling around about that disk," he called after me.

"I'm getting it for you now," I yelled over my shoulder. I unlocked the outside door and ran down the seven steps to my apartment. The disk was in the toaster. I flipped the lever, and it popped up.

The car was still running when I went back outside.

"Here it is." I passed it to him through the window.

"Thank you." He put it on the seat beside him. "I appreciate your co-operation."

"Right," I said. "And while we're being sarcastic, I should tell you that your undercover disguise looks very natural. Particularly your brush cut. Nice touch. If I didn't know you were a cop, I never would have guessed."

He stared at me for a moment, said, "I wasn't being sarcastic, Edna," then roared off in a cloud of pale exhaust fumes.

I stood on the doorstep and watched his car turn the corner at Briar Hill. He looked back at me before he disappeared. I glanced away.

Away happened to be in the direction of the juniper bushes next to the door. I did a double-take. A hand was poking out of the bush. It was waving at me.

"Edna," hissed the voice that belonged to the hand, "is the coast clear?"

"You idiot!" I said loudly. "Where the hell have you been?"

There was a slight rustling, some nasty swearing and a sharp tearing sound, and then Gerald Fineberg squeezed out from behind the bushes, scratching his arms. He had a prickly rash on his face and the top of his head. His toupee had come off, and there was a rip in the front of his shirt. His knees were dirty.

"Well — " I glared at him " — if you didn't already look so miserable, I'd punch you in the nose."

"Edna," he said in a whiny voice, "you have to help me."

"I certainly do not." I took a giant step backwards. "Did you kill Grobbelaar?"

"No! I swear!" He looked around wildly, then crouched near the shrubs again.

"Then what were you doing with Grobbelaar's disk?"

"How do you know about that?"

"Did you see that policeman who just left? He has it now. And, boy, are you ever in trouble!"

"Let me come in for a minute. I can explain."

"No way. But I'd be happy to call the police if you need an escort home."

"No!" he whispered loudly. "I'm not ready to turn myself in yet."

"*Yet?*" I shouted.

"I've been having some financial difficulties."

"No kidding!"

"Edna, please give me a chance to explain."

"Go ahead," I said with a thin smile. "I'm dying to hear you talk your way out of this."

"I won't mess around with you, Edna. These are the facts. I owe money — lots of it — to some . . . private financiers. The payment deadline is the day after tomorrow. If I get myself arrested now, I'll never have a chance to pay back these gentlemen, which will be very disappointing for everyone concerned."

"You mean they'll probably shoot off your knee-caps," I said.

Gerald closed his eyes. He seemed to be losing colour fast. "Listen, Edna. You're my only hope. I need you to get something for me, something very important. If you can do it, I promise I'll turn myself in to the police."

"Forget it," I said flatly. "I'm not doing anything for you. As far as I'm concerned, my days with you ended the minute the gallery went under. I don't trust you, Gerald. I think you set me up. You knew Grobbelaar was dead, even if you didn't kill him yourself. You went in there Tuesday morning to talk to him, and when you saw that he was dead you took his disk. Am I right?"

"I'm sorry, Edna. I was scared."

"What do you think I was? Enraptured? What was he doing, anyway? Blackmailing you?"

Gerald sighed. "He found out that I sold a fake Matisse to the AGO. He gave me a printout with the proof. But I swear I didn't kill him. I only took the disk because I knew the police would think I did."

"Well, the police think you did it anyway, Gerald. And you sure have put me in an awkward position. So I'd appreciate it if you'd just go away now and leave me alone."

"Edna," said Gerald. He was actually beginning to cry. "If you don't help me I'm dead. And I really mean dead. I have to be honest with you, Edna. If you don't get this thing for me, they won't just go for my knee-caps." He gave a tremendous sob. His whole body heaved.

"Oh, Gerald!" I sighed. "Straighten yourself out! Can't you see what a mess you are?"

"I can only see what a mess I'm going to be."

I looked down at him. He looked back, his eyes magnified and quavering behind his tears, his bald head glowing fiercely with its juniper rash.

I asked, "What is this thing you want me to get?"

"A box," he said. "Just a box. That's all. All you have to do is get it and bring it to me."

"Where is it?"

"In Grobbelaar's shop."

"I should have guessed. It's Grobbelaar's."

"No! I swear it's mine. I only stashed it there for protection. There's something very personal inside. I would have taken it out the other day, but I couldn't because the police were hanging around and I knew they'd think I was stealing it. But, Edna, I swear to God it's mine. All you have to do is go in there and get it. It's a chocolate box. About a foot long, six inches deep. It says 'Bruno's extra hard, extra thick, dark chocolate' on the lid."

"Of course it would," I said. "Where is it?"

"At the back of the second shelf from the bottom, in the female-body-parts section. Behind a box of knees."

"And just how do you suggest that I get into the store? Don't you realize that the police are probably watching it?"

"I'll leave that up to you," said Gerald. I noticed that he had stopped crying. The gleam was back in his eyes.

"And after I give you the box, you're going to pay off your debts and go immediately to the police?"

"Yes," he said with a sparkling smile. "Oh, thank you, Edna. I promise you won't regret this."

I shook my head. "This is the greatest act of insanity I've ever committed. Where am I going to meet you?"

"How about here on Sunday?"

"No. I don't want you coming here again. How about at the Lytton tennis courts at ten o'clock Sunday morning?"

"Yes. Oh, yes. Thank you, Edna. I kiss your feet."

"Back in the bush, Gerald," I said sternly.

I went inside and got out my phone book. There were about thirty Cipollones listed. Mrs. Cipollone cleaned from six until ten Monday and Friday evenings. We had often spoken when I stayed late at the gallery to hang shows or make up invitations. I knew that she lived near St. Clair and Dufferin because she had talked to me about her neighbourhood on several occasions. There were three numbers in that area. The first was an old man who had trouble understanding me and eventually hung up in exasperation after shouting something incomprehensible but probably vulgar. At the second Cipollone household a younger man answered.

"Hello," I said. "I'm looking for Mrs. Giuseppina Cipollone, the lady who does the cleaning on Hazelton Avenue."

"Just a minute. She's just getting ready for work." I

heard him call out, "Ma!" and then something in Italian.

A few seconds later Mrs. Cipollone picked up the receiver. "Allo?"

"Mrs. Cipollone?"

"Ya?"

"Hello, Mrs. Cipollone. This is Edna, from the Fineberg Gallery. How are you?"

"Oh, it's okay. Havar you, Edina? You no work dere no more, eh?"

"No, I don't, I'm afraid."

"Dat's too bad. *Ma*, maybe we still gonna see you somatime, anyway."

"Well, actually, that's why I'm calling," I said carefully. "In fact, I was hoping that you'd be able to do me a favour."

five

BY EIGHT O'CLOCK HAZELTON Avenue looked as though it had been evacuated. The sky was green and threatening rain, and only the few people who came after work to dine and drink at the hoity-toity restaurants and cafés remained, mincing with their furled umbrellas along the interlocking brick walkways, intent on nothing but their own reflections in the darkened store windows. If they passed me, I wouldn't even have registered.

I knocked on the back door of Grobbelaar's building. Mrs. Cipollone opened it and pulled me into the tiny hallway. "You come in quick. I no want nobody to see."

"I really appreciate this, Mrs. Cipollone," I told her in a low voice.

"Oh, it's okay," she said with a smile. "You, I like. *Ma*, Edina, tell me why you wanna go up dere anyway. You a nice girl. Why you wanna be looking around dere?"

I wondered whether I should tell her the truth: that I had never before been a part of anything as exciting as a murder investigation. But I thought she might not appreciate that. From my past conversations with her I knew that Mrs. Cipollone's biggest concerns were how to remove greasy hand prints from glass and how to get her adult son, Michael, to move out of her house. So I said, "I heard that Grobbelaar had a collection of antiques up there, and I was hoping to take a look at it before someone clears it all out."

"Huh," she said, rattling around with her keychain. "Okay, but you be careful, eh? De poleetz, dey tell me no go up dere." She winked and handed me a brass-coloured key. "*Ma*, dey never say I no can let nobody else go."

I smiled and looked quickly up the stairs. Spanking clean, as if a body had never lain there and pumped rich red onto the mock marble. "Did you have to clean up that mess?" I asked.

"Oh, no," she said without looking. "I tink de poleetz make clean like dat. Maybe dey hev some spaychal cleaning stoff jiust for blood."

"Maybe." I shrugged, marvelling at our ability to discuss these details so casually.

"Okay," she said, heading into the broom closet at the bottom of the stairs, "I go clean now. I see you in forty-five meenoots, okay?"

"Okay. Thank you very much. I really appreciate this."

I pulled on a pair of gloves. They were the stretchy black evening variety; I had bought them from a vintage clothing shop to wear to a Hallowe'en party. I had no idea whether the police would return, but I didn't want my loops and whorls hanging around after I had gone.

I went up the stairs, unlocked the door and pushed it silently open.

I don't know what I'd been expecting. Rooms dressed like tarted-up women, tasselled and over-coloured? Maybe the scent of some pseudo-exotic fragrance or the glitter of rhinestones? At least a few posters of a seventies Ellen in some vulgar get-up, or worse, in nothing at all. But whatever picture I had in my head was nothing like Heinz Grobbelaar's apartment.

There were two art deco lamps plugged into timers that whirred faintly. The light they gave off was dim, but there was enough of it to ascertain that either Grobbelaar had known a great decorator, or I had sorely underestimated his level of taste.

The walls were hung with needlework tapestries suspended under glass by invisible threads. They were worked so finely that the stitches were barely visible until I stood up close to them, and when I did, I could see that the edges were crumbling and brown like old paper. The images were faded: tender Madonnas clasping haloed babies to their breasts, bearded saints raising their hands in blessing, shaven-headed men in black robes, marching in a long line up towards an angel whose pointed toes rested on a perfectly symmetrical cumulus. They were breath-taking. I must have stood for ten minutes, gaping at them.

I went to the glass case that stood against the far wall, floor to ceiling, softly lit from behind, and filled with what looked like museum pieces. There were sculptures in marble and wood, bas-reliefs in blackened metal, and urns of mellowed silver. One of the doors was half open, and I looked more closely, careful not to touch it. There was a faint film of dust on the shelves, and between one of the crucifixes and a marble Madonna I could see a clean area where something round had sat.

I crouched down on the silk carpet and peered under the couch. No monogrammed hankies. No eye charts. No drawing pencils or squashed water-colour tubes. Not even a cracker crumb. The rug itself seemed to have been freshly vacuumed. The ashtray on the inlaid coffee table was empty.

How was I supposed to know who had been there if there were no traces of a visit?

I went through to the kitchen, which was tiled from floor to countertop in black and white hexagons, like the old bathroom in my parents' house in Elegance. But these were clearly a more recent installation. There was nothing on the counter except a mug containing half an inch of water. In the sink was a large soup spoon with a fuzz of mould sprouting near the handle.

I looked in the cupboards, wondering what Grobbelaar had liked to eat. There were cans of sardines and herring, one of eel, a jar of marinated artichokes, a dented and rusting pail of honey, boxes of cheese wafers, a chocolate cake mix, a foil pouch of instant pasta and sauce, and three faded boxes of Kraft Dinner. Most of the containers were coated in grey dust, as if he hadn't looked at them in months.

I closed the cupboards and opened the fridge.

Cheese, salami, and three packs of bacon well past their Best Before dates, a dried-out loaf of pumpernickel, a slimy tub of something green in brine, a fetid piece of uncooked pork, and a carton of eggs. Beer in the door. The freezer was filled with ice cream. There must have been a dozen cartons of it. Häagen Dazs. The smell of the rotting pork was wafting into the room, even through the freezer. I closed the door quickly.

The bathroom was small and ordinary. Heinz couldn't have been much of a bather. It would have been a tight squeeze for him, getting into that tub. There was the same rust-coloured ring inside the toilet bowl that I'd seen in the Fineberg bathroom, and the faint, sweetish smell of urine. I shut the lid. Grobbelaar's razor and foam were in the medicine cabinet with a single Band-Aid, a box of seltzer tablets, and a large brown bottle of aspirin.

The huge bedroom was a study in asceticism. It was painted a deep turquoise, and contained only a simple wooden four-poster bed with a plain wool mat beside it, a dark wooden dresser with a mirror attached, and a single small ink drawing on tinted paper beside the light switch.

I opened the closet, where I found three grey suits

and a black one, seven shirts, and eight ties. I checked all the pockets and found only a crusty, yellowed Kleenex and two pennies. There was nothing but clothing in the dresser.

I had five minutes to examine the study. This room was more like the first one I'd been in, filled with rich-looking antiques and decorated with nineteenth-century watercolours and what looked to me like an Otto Dix oil. The computer on its stand seemed like a whimsical anachronism. There were no disks in sight. I sat down in the leather chair at the oak desk and opened the top drawer. There was an appointment diary inside, bound in shiny blue leather. There was nothing written in it except Heinz's name and address in German-looking script inside the cover.

I shoved it back in the drawer and pulled out a box of postcards. These were written in German, but not in the same writing that was in the appointment book. There seemed to be no salutation on any of them. Just Grobbelaar's name and address, and a short message on each. No signatures, either. That fingerprint detective at Fifty-two should have been reading them. But perhaps he already had and didn't think they were worth taking.

There were two dozen of them, and they'd been mailed from different places around the world: Australia, New Zealand, France, Belgium, Italy, Greece, Britain, Germany, Venezuela, Uruguay, the States, Montreal, Vancouver, Sault Ste. Marie, Timmins, Halifax, and Calgary. There were three postmarked Toronto. They were mostly tourist cards, scenes of bridges or lakes or mountains, but one of the few that had been mailed in Toronto two years earlier was a black-and-white photo of the kind that Heinz sold downstairs in his shop. It featured a hairless, muscle-bound man in a G-string and black eyepatch, with a ball and chain attached to his left ankle. His tongue was hanging out, and he was grinning at the camera. On the back of the card was a credit to the photographer and a brief hand-written communication in German. I decided that since there were so many others, it wouldn't hurt to keep that one card. I put it in my purse and stuck the rest back in their box.

When I checked my watch it was almost quarter to nine. I hadn't even had a chance to burglarize the filing cabinet. It was locked, but when I tapped lightly on one side, it sounded hollow. Its contents were probably what Ellen had seen the police carrying away in boxes on the first day.

I shut out the lights that I'd turned on and went back out the door and down the stairs. The broom closet was still open, but Mrs. Cipollone hadn't yet returned. I noticed that she had hung a plastic crucifix above the inside of the door. Her street dress hung on a hook beside the mop and a pair of rubber cleaning gloves. Her black purse was sitting on the floor.

When I came back out of the closet, I could see a bar of light under the door that led to the shop. An angular shadow was moving back and forth across it. Figuring that Mrs. Cipollone was probably washing the floor, I pulled the door open.

But instead of being down on her hands and knees with a scrub brush, Mrs. Cipollone was crouched down, apparently examining the bottom shelf of a display of chocolate penises, the dimensions of which could only be described as implausible. When she heard me opening the door, she sprang up and instantly put her feather duster to work, flapping it at a great rate back and forth over the merchandise.

"Mind if I take a look around here?" I asked casually.

"I no mind," she said without looking at me. "You see everyting up dere?"

"Well, not quite. But I think I saw what I needed to see."

Once she realized that I wasn't going to comment on her earlier posture, she began to look me in the eye again. "He got a nice place, eh?"

"Quite nice, yes." I gave her the key and thanked her. I looked out at the store. Only half of the lights were on, but anyone looking through the windows from the street would have been able to see both of us clearly. I stepped behind a shelving unit displaying something called 4-Her Inner Rinse. A flashy sign informed me that this product was now available in seventeen exotic flavours. Mrs. Cipollone went back to her dusting, and I began to take a good look at the place.

Besides chocolate body parts, the shelves were stocked with fruit-scented edible body gels, licorice-flavoured undergarments, and cans of pressurized whipped cream with amusingly shaped spigots. Resting on a sumptuously overstuffed velvet-and-gilt settee was a pink wicker gift basket for hostesses or brides-to-be, overflowing with cream-centred chocolate penises, glow-in-the-dark peppermint condoms, Sta-Firm prolonged pleasure ointment, musk-scented candles in ambitiously large phallic forms, and a bottle of champagne with two flute glasses.

I had never purchased anything from this store, although I had once seen a light switch for golfers — the functioning part of which involved a movable piece of a cartoon golfer's anatomy — that I had almost bought as a birthday gift for my father, until a vision of my mother's face brought me down to earth. But the price per kilo on the chocolate items was way over my budget. Not that I'd ever known anyone I'd felt the urge to give a candy body part. And I certainly couldn't see myself sitting at home alone, munching on a finger or a toe or God knows what else with my after-dinner coffee.

I made a dash to the other side of the store, ducking behind a felt-covered partition that had a selection of brightly coloured animal-shaped party balloons stapled to it. When I examined them more closely, however, I realized that they weren't really balloons at all, but speckled, spotted, and striped condoms with eyes, ears, and half-inch snouts. Most of them seemed to be grinning deliriously, but the illusion may have been augmented by the fact that they'd been, quite literally, blown out of proportion.

Directly in front of me was the female-body-parts section. The top shelf contained facial features such as mouths, ears, and noses. The second one down was for shoulders, breasts, and elbows. Navels and vulvas were next, then leg parts, and finally, at the bottom, ankles and toes. I knelt down in front of the legs and began to hunt through the boxes of chocolate knees. At the very back was a box labelled "Bruno's extra thick, extra hard dark chocolate." It felt heavy, but I didn't waste time looking inside. It was almost nine o'clock, and I knew that Mrs. Cipollone would be almost finished her work. I pulled it out and wedged it into my large purse.

Next to that section was the stairway that led to the lower level, where Grobbelaar maintained his rental department. I went down. I'd been in this section once before, during the same shopping expedition that had ended in my reluctant rejection of the golfer light switch. At that time, it had been filled with videos, camcorders, photographic lights, binoculars, and telescopes, inflatable PVC virgins in three choices of colour, and bake-your-own cake tins and jelly moulds in shapes that you'd never find in a *Better Homes and Gardens* mail-order catalogue. Tonight, however, it was practically empty. It looked as though a band of thieves had swept it clean. The only things left were the kitchen utensils and the videocassette display rack featuring take-out items such as *Naughty Nadia's Night Out* and *Olga, She-Nazi of the Fourth Reich.*

"Mrs. Cipollone," I asked when I went back upstairs, "when was the last time you were down in the basement?"

She looked up from her vacuuming. "Monday past, when I come for clean."

"And what was down there?"

She shrugged. "I no know. All kind of camera. You know. All de stoff for make de movies."

"Aha!" I cried, feeling a surge of excitement. "That's what I thought. Did you know it's all gone now?"

"I know," she said, calmly nodding. "De poleetz tell me dey take alla de stoff from down dere. Maybe dey want for de stamp you make wid you hand."

"Fingerprints?" I suggested, feeling disappointed.

"Ya," she said. "Fingerprints." She smiled. "Well, I tink maybe I go home now. I finish early tonight because I no hev to clean up dere." She unplugged her vacuum cleaner.

I watched the cord retreat automatically back into the machine before I said, "Mrs. Cipollone, I want to thank you. I know I've put you at some risk, asking you to let me in."

"I no tink so," she said with a shrug.

"Well, it *was* breaking the rules."

All at once she frowned, and her eyes seemed to darken. "Hey," she said softly. "You no tink dat man never break no rules?" She turned to pick up a bottle of Windex and a rag.

"What do you mean by that?" I asked, staring at her plump floral-printed back.

She turned again and glared at me. "He was a very

bad man. Believe me. I know. You not de only one who look at his stoff. You tink I spend alla my time waxing floors?"

I suddenly imagined little Mrs. Cipollone on her own personal espionage mission, riffling through Grobbelaar's files, murmuring in disgust over what must have been there before the police arrived. I kept myself from smiling by studying the flecks in the floor tiles.

"Hey," she said. "You are a nice girl. You no worry about stoff like dis. Dis for de poleetz. What you do for work now?"

"I haven't got another job yet. But I'll be looking soon."

"You no married, eh?"

"No."

"Jiust like my son. He work all de time, never go out of de house except for work, never tink about getting married. You should come to my house and meet him. Maybe you like, who knows? He no look like me. You no worry."

I laughed. Mrs. Cipollone was always fretting over her son. I was beginning to fret over him myself. But I wasn't eager to meet him because something told me he wouldn't be my type. Not that I have a type.

"You are a nice girl, Edina," said Mrs. Cipollone. "You geev me you phone nomber. Somatime maybe you come for deener."

I had become quite fond of Mrs. Cipollone. She seemed more sincere than many of the people I'd met in the city. Maybe when all this was over it would be nice to see her again. So I tore a page out of my notebook and wrote my number on it. "Let's keep in touch," I said.

"Ya," she said. "I like dat very much."

I SAT in the flickering light of the northbound subway car, full of the relief of knowing that I had gotten safely out of the store with Gerald's box. I considered the evening, trying to decide whether I'd wasted my time in Grobbelaar's apartment. On the one hand, I hadn't found any evidence that I knew for sure was connected to the murder. On the other hand, I had seen his fantastic collection. Minus whatever circular thing had been inside the open cabinet door.

I climbed out of Eglinton Station and walked west. Although the sky had darkened, I could see a patch of purplish storm clouds moving from the east. I walked quickly, feeling the pressure like a thick breath of hot air against my back.

There was a book and magazine store about halfway between Yonge Street and Avenue Road that stayed open until eleven on Fridays and Saturdays. I pushed the door open just as the first crack of lightning ripped across the sky.

"Nice night," commented the girl at the cash register.

I smiled and said, "I need a German-English phrase book. Do you sell those here?"

She stood up, and I followed her to the middle of the store. "This is a good one," she said, picking up a paperback entitled *Let's Visit Germany*. On the cover was a picture of a stone castle overlooking a reflecting lake.

"Is this the most complete one you have?" I shouted as a boom of thunder vibrated the bookshelves.

"I'd say so," she replied. "It says here, 'Over one thousand German phrases demystified.'"

"I'll take it," I said, glancing out the window. Another flash of lightning lit up the street.

I paid for the book and left the shop. The rain had still not begun to fall, but the wind had picked up, and although it wasn't exactly howling it did have an unmistakably plaintive tone to it. I walked as fast as I could, with my weighted-down purse hanging over my shoulder and the plastic book bag flapping at my side.

When I arrived at the door to my building I stood for a moment, fumbling with my keys. The light over the entrance was out, and the nearest street lamp was on the other side of the road. As I turned and held the keys towards it, another brilliant streak of lightning in the east turned them into a sudden silhouette.

The next thing I knew, I was grabbed from behind and shoved face first against the door. The keys, my purse, and the book bag fell to the ground. My left arm was pinned to my back and bent up at the elbow so that my shoulder blade felt as if it would pop right out of my back. What I imagined to be a knee was pressed against my right leg. I screamed, partly in pain and mostly in terror, but unfortunately just as there was another great clap of thunder.

"Shut up," said my assailant, and he put a hand over my mouth. It smelled like mushrooms that had been left in a plastic bag too long. "Are you Heathcott?" He was talking quietly, almost in a whisper.

I tried to speak, but I was having enough trouble just breathing. One of my nostrils was squashed up against the door, and the smelly hand was unrelenting. For some reason I thought that if I said no he'd leave me alone. I shook my head as vigorously as I could.

"I think you're lying," he said softly and pulled up, just slightly, on my left arm. "I don't like liars. Are you Heathcott?"

Suddenly I realized, with horrified fascination, that the hand over my mouth was missing its thumb. Out of the corner of my right eye I could see a little shadowy stump, and I could feel it, not like a real thumb, against my cheekbone. He pulled up further on my arm. I was afraid it would break. I nodded, keeping my eye on the little stump. Even in the dim light I could see little puckers in the skin, like the mouth of a sack drawn closed with a string. Scar tissue.

"All right," he said. "I have a message for your boss. Tell him he's not going to get away from us. Tell him that Cyrus knows how to find him. Do you understand?"

I didn't move. I noticed that a soft rain was falling.

"Do you understand?" he repeated. "Tell Fineberg that when we get him — which we will — we're going to cut him into little pieces and make him eat himself. Get it? Make sure he knows. Now don't turn around until you count to ten."

I didn't count to ten. I counted to twenty. And then I started to cry.

"CAN YOU DESCRIBE HIM TO ME?" Detective Owl asked a half hour later. We were sitting in my living room, side by side on my couch. All the lights in my apartment had been turned on, and the curtains were clothespinned shut.

"He smelled," I said. My tongue felt thick, almost paralyzed. "Like fungus."

He shook his head and tapped his notebook with his pen. "I don't want to know how he smelled. What did he look like?"

"I have no idea. I told you, he came up behind me."

"How tall was he?"

"How should I know?" I said angrily, as if the whole incident had been his fault.

He sighed. "When he threatened you, where was his voice coming from? Above your ear? Beside it? Below it?"

"Maybe a little above. Maybe a few inches above."

"So that would make him, say, six feet tall?"

"He could have been leaning over."

Detective Owl frowned. "So you're saying he could have been over six feet tall, then?"

"How do you know he wasn't wearing platform shoes?" I shouted. "Maybe he's only five foot six."

"Fair enough," said Detective Owl. His voice was quiet. I supposed that he was trying to calm me down. I wondered if he could hear my teeth chattering. "Okay," he continued. "Now about this hand. Other than the fact that it was missing the thumb, can you describe it?"

"I don't know," I groaned. "What else do you need? Isn't a missing thumb enough?"

"Ms. Heathcott," said Detective Owl, shifting slightly, "I don't have to tell you that you're not being a particularly brilliant witness, especially considering that you make your living thinking about how things look."

I shook my head miserably. "I'm sorry. I really am trying to remember."

"All right," he said. He wrote something in his note-book. "Was it hairy?"

"What?" I cried.

"His hand," Detective Owl said patiently. "Was it a hairy hand?"

I closed my eyes and tried to think. All I could see was the stump. "I really couldn't tell. It might have been. There weren't any hairs poking into my face, if that's a help."

"Fat or thin?"

"Thin, I guess. Hard. It could have been callused."

"Good," he said, and made a note. "Did you touch him?"

"No," I said, feeling sick. "He did all the grabbing."

"Unfortunate. We could have done a fingernail scraping if you'd tried to scratch him. We might at least have had a skin sample."

"I'm sorry. I didn't think of it at the time."

"All right. How about his voice. Low? High?"

"Fairly low."

"Any accent?"

"No. And his grammar was commendable for a thug."

He smiled faintly. "And there's nothing else you can remember about him?"

"I'm sorry. No."

He leaned towards me and said quietly, "Well, I hope you've learned something from this."

"Like what?" I retorted. "Not to stay out after dark?"

"Ms. Heathcott," he said sternly, "it seems you still haven't realized that you may be dealing with a dangerous group of people here. My bet is that guy didn't lose his thumb in an industrial accident. And unfortunately it sounds as though we're not the only ones looking for Fineberg. I'm sure we'll find him. But until we do, I don't want you trying to make any kind of contact with him."

"I haven't been trying to," I said indignantly.

Detective Owl frowned. "Be that as it may, I should warn you that he may try to make contact with you."

"Why would he do that?"

"You might know the answer to that better than I."

"Just what are you implying?" I asked sharply.

"I'm not implying anything. I'm merely stating a fact. Gerald Fineberg is up to his ears in hot water, and he'll probably try to seek assistance wherever he thinks he can get even the slightest hint of sympathy."

"You think I have sympathy for Gerald?" I asked, wondering if I was overdoing the volume. "That man gave away the best job I ever had. I don't care if I never see him again."

"That's good. Because I know Mr. Fineberg is an extremely manipulative person. And that's why I'd like you to stay as far away from him as possible. Don't give these people any reason to think you may be connected to his financial affairs. I'm hoping that they were just looking for a convenient messenger service tonight, and you happened to make yourself available. But if you feel you need protection, we may be able to help you out."

"I'll be fine," I said. "Please don't worry about me."

He stood up. "All right," he said and gave me a quick pat on the shoulder. "As long as you're sure." He went to the door and opened it. "Make sure this is locked. And remember: no more sneaking around like Nancy Drew."

"What?" I said hotly.

"You know what I mean." He smiled and closed the door.

I got my purse, which was sitting on the floor nearby, and took it into the bathroom. It was the only room in my apartment that didn't have a window. I locked the door. Then I squatted down, opened my purse, and took out the "Bruno's extra thick and hard" box. I put it on the floor and lifted the lid.

For a moment I thought that I was going to stop breathing permanently. Inside the box was a ten-inch-high goblet, unquestionably of pure gold, with a dozen glittering jewels set into the round base. There was an empty setting for a thirteenth stone, which would have been slightly larger than the others.

I knew at once that Gerald had been lying. The goblet could only have come from Grobbelaar's collection. But it wasn't the obvious age and quality of the piece that made me realize this. It wasn't even my memory of the clean, circular mark in the dust on Grobbelaar's shelf. It was the stain of blood, almost as dark as chocolate, which had dripped down and dried on the inside of the rim.

six

I DECIDED THAT THE WORST THING I could do was panic and jump to conclusions, so I hid the goblet behind a box of Cheerios in the cupboard over the fridge. I figured I'd stay calmer if I didn't think about it, at least until Sunday morning at ten o'clock. Then I could ask Gerald Fineberg what the hell he was doing with a bloodstained goblet belonging to Heinz Grobbelaar.

I didn't sleep very well. The thunderstorm seemed to go on for hours, and I was afraid to get undressed and under the covers in case the one-thumbed messenger returned and I had to run into the street screaming for help. So I dozed on the couch, facing the chained door, and waited until morning.

By the time the sun had risen to a decent position, I was beginning to wonder if I should change my name and start looking for a new apartment. I showered and got dressed and was poking at a fried egg on toast when the phone rang.

"Hello?" I said quietly.

"Edina?"

"Mrs. Cipollone! How are you?" Awkward was how she sounded. I hoped that she wasn't calling to tell me that someone had found out that she'd let me into Grobbelaar's apartment last night and she'd lost her job.

But she only said, "Oh, it's okay. Maybe you no beesy tonight?"

"Tonight? No, I'm not busy." Unless she wanted to count fleeing from dangerous criminals.

"Ah." She hesitated. "Maybe you like to come for deenner. I make a barbecue. You like barbecue?"

"Yes," I replied slowly. "I do."

"Good." She sounded relieved. "You come den. Five o'clock."

Boy, I thought. She didn't waste any time. Her son really must have a major social disability. But her offer couldn't have been more opportune. "I'll be there," I said. "Tell me where you live."

She gave me her address, and I hung up the phone, wondering what I had got myself into. But at least I wouldn't have to spend the evening alone at home.

In the meantime, I realized that the safest place for me would be in a crowd, and I couldn't think of anything more crowded than a shopping mall on a Saturday. I put my fried egg in the fridge and went up to Yorkdale where I spent the day practising furtive glances and cunning dodges. I even found a pair of sandals on sale. Then at four-thirty I got back on the subway and headed south to my dinner engagement.

I WAS MARRIED WHEN I WAS NINETEEN, partly because he had a great body, and partly because I thought I'd never find anyone else my own age who wanted a wife named Edna. Also, my mother approved. It was a great way to keep me living just around the corner. There weren't too many girls my age who stuck around town once they'd finished high school. My father's favourite joke at family gatherings was "Edna's the only one of my kids who's got any sense. She's going to live in Elegance for the rest of her life."

And I would have, too, if I hadn't found out two years later that my husband had been carrying on with the cashier at the L and M for the past three. Apparently, he'd felt that there was enough of his great body to go around. But I was the one who knew how to make a macaroni-and-cheese casserole that tasted just like his mom's. "So why didn't you stay with your mother?" I'd demanded. Because he couldn't sleep with his mother, could he? "Nothing would surprise me any more," I'd told him.

Ever since then I'd been unable to stomach either macaroni-and-cheese or men with great bodies, so it wasn't without a measured sense of foreboding that I sat down to eat pasta carbonara and grilled lamb with Mr. and Mrs. Salvatore Cipollone and their well-built son, Michael.

However, if I was feeling less than receptive to Mrs. Cipollone's beaming enthusiasm, it was clear that her husband and son were absolutely impervious to it. Apparently she'd told them as much as she knew about me, and they were just about as thrilled to have me there as they would have been if she'd invited the moderator of the United Church of Canada to tea.

After the first few minutes, during which we told each other how nice it was to have finally met and listed all our living relatives and their respective ages, there wasn't much more to say than "Pass the cheese, please." Between bites, Mrs. Cipollone smiled at me with a sort of kindly encouragement, and Mr. Cipollone adjusted the position of his false teeth. Michael just looked through the sliding doors out to the grapevine-covered patio. At least he was interesting to watch. I was fascinated by the deliberate way he ate: biting, chewing, swallowing, wiping his mouth. He never hurried. He seemed to savour every morsel. I was almost afraid to imagine how that might carry over into other pursuits.

I thought of a number of provocative questions I could have asked to break the silence. To Mr. Cipollone: How has wearing dentures affected your ability to chew food with your mouth closed? Or, why do you keep staring at my hands? To Michael: Have you ever been involved in a weight-lifting program, or have your genes done all that work by themselves? Or, why are you still living at home, anyway? But I didn't feel that I could ask and still expect to be welcome for dessert.

I looked above Mr. Cipollone's head to the sideboard. It was a walnut-grained plastic laminate affair with rose-etched sliding glass doors and imitation brass knobs. Its crocheted doily-covered shelves were stocked with unmatched tea and coffee cups, souvenir spoons with tiny crests and icons on the handles, two glasses in the shape of the CN Tower, and espresso makers in three sizes. Wedged between the doors and the shelves were several photographs of people I imagined to be relatives, mainly well aged, standing in groups and squinting at the camera. A pink, unfocused finger covered the bottom third of one. Taped to the left-hand door was an Italian calendar featuring a gently smiling Pope looking hopefully toward some point off camera, as if to say Follow me, my lambs. There's better pasture over the hills. Someone had hand-drawn the phases of the moon onto the appropriate days, and my own name was written under today's date: *Edina*.

There was a small television on top of the refrigerator, and I caught Mr. Cipollone's eyes wandering upwards a couple of times. He was probably missing his favourite game show. I would gladly have jumped up and turned it on for him if he had asked, but suddenly he pointed his fork at me and said, "So, you de one who find de body of dat sex-store man," in a tone of voice that indicated he felt I was likely reponsible for having killed Grobbelaar myself.

I looked at Mrs. Cipollone, expecting her to remind her husband that it was unmannerly to discuss throat-slashings during mealtimes, but she was blithely twirling another forkful of pasta against her spoon and smiling expectantly at me. Even Michael looked up from his plate and was watching me with what I took to be interest. At least both his eyes were completely open.

I swallowed a mouthful of tagliatelle and said, "Yes, I was."

"Hmph," Mr. Cipollone grunted. "Bad beezneess."

I didn't know whether he meant the murder or the shop itself, but it was apparent that he wasn't going to elaborate. He stuck another forkful of pasta into his mouth and chewed thoughtfully.

Well, that's the end of that foray into the wondrous world of conversational dining, I thought gloomily as I ate my last bite of pasta. But Michael passed me the salad tongs and said, "Have they caught the guy who did it yet?"

I put a few chunks of tomato on my plate. "Not as far as I know," I said.

"What about the guy you worked for? I thought he was under suspicion." He took the tongs out of my hands and ladled a mound of tomatoes and olive oil over a piece of bread in his pasta dish. Then he stuck his fork into the middle of it and began to make slicing motions, breaking up the bread into bite-sized pieces.

I noticed that Mrs. Cipollone was watching this procedure proudly. I suppose I would have, too, if I had had a son who looked as good as he did, even considering what he was doing to his food.

"Yes, he is," I said, trying not to stare at the pieces of bread and tomato disappearing into his mouth. "He took off before the police had a chance to question him."

"Do you think he did it?" Michael asked, wiping olive oil from his chin with a serviette.

I hesitated before I answered. "At first I didn't think so. But now I'm not so certain. I know he was in big debt to some loan shark. He owed so much money that he was afraid for his life." I wondered why I found myself speaking of Gerald in the past tense.

Michael frowned and thrust his fork into another chunk of tomato. "How do you know that? Does your boss usually tell you these things?"

I blinked. "Well, no. Not usually. But these were rather unusual circumstances."

He didn't get a chance to respond, because Mrs. Cipollone passed a large platter of barbecued lamb to me and said, "Here, Edina. You take a big piece. I make lots."

I did. Although by then Michael was watching me curiously, and I wondered nervously whether I'd be able to cut the lamb without sending it sliding off my plate and onto his lap.

"My mother tells me you lost your job," he said, just as I managed to get a piece of meat into my mouth.

I attempted to murmur a perspicacious response, but I had to keep my lips closed so I wouldn't spray a mouthful of semi-masticated lamb across the table.

Michael didn't seem to notice. "What exactly did you do at that art gallery?" he asked.

I forced the lump of meat down my throat and said, "I answered questions about the work we exhibited, made phone calls, sent out invitations. But my main job was doing appraisals, particularly of paintings from estate collections."

"I don't know very much about paintings," he said, motioning to the wall behind him. I noticed that he had a faded ink stain on the side of his hand. "Look at what we have here. My parents' idea of a picture to hang on the wall is a postcard of a crucifix we got from Italy. I guess you must know a lot about paintings."

"I know what people are interested in buying. I also know something about what goes into a good painting or sculpture. I went to art college for a couple of years."

"So you're a frustrated artist, then."

I cringed. "No. Definitely not."

"Not frustrated," he asked softly, "or not an artist?"

"Neither," I said steadily. "I knew all along I'd never be a painter. But I love looking at paintings. I always knew that whatever I ended up doing would have to have something to do with art. So I wanted to learn everything I could, even from the artist's point of view. That's why Gerald hired me. He needed someone who'd sound reasonably well informed to collectors. He's really just an entrepreneur. At least, that's what he thought he was."

He nodded. "So, now what are you going to do?"

I shrugged. "There are plenty of other galleries in Toronto. Some of them would be worth working for. I'm not going to work at McDonald's, if that's what you mean."

Mr. Cipollone, who had been busy watching his wife cut his lamb into tiny, baby bites for him, broke in. "Why you no married? You need a hosband. Every woman need a hosband."

Michael shook his head and went back to his dinner.

"Oh, I'm quite capable of looking after myself," I said. I could tell by the way he was looking at me that he attributed my unmarried state to some disastrous personality flaw or a grotesque but well-hidden physical deformity. But I didn't feel up to giving out my entire personal history. After all, no one was bending over backwards to explain what Michael was doing still sitting at his mother's kitchen table, eating her hand-cut tagliatelle.

Mrs. Cipollone smiled comfortingly. "You like to see my grenddaughters?" she asked. "I show you a photograph." She told her husband to get the picture out of the sideboard, and he passed it over to her.

I looked at the photograph of three girls in matching red-and-white velvet dresses and black-patent-leather shoes. "They're beautiful," I said. "You must be very proud of them."

"Oh, ya," she said, nodding. "Dis one, she look jiust like me when I hev de same age." She pointed to the eldest.

The girl had a dark oval face and glowering black eyes. If she had put on a nylon dress and hairnet, she would have been a perfect miniature Mrs. Cipollone. Next to her, the other two looked like grinning imps in ribbons and pigtails. I passed the photograph back to Mrs. Cipollone.

"My son no is married," Mr. Cipollone said to me. "Maybe you want for marry him."

I looked at him, speechless, while Michael slapped the table with his hand and said, "Pa, what are you doing?"

His father shrugged. "You no hev notting wrong wit you. Maybe she like."

Michael said something in loud Italian. Mr. Cipollone said something even louder. His face had turned a deep shade of red, and his dentures were making a peculiar squishing sound against his gums. Over the racket, Mrs. Cipollone shouted, "You want coffee, Edina?"

"Yes, please," I said, pushing my chair back as fast as I could. The chrome legs screeched against the tile floor. "Can I help you?"

"No. You stay dere. I make espress'. You like?"

I stood up anyway.

"Please sit down," said Michael. "We won't argue in

front of you. My father knows he was out of place. He's just trying to be helpful. I'm sorry if he embarrassed you."

Mrs. Cipollone brought the coffee to the table in four small cups. She added three spoonfuls of sugar to her own, and passed the bowl to me. I took one. Michael took two. Mr. Cipollone took three and a few drops from a green, straw-covered bottle labelled Centerba.

"You want some?" he asked, nudging the bottle in my direction.

I declined, noting the seventy-proof warning on the label. We drank our coffee and ate an anise-flavoured sponge cake with the same tiny spoons we had used to stir the espresso. The conversation returned to its pre-Grobbelaar discussion. The Cipollones glared at each other, and I gazed intently at the rose pattern around the edge of the dessert plate.

"Well, that was certainly a delicious dinner," I said, after we had all refused offers of second slices. I looked at the clock hanging above the sideboard. It was only six-thirty. I wondered what we were going to do for the rest of the evening. Maybe they expected me to leave now. Mrs. Cipollone had said, "for deener," but she'd never mentioned follow-up entertainment. I wondered fleetingly if I should offer to sing them my father's version of "Funiculi Funicula," which contained verses hitherto unknown in polite circles.

"You like ice cream?" Mrs. Cipollone asked suddenly.

"Yes," I said warily. Perhaps we were just going to sit at the kitchen table for the rest of the evening, cramming more and more layers of food into our stomachs.

"Maybe Michael take you to Sanglair for ice cream," she said, stretching her lips across her teeth at him. I paid careful attention to his expression, watching to see if he was being prodded in the shins by an orthopedic shoe. But he seemed to be as relieved as I was at the thought of getting up from the table.

"Good idea," he said, looking at me.

"We don't have to," I told him. "Maybe you have something else you'd rather be doing."

"He no hev notting to do," said Mrs. Cipollone. "You go for eat ice cream."

"Come on," said Michael. "You don't want to sit here talking to my parents for the rest of the evening, do you?"

Instead of looking fatally wounded as my mother would have if I'd said anything like that, Mrs. Cipollone nodded and said, "Dat's right. You go pass a good time."

"Okay," I said, and Michael stood up. I got another fast look at the lower half of his body. He was wearing a pair of faded grey shorts, and he had the most incredible legs I'd ever seen in real life. He probably knew it, too, I thought dimly as I turned to thank Mrs. Cipollone for the dinner.

"I am very happy you come to my house," she said, kissing both my cheeks. "You come beck again soma-time soon, eh?"

"I will," I said, not unconvincingly.

We walked up Dufferin Street and turned left at St. Clair Avenue where we immediately had to sidestep an outdoor fruit display. I could smell the warm, sweet scent of figs wrapped in purple paper and plums and oranges stacked on lime green plastic stands. We passed wedding shops flaunting six-foot plaster brides in hand-beaded gowns who clutched the black-jacketed arms of their plaster grooms with cracked, flesh-tone hands. In narrow, darkened restaurants with tiny, white-clothed tables, dark-haired people dressed like pages from *Vogue* ate spaghetti *alla bolognese* from imported dinnerware. Groups of short, pot-bellied old men, who looked startlingly like Mr. Cipollone, gathered to smoke and argue outside a billiard hall, while a conference of taller, younger, pony-tailed men in rumpled silk suits and ties huddled outside a corner café, speaking Italian in low, secretive voices. They were probably striking a business deal. They looked as though they could have been the board of directors for some cocaine-importing syndicate.

"I'm sorry about my father," Michael said after we had walked a few blocks.

"It's quite all right," I replied. "My mother's been known to be a lot more personal than that."

"One thing I want to know," he said, "is how you got roped into this. Don't look at me like that! You know what I mean. You seem too independent to let a little Italian lady force you into something you don't want to do. She can't scream that loudly. Do you owe her money or something?"

I laughed. "I came over because I like her, and I thought I'd have a nice time. I didn't come over just to meet you, if that's what you're worried about."

"I'm not worried about it," he said. He started to walk faster. Either he really wanted the ice cream badly, or he was hoping that I'd collapse with exhaustion and get lost in the crowd.

I stepped up my pace. "You don't have to buy me an ice cream, you know."

"That's not why I was asking," he said. "I'd like to take you, if you really want to come."

"Sure," I said, and shrugged casually, hoping that he wouldn't think I was too eager.

"What exactly did my mother tell you about me?"

"Not too much." I considered adding, Only that she wants to get you out of the house for once, but refrained. I said, "Just that you don't look anything like her. She was right. You're much taller."

He laughed. "Did she tell you what I do for a living?"

"No. What do you do for a living?"

"I plan green spaces for factories and office buildings. I'm an industrial landscaper. I own my own business. I have six people working for me."

"You do?" I said, in a tone of surprise that probably exceeded the parameters of polite inquiry by several degrees. I'd never known a landscaper before. That is, unless you counted the four elderly ladies from the Elegance Horticultural Society who filled the concrete planters along the main street with scarlet geraniums every summer. "Is it an interesting job?"

"Very interesting. To me, anyway. I don't know how you feel about parks."

I didn't get a chance to answer. Michael said, "Well, here we are," and we stopped at an aluminum window in the side of a small café. There was an old man behind the glass wearing an ice-cream-stained apron over a green T-shirt with a hole in one sleeve. We ordered our flavours and carried them to a wooden bench overlooking the community centre pool. We sat at opposite ends with my purse in between.

I looked into the turquoise water and tasted my ice cream. "It's good," I said. "Even though I'm already full from dinner."

"You have nice hands," said Michael.

I put the spoon down. "Is that why your father kept staring at them?"

He snickered. "Oh, that. Don't take it personally. He does that to everyone. He has a thing about hands."

"A fetish?" I had a sudden, terrible picture in my mind of Mr. Cipollone secretly drooling through his dentures over the memory of the way I had held my fork over his wife's specially marinated lamb.

"No. He thinks he can tell what a person is like by looking at their hands. It's probably the gypsy in him."

"And can he?"

"I don't know," he replied with a straight face. "I prefer to look at the whole body."

I didn't know if that was a pass or not, but I responded immediately and wittily. "Hunh?"

Michael gave me a slow smile. I wondered if he'd practised it in front of the bathroom mirror. It looked good enough to win a contest. "Come on, Edna," he said. "Lighten up. You're sitting there like a salami with your ends tied too tight." He reached over and set my purse on the ground.

I put another spoonful of ice cream into my mouth and tried to swallow it, but I couldn't seem to get my tongue to co-operate. As I watched him, unblinking, I made the sensible decision just to let it melt and trickle down my throat.

Michael put his knee up on the bench where my purse had been and slung his arm over the back in a casual pose. Then he licked his ice cream spoon and asked, "Are you seeing anyone right now?"

"Why?" I asked, feigning a casual air.

He looked away. "I could be wrong," he said, "but you seem to be a little on edge since we came outside. I noticed that you kept looking behind you as we were walking. I figured you thought someone was following you."

I stared at him. "Following me? Why would someone be following me?"

"Jealous boyfriend?" Michael suggested.

"Jealous boyfriend?" I scoffed and looked down at my melting ice cream. "What an idea!"

"That doesn't sound like an answer to the question, Edna. Are you already involved with someone? Because if you're not, I'd like to see you again."

"Look," I sighed, glancing hastily over my shoulder. "I'm not seeing anyone right now, and I certainly don't think anyone is following me, but I should tell you that I don't particularly like this situation." Right. The worst thing that had ever happened to me was sitting on a bench with a man built like an ancient Greek marble in Italian shorts, telling me he wanted to see me again.

"What?" said Michael. "What situation? Sitting in front of this pool?"

I nearly choked on my spoon. "No! I just don't like thinking that you've been set up. Or that you're just being polite." I finished my ice cream and crumpled the cup with the wooden spoon inside.

"Edna," he said, moving to the centre of the bench, "it's impossible to set me up. And I'm never just polite."

I stood up quickly and headed for the nearest garbage can. "I'll bet you're not," I said into the chute marked Thank You for Not Littering.

"Hey, Edna," said Michael. "Would you like to see a movie tonight?"

"Which one?" I asked more suspiciously than I'd intended.

"I was thinking about *Rear Window*," he said. "Do you like old movies? I think it's on at the Kingsway."

"*Rear Window*? You want to see *Rear Window*?"

"Have you already seen it?" he asked.

"Yes," I said, bending down to pick up my purse.

"Oh." He was obviously disappointed. He threw his ice cream cup into the garbage can. "Well, we'll have to check the paper, then."

"I've seen it six times," I said as I straightened up.

"Oh!" He began to smile again. "Would you like to drive or take the streetcar?"

ONE GOOD THING about being taken to a film that I'd already seen six times was that I could spend the hour and three-quarters thinking about the Heinz Grobbelaar business and yet still be able to carry on a reasonably sound critical analysis of the movie afterwards. Also, I could stare at Michael Cipollone out of the corner of my eye while giving the outward impression of being enthralled by the shade of Grace Kelly's gown.

I preferred not to think about the goblet in my cereal cupboard. Instead, I sucked quietly on the Smarties I'd bought for us and tried to figure out whether the fact that Grobbelaar had received a pornographic postcard mailed in Toronto had anything to do with his murder. Surely, I thought as I let melted chocolate coat the roof of my mouth, the police would have taken the cards if they'd had any significance. But still, I wished that I'd brought the whole box home with me. The more I thought about them, the more peculiar my feeling about them became.

"Smartie?" I whispered to Michael.

He held out his hand without looking away from the screen. If he thought that I had nice hands, then he should have heard what I thought of his. They looked as though they should have been holding a stone and a sling in the Accademia in Florence. Or maybe grabbing a pair of shoulders or some other willing part of the anatomy lower down. I dumped a few Smarties into his palm and stuck another one in my own mouth.

I wondered if Mrs. Cipollone would let me back into Grobbelaar's apartment when she went to clean on Monday evening. She might be more willing if Michael told her what a great date I'd been, but I didn't think she'd go for letting me walk out with a box of postcards under my arm.

I concentrated on the movie for a few minutes, and then on the shape of Michael Cipollone's profile, which was not quite perfect. Under normal circumstances I would have been feeling less than enthusiastic about letting my mind drift into active self-delusion, but since

Jimmy and Grace were having such a high time up on the screen, I felt that it wouldn't hurt to let my own images of Michael and Edna develop with photographic precision inside my head. And I wasn't envisaging scintillating table talk.

I can't say that my fantasizing wasn't tempered by the knowledge that there were probably 194 other women in the world who were simultaneously engaged in the same activity — from Michael's secretary, if he had one, to the dyed-blonde woman in the ticket booth out front, who had taken what I thought was an inordinate length of time to make change for Michael's ten. Not only that, but I still hadn't been able to completely extinguish the inevitable sense of panic that accompanied any flights of fancy I ever took over men who were even slightly better looking than a lowland gorilla.

So it stood to reason that my concentration on an unlikely scenario — in which Michael and I were accidentally locked into the Kingsway Theatre broom closet for the rest of the weekend — would eventually dwindle in favour of paying attention to the non-arousing problem of the Grobbelaar postcards. The solution, as it turned out, came to me in a literal flash as Jimmy Stewart zapped Raymond Burr out of the darkness with his photographic lights: take pictures. It was the same old trick used in every spy movie I'd ever seen. But I figured that if it was such a common procedure, it really must work. I even had a 35 mm camera with a close-up lens.

I began to munch on the rest of the Smarties with true gusto, and it wasn't until Michael put his hand on my leg and began to move his fingers in counterclockwise circles over my kneecap that I threw caution to the wind and let my mind slip back to the Kingsway broom closet.

seven

I WASN'T LOOKING FORWARD TO
seeing Gerald. I was, however, looking forward to finding out what he'd been doing with the goblet.

I figured that he'd probably tell me. Gerald was the
kind of person who was proud of his lapses into the
shady side of life, and I imagined that this was just
another in a long succession of what he would consider
simply ticklish little misadventures. He had always
gotten a thrill out of trying to scandalize me with tales
from his repertoire of big-city hustles. And he had a
sackful of those.

Before becoming a dealer in fine art, Gerald Fineberg
had been everything from a circus barker to a blackjack
dealer. His move into the world of painting and sculpture had not been a step towards cultural self-reform. I
was certain that Gerald had only opened his gallery to
gain easy access to the wallets of the wealthy. Art was
the perfect merchandise for Gerald. He had a knack for
convincing people that buying a painting was akin to
buying into immortality, and that wasn't an easy thing
for the affluent or would-be affluent to refuse. You
could practically see the saliva running from their
mouths when Gerald got talking about bequests to
public collections. If they couldn't afford to get an
opera house named after them, they could at least die
knowing that their names would be etched in perpe-
tuity on a brass plate tacked to a gilded frame in the

museum of their choice. And all that in easy monthly instalments.

Unfortunately, Gerald also had a knack for spending more than he earned. He had never been able to kick his gambling habit, so even after he was making enough money to actually afford the Jaguar and the raccoon coat, he was deeper in debt than he had ever been before. He'd never come out and told me this, but I had often watched him through the glass walls of his office, shouting into the phone and flailing his arms like a drowning man in a silent movie. Gerald had been frequently pestered by his creditors.

The only thing I couldn't fathom was why I hadn't realized how dangerously far Gerald had fallen into the hole. Maybe I wasn't quite as good at reading lips as I'd thought I was.

At ten o'clock on Sunday morning I climbed down the creosoted timber steps to the Lytton tennis courts. Gerald was nowhere in sight. I sat, twitching nervously, on a bench near the chain-link fence surrounding the court and watched a couple whacking a bright green ball to each other. I had been careful to make sure that I wasn't being followed, but every few seconds I glanced up towards Avenue Road, just to find out if anyone was peering down at me with a violin case in hand.

The day was oppressively humid, and the tennis players were both glowing. I probably would have been glowing, too, if it hadn't been for the block of ice I could feel in my stomach. I noticed that the veins in the backs of my hands seemed to have shrivelled, and my nails were a faint bluish colour. I clutched my purse on my lap and tried to remember the lyrics to "Whistle a Happy Tune."

By ten-fifteen there was still no sign of Gerald. My mouth was dry, and my tongue seemed to be sticking to my palate. I moved warily over to the fountain and had a drink, heedful of a middle-aged man walking a St. Bernard on the Alexandra side of the park. He was eyeing me with what I hoped was only lecherous intent, but after my escapade the other night, I wasn't prepared to make any rash assumptions. If he was out to kill me, I wanted to see him coming. Instead of returning to the bench, where my back would have been exposed, I stood under the covered area outside the changing rooms and glared at him. After a few more minutes the dog left an enormous deposit at the top of the hill, and the man departed with a wink in my direction.

It was nearly ten-thirty. I wondered how long I was supposed to wait. I couldn't imagine why Gerald would be late. Surely he hadn't forgotten. I decided to give him ten more minutes.

At twenty to eleven I made my way back up the steps, walked north to the lights at Glengrove, and crossed over to the west side of Avenue Road. I took note of the fact that a blue Fiat, which had been parked on Alexandra while I was watching the man with the St. Bernard, was waiting to make a left turn onto Glengrove. The driver was a woman in her thirties, with short red hair and dark glasses. Her lipstick was scarlet. As I passed the car, I stared at her expressionlessly for as long as I could without breaking my neck. She looked back with what I took for disdain. I considered sticking out my tongue.

Gerald's house was only a short walk from there, on a winding street with a dark canopy of maples. Although it was a large home, it was not ostentatious, and the only hint that there might be something extraordinary hidden inside was the series of simple cast-iron bars across the basement windows.

Trying to ignore the presence of the blue Fiat, which was parked about thirty metres away and slightly hidden by the curve in the street, I stood on the porch and rang the doorbell. No answer. I rang again. I could hear the chimes faintly through the heavy oak door. There was a sheer curtain drawn into tight little gathers over the window above the lion's-head door knocker, and not even the keenest eye could have discerned whether there was any movement within. For all I knew, Gerald could have been standing on the other side of the door. I waited another minute and then headed back down the steps. I couldn't see whether the red-haired woman was still in the Fiat because there was a reflection of pale sky on the rear windshield.

The gate between Gerald's house and the one next door was unlocked. I pushed it open and walked down four flagstone steps into the garden.

The first thing I noticed was the William McElcheren bronze on the lawn. The second was the fact that the grass was so long that it was bending over, and under the silvery dew that still hadn't evaporated in the damp air, it looked like grey-green waves on a surging ocean. The third thing was the group of dark green footprints over the ocean that cut a path from where I was standing, around the McElcheren, over to a Fafard cow, and across to a Maritime folk art weathervane that was mounted on a concrete pedestal. The footprints mingled, then moved back towards the flagstone steps that led up to the gate.

I walked down among them and tried to decide whether they were Gerald's. One set could have been, although the other seemed to have been made by a pair of pointy women's shoes. Wet grass wasn't the best medium for holding impressions of feet, but it almost looked as though there could have been two men and a woman touring Gerald's little sculpture garden. And I had a pretty good idea of who they might have been.

I glanced swiftly towards the back of the house to see if Ms. Pistachio Nails and her two bodyguards were looking out the window. But there was no sign of anyone. They had probably just been in the garden taking inventory.

The blue Fiat, I noticed with relief, was gone. Not that I could imagine the red-headed woman being one of Gerald's disgruntled financiers. But she'd had a particularly nasty twist to her mouth that even bright red lipstick couldn't hide, and knowing she might have been watching me gave me the creeps.

I didn't see any sign of her as I headed home, but that might have been because I was trying to keep my head down to avoid the rain, which had begun to fall. I didn't mind getting soaked. I felt that it was a fitting end to the morning.

What I did mind, however, was finding a set of wet, pointy-toed footprints on the stairs that led down to my apartment and a white envelope from the Payco Loans Company stuck through the letter slot in the door. I must have just missed them.

Dripping rainwater onto my kitchen floor, I stood reading it:

Dear Ms. Heathcott:

Re: Fineberg Gallery Audit

Our records show that the balance of payment equalling $1,572.00 for a graphite on paper drawing by Stanley Spencer is still owing by you. This balance must be paid on or before June 30. If we have not received payment by this time, we are authorized by law to repossess the drawing. We anticipate your full co-operation.

Thanking you in advance, I am

Yours truly,
Cynthia Weid
Auditor

CW/jp

I nearly threw up. It was bad enough knowing the woman had been all but over my threshold, but the thought of her sitting at her desk, dictating the foul little note to jp, whoever that was, was really sickening. And she was no more mine truly than Heinz Grobbelaar was.

I made sure that the kitchen curtains were still clothespinned shut before I took the box containing the goblet out of my purse and stuck it back in the cereal cupboard. Then I removed my wet clothes and wrung them out in the sink. After I'd dried myself with a tea towel, I went into the bedroom to get a fresh pair of shorts and a T-shirt.

I sat on my couch and looked at the drawing. It wasn't the best Spencer I'd ever seen, but it was the best I could afford, and it was the first in what I'd hoped would eventually develop into a pretty fine drawing collection. Although I wasn't exactly rolling in dough, I realized that it wasn't actually paying off the drawing that bothered me. I would have had to do that anyway. It was the thought of Cynthia Weid cackling with lascivious glee as she grasped my cheque — which probably represented less than one ten-thousandth of what Gerald owed — in her greedy little hands. But I supposed that I would rather deal with that thought than have her gloating over my inevitable defeat in small-claims court.

I made up a cheque for the whole amount and post-dated it to the thirtieth. Then I wrote a brief note on pink vellum with yellow tea roses printed in the margin:

Dear Ms. Weid:
Just wanted to thank you for your delightful, newsy letter. I hope this finds you in good health. I am happy to enclose a cheque for $1,572.00, representing the balance owing on the Spencer drawing. Thank you again for your kind interest in my financial affairs.

Yours faithfully,
Edna Heathcott
Unemployed

I sealed the note with my cheque in a matching rose-lined envelope and addressed it to the attention of Cynthia Weid at the Payco Loans Company. Then I huddled on the sofa and tried to figure out why Gerald hadn't shown up. For all I knew, I thought dismally, he could have been lying dead in some back alley, after having confessed to the loan sharks that he had sent me to get his precious package. I knew that I should never have brought it back to my apartment. I had to get rid of it.

But I couldn't just dump a fifteenth-century goblet in the street. And I sure didn't want to have to explain to Detective Owl why I had it. The only way out of the mess was to put it back where I'd found it as soon as possible.

I decided to distract myself by making some more phone calls. I put on my raincoat and walked stealthily out to the phone booth. But there was no answer from either the Birches or Anna Dellarosa. Gwen Tattersall's answering machine came on, offering to take my message, but I hung up without even a whisper and went back inside.

There was still another person on my list whom I hadn't yet tried to contact: the art critic, John Henderson.

I had met John Henderson. He was a tall, slim, frenetic man with silver hair that rolled back from his forehead to his crown in three smooth ripples. He wore thick, dark-rimmed glasses that magnified his eyes into frightening proportions. He had started out his working life as an oral surgeon, but had quit that long ago and now wrote a monthly column for *Art in Canada*, which no one I knew could understand.

But he didn't make all his money sitting at a type-writer. He also had a ton of investment income that had originated in an inheritance from his grandmother. To look at him you'd never know it, because he obviously didn't spend a dime on clothes. His Great Dane, Rita, wore an eighteen-carat gold chain, but John Henderson ran around all year long in beige polyester bellbottoms and an olive green Harris tweed jacket. Yet I'd heard him say to Gerald on more than one occasion, "Get me whatever's interesting for two-hundred," and he wasn't talking two-zero-zero.

He had a collection that any one of the B-level museums in the province would have killed for. I'd never seen it all together, but once in a while John Henderson would lend out a portion to a travelling exhibition, and his name was always appearing in the acknowledgements section of books on twentieth-century figurative art.

I couldn't imagine what he might have done to invite the attentions of a blackmailer. Unless there was some crazed pervert lurking inside the polyester slacks. But even if there was, I doubted that I'd find out over the phone. He was far too shrewd to give away secrets to a stranger, even one who mentioned Grobbelaar's name. I would have to see him in person. But what was I going to do? Call him up and ask to see his water-colour collection? He'd laugh me off the line. At least if he'd still been a surgeon I could have phoned up his secretary and made an appointment to have my jaw realigned.

The frustrating thing was that I could actually see him putting the knife to Heinz's throat. He might even have had the proper tool for the job, something left over from his surgical heyday still hanging around the med-icine chest. He would have known how far below the jawline to strike, how much force to put behind the knife, in which direction to jump in order to avoid the splatter.

I was lost in this grisly speculation when the telephone rang on the couch, right next to the cushion that was supporting my head. My heart immediately leaped into double time, and I narrowly escaped swallowing my tongue. I let the phone ring twice more before I picked it up, using the time to sit up and recompose myself.

"Hello?" I said in a reasonably good imitation of my usual self.

A man was whispering, "I want to see your body."

An obscene caller. Or Cyrus, the grammatically correct, one-thumbed thug, checking back?

I couldn't help it. Even though I was certain that no one was watching, I glanced over at the kitchen windows to make sure that the curtains were still drawn. Then I said as firmly as I could, "Get lost, you pervert," and slammed down the receiver. Maybe Zylie Wedge had had the right idea. If I'd been wearing a whistle, I could have used it.

I stared at the phone. If it had been a random dialler he'd never call back. But if he had found my Heathcott E A in the phone book, I was in for a repeat performance.

It rang.

This time I picked it up after the first ring and held it to my ear without saying anything.

"Edna? Are you there?"

Michael.

"Was that you?" I said in disgust.

"I'm sorry. I thought you'd realize." He wasn't sorry. He was snickering.

"Thanks a lot. How was I supposed to know it was you?"

"You mean you get a lot of requests for your body?"

"Don't be sarcastic."

"I'm not. Can I see you?"

"Already?"

"It's been twelve hours. I've had time to think about it, and I'm convinced that I'm in love with you. Would you like me to come over?"

"Sure, I guess so."

"Don't sound so thrilled.

"I *am* thrilled," I said truthfully. "I'm just surprised."

"At what?"

"I don't know. Your eagerness, I guess."

"You haven't even seen eagerness yet," he whispered in his obscene-caller voice. "I'll be there in fifteen minutes."

I went into the bedroom, put on some makeup, and spent five minutes trying to do something interesting with my hair before giving up and sticking it into a ponytail. I spent a few more minutes plumping cushions and blowing dust out of corners, back into the air. Then I took the clothespin off the kitchen curtains, reopened them a crack, and stood at the sink waiting for the great legs to arrive.

He had roses.

"I cut them through the neighbour's fence," he said when I thanked him. "I hope you realize that I nearly lost an eye when she blasted me with her aphid spray."

"She didn't," I said, trying to find a vase.

"No," he said. "But I thought you might appreciate them more. What's with the clothespins?"

"There's been a peeping Tom in the neighbour-hood," I said quickly. "Would you like something to drink?"

"No, thanks. I just came over to seduce you." He stood behind me and put his arms around me. "Did you dream about me last night?"

No. But I'd lain awake half the night thinking about his thighs. I said, "I don't remember."

He nuzzled the back of my neck. "You smell great."

"Acid rain," I murmured, pressing my ponytail against his throat. "Did you remember to ask your mother about tomorrow night?"

"Edna." He pulled away and turned me around to face him. "Am I boring you? You don't seem too responsive."

Good thing he didn't have a humidistat down my shorts. "I just wanted to get that one thing out of the way," I said. "Then I'll be extremely responsive."

He smiled. "My mother said it was okay, and to meet her at the same time again."

"Good," I said, thinking with relief that by tomorrow evening my involvement with Gerald and the goblet would be finished. "Now, let's sit down."

We went into the living room, and somehow I ended up flat out on the couch with Michael on top of me. He put his face close to mine and said quietly, "I'm going to kiss you."

But before I could even part my lips and get my tongue ready, he had rolled both of us down onto the floor and was undoing my shoelaces.

"Whatever happened to kissing?" I gasped.

"We'll get to it, Edna. Be patient." He pulled off my running shoes and my socks, and then he took my right foot into his hands and began to accomplish things with my toes and his mouth that I would never have imagined possible if I hadn't already seen how he ate tomatoes. When he was finished with the toes, he lingered for a while on the tops of my feet, moved to the ankles, and then doubled back to the soles.

After he had more than competently entertained my right foot, he carried on with the left, and then moved leisurely up to my calves. I was beginning to forget about wanting my mouth kissed. When he got to my knees he whispered, "Do you like this?" and I could hardly croak out a reply. I thought for certain I was going to pass out.

And then the door buzzer sounded, three times.

Michael's head shot up. I could actually see his pupils contract. "Are you expecting anyone?" he asked.

"No," I said hoarsely. I raised my leg a little, just to get his mind back on the affair at hand, but he sat up against the couch.

"You'd better see who it is," he said. I was impressed by how steady his voice was. It occurred to me that perhaps he hadn't been as carried away as I had.

"No," I said. "Ignore it."

Michael stared at me curiously. The buzzer went off again. "I think you should answer it. You never know. It might be important."

Somehow I managed to stand up and get to the door without collapsing. I unlocked it and pulled it open, thinking vaguely that if the thug had come back to threaten me, I could get Michael to threaten him.

"Ms. Heathcott? May I come in?"

I stood back to let him walk by me. "Detective Owl," I said with stunning composure, "this is my friend Michael. Michael, Detective Owl. Back in civilian clothes, I see."

"Pleased to meet you," said Detective Owl, offering his hand to Michael. "Stephen Owl."

"Stephen," I said. "But I get to call you Detective."

Michael raised his eyebrows, but he moved my shoes and socks out of the way and offered half of the couch to Detective Owl.

"I hope I haven't caught you at a bad time," said Detective Owl, staring at my shoes.

"Oh, no," I said. "Would you like a drink? I think I'm going to have something very cold. A glass of juice and soda water."

"That sounds good," said Detective Owl.

"Make it three," said Michael.

I went into the kitchen and got out a can of apple juice and a bottle of club soda. I mixed three drinks with ice cubes and carried them back into the living room.

"So, you're the man in charge of this Grobbelaar business," Michael was saying.

"Yes." Detective Owl nodded. "That's me."

"Have you got the guy yet? The one who did it?"

"Not yet. "But we're making good headway, I think."

"Tell us about it," I suggested as I passed out the juice.

He smiled tightly. "You know we've discussed this already."

"He has special rules," I explained to Michael. "He's not allowed to give out clues until he's got the whole thing wrapped up. Otherwise we might figure it out ourselves and warn the murderer to escape."

Detective Owl gave Michael a look that said, She's flipped her lid, but we'll humour her until she talks herself to death.

Michael folded my socks.

"The reason I'm here," said Detective Owl in his polite-in-front-of-company voice, "is that I need your help in a related matter, Ms. Heathcott, and I was hoping that you'd feel up to giving us a hand."

The only person I was up to giving a hand to at that moment was Michael, but I would never have said so. "What's it about?" I asked with a slight smile.

Detective Owl glanced over at Michael.

I winked at Detective Owl, and said, "It's okay, he can be trusted. He's one of us."

I noticed Michael's shoulders twitching.

Detective Owl spoke to my original Spencer. "Someone has come forward with a claim on the Heinz Grobbelaar collection."

"Aha." I nodded, feeling a sudden pang of anxiety.

"The fifteenth-century religious artifacts." I somehow kept myself from glancing at my kitchen cupboard and rubbed my hands together, as if in glee, but really to keep them from trembling.

"This man is a rather important person," Detective Owl went on, "and I'm afraid I can't mention his name."

"Of course not," I murmured, nodding again. "I understand completely. How is it that I can help you?" I sipped my juice.

"I wouldn't ask," said Detective Owl, somewhat nervously himself, I thought, "except that I've learned you're something of an expert on Renaissance artifacts." He took several quick swallows from his glass and emptied it.

"You are?" said Michael, breaking into a broad grin.

"Sort of," I said modestly. "My special interest at university was the recovery of art treasures taken by the Germans during the Second World War."

"So I've found out," said Detective Owl. "And what I need to know is whether you could give me your impression of where this collection might have originated."

"So if what I say clicks with what this other guy says, then you'll know he's on the level."

"Exactly," said Detective Owl, looking rather relieved.

"Well," I said, banging my glass down on the coffee table, "you sure have a lot of nerve!"

"Edna," Michael said gently.

"It's all right," said Detective Owl. "I think I understand her frustration."

"Sure you do," I said loudly. "You refuse to give me even one speck of information to help with my investigation, and yet you expect me to fall all over myself telling you everything I know."

"*Your* investigation?" said Michael.

"She's playing Miss Marple," said Detective Owl, shrugging.

"I am not!"

"It's quite a normal reaction," Detective Owl continued calmly. "Very often we find that people who discover a murder feel inexplicably responsible for seeing the case to its conclusion."

"I see," Michael said thoughtfully. He raised his glass to his mouth and drank some juice. I could see his throat moving.

"No, you don't," I said. "He's belittling me. Don't listen to him."

"Of course I'm not," Detective Owl said, crunching an ice cube between his teeth. "I'm simply stating a fact. Edna is over-reacting now because of some earlier run-ins we've had."

"Run-ins?" said Michael. He set his half-empty glass on the floor beside my shoes.

"This is crazy," I said. "I'm certainly not going to help you. I'm under no legal obligation here. Find someone else who can do it."

Detective Owl shook his head. "I guess I forgot to mention the consulting fee." He took out his notebook.

"Consulting fee?" I repeated stupidly.

"Of course. What do you usually charge for a consultation of this kind?"

"Oh." I looked at the Spencer and smiled. "Fifteen hundred and seventy-two dollars."

Detective Owl opened his notebook. "That shouldn't be a problem. I have a fairly reasonable expense account."

"Well," I said, picking up my glass. "Who wants more juice?"

eight

Dr. Harold Cunderlik's office was in a large old house on St. Clair Avenue near Forest Hill Road. It had been converted into ten suites for optometrists, family practitioners, and dentists. A wide central staircase led up to the second floor, where there were benches with their backs to the railing to seat the waiting patients. Dr. Cunderlik's office was 2C, the erstwhile master bedroom.

A window had been cut into the wall beside the door, and a receptionist sat behind it. The wheels of her swivel chair clicked as she rolled away from her typewriter to greet me.

"I'm Edna Heathcott. I have an appointment with Dr. Cunderlik."

"Oh, yes," she said. She looked as though she'd been caught in a time warp. Her face was coated with pink powder, and she was wearing a pair of old-fashioned cat's-eye glasses. She looked at her appointment book. "Oh, yes," she said again. "You're our nine-forty-five. Have you seen Dr. Cunderlik before?"

"Not as a patient. As I explained to you over the phone last week, my regular optometrist is on vacation, and I — "

"Oh, that probably wasn't me," she said, patting her ash-coloured beehive. "I'd remember your name. When did you make your appointment?"

"Friday. Last Friday."

"Well, that definitely wasn't me, then. I used to work only Mondays and Thursdays. Now, of course, I'm on full-time." She pulled a file card out of a box on her desk and handed it to me with a pen. "Fill this out. Name, address, OHIP number. Can you see it all right?"

"Well enough," I said, affecting a squint for her benefit.

"It's a real tragedy," she sighed, wheeling back to the typewriter. "I don't suppose you knew Miss Dellarosa if this is your first time here. I never actually knew her myself, her being here on Tuesdays, Wednesdays, and Fridays and all, and me being here on Mondays and Thursdays. You know?"

I was so astonished that I was barely able to nod in agreement. Anna Dellarosa had been Harold Cunderlik's receptionist?

"But it just horrifies me," the woman went on, "to think that here I am, typing where she typed, sitting where she sat. I even found a box of her cookies in the file cabinet this morning. Poor Anna. Makes my hair stand on end, almost."

Not under all that hair spray, I thought. "What," I asked, noticing that all of a sudden my own was not exactly lying flat, "happened to Ms. Dellarosa?"

The receptionist folded her spotty hands on her lap and leaned slightly forward. "Killed," she whispered.

"Killed?" I repeated in the same hushed tone. No wonder she hadn't answered her phone yesterday! I swallowed. "How did it happen?" I would have bet a thousand dollars that she was going to say exposure of the throat to a sharp object.

But she whipped out a turquoise Kleenex, blotted her eyes, and said, "A bicycle accident. A bus . . . a bus squashed her."

"Oh, my God," I murmured. It couldn't have been murder, then. Unless the killer was becoming more daringly original in his approach. "The poor woman! When did it happen?"

The receptionist seemed to find nothing unusual in the fact that I wanted to know more. If anything, she seemed delighted that I was showing an interest in more than just the latest thing in bifocals. She leaned back in her chair and put her hands on the armrests.

"Saturday afternoon, it was. Late afternoon. She was on her way home from somewhere. She was only two blocks south of her apartment building, riding her bicycle north. That's how they figured out she was going home. Anyways, she was going to turn the corner, onto her street, you see, a right-hand turn? And, ohhh, I guess the bus driver didn't see her. . . ." She sniffed and straightened herself up. "Well, you'd better get that form done. Dr. C. will be ready for you in a minute."

I nodded and began to fill out the card, but I could hardly concentrate. What if Anna Dellarosa had been Heinz Grobbelaar's killer and, in a sudden fit of remorse, had turned her bicycle into the path of the biggest vehicle available?

"He never even stopped, either," the receptionist said suddenly.

"What?" I looked up from my card.

"The bus driver," she sighed. "He drove three blocks before he realized that he was pulling an extra load behind the back wheel. It was her bicycle, though. Not her. Oh, my! Did you think I meant . . . ? Oh, no! She was still back there, stuck to the pavement."

"That's dreadful." I passed the card back to her.

She stood up and opened the door to let me into the examination room where she motioned to a thickly padded chair in front of an eye-examining apparatus.

"The doctor will be right in," she said, and left.

I looked around the room. It was painted pale blue and had grey and blue linoleum tiles laid out in a checkerboard on the floor. Around the chair were scuff marks where, I presumed, Dr. Cunderlik did most of his standing and adjusting. The lens apparatus was a horrific-looking thing, like something you'd see at Madame Tussaud's for popping out eyeballs. I glanced towards the receptionist's door. I could hear her typing. That meant that she could also hear me in case I had to scream.

Then Dr. Cunderlik came in. He was reading my card.

"Good morning," I said.

He looked at me and frowned, and I shrank back a little in the chair. But then suddenly he broke into a smile and said, "Ah! Now I remember. I knew your name was familiar. Fineberg's, right?"

"Right." I smiled weakly. "The ex-Fineberg's."

"Oh, yes. I heard about that. Most unfortunate."

Not as unfortunate as losing your receptionist under the wheels of a bus, I wanted to say. But I shook my head and agreed. "Most."

He pulled on a pair of rubber gloves as he approached. They were yellowish and powdery, and they made the black hairs on the backs of his hands and fingers look like some vile parasite burrowing under his skin.

"Don't mind these," he said, wiggling his fingers at me. "I don't think we can transfer germs through finger-to-eye contact, but I have a slight abrasion on my palm, and I'd rather play it safe. Actually, I don't really have to touch your eyes at all."

Thank God for that, I thought, wondering what I had got myself into.

"Shall we get started?" he asked.

The first thing he had me do was read the eye chart on the wall. He turned the chair around and stood behind me, offering banal little bits of encouragement as I got down to the lower lines.

"Well, it certainly looks like you need reading glasses, anyway," he clucked.

"I do?"

"We'll see if there are any other problems," he continued cheerfully. "Getting lots of headaches?"

"No," I said glumly. "I never get headaches."

"Lucky you," he said, spinning the chair around so that my eyes were lined up with the eyeball-extracting machine. "Now, I want you to tell me when it gets easier to see." He began to turn some dials so that different lenses fell into place in front of my eyes. I decided that since my mouth was still free to move, even if the rest of my face wasn't, I might as well start trying to find out what I wanted to know.

"Too bad about Mr. Grobbelaar, eh?" I said chattily.

He paused for an instant before he flipped another lens into position. Then he said rather loudly, considering that his mouth was only about two feet away from my face, "Yes, it certainly was a shock. Never knew the man myself, of course." He turned his back on me, and I thought that would be it, but then he chuckled. "My wife, now, there's a different story. Do you know she used to do half of her Christmas shopping at The Chocolate Box? Got me a great pair of binoculars last year. I'm a birdwatcher, you know."

I'll bet you are, I thought. But I said politely, "Are you really? Now, that looks much clearer."

"Figured it would," he said. "You also have a slight astigmatism in your left eye."

"Is it serious?"

"You'll need a pair of glasses," he said. "But it's not contagious, if that's what you want to know." He made a sound that was frighteningly close to a giggle.

I said, "Glasses. Well."

Dr. Cunderlik cleared his throat. He seemed suddenly agitated. "Since you're here, Edna, I've got a little story you might be interested in."

I pulled my head away from the lens apparatus. "Really?" I breathed, feeling certain that I was on the verge of a major breakthrough in my search for the Grobbelaar killer.

But Harold Cunderlik proceeded to spend the next few minutes telling me — his eyebrows waggling frenziedly — that if he could only scrape together the dough, he'd found someone who was willing to part with an early Milne, privately. I tried to wheel the conversation back to the subject of Grobbelaar, but he seemed to take no notice. The guy was an art addict. He was fortunate that his wife was both extraordinarily wealthy and fond of him.

I decided to take a different tack. "I was very sorry to hear about your receptionist."

"Oh, God, yes," he muttered, walking around to the other side of the lens machine. "Did you see the picture in the paper?"

"Of the accident? They printed it in the paper?"

I could see the top of his balding head over the machine. He was shaking it. "Those tabloids! You never know what they're going to come up with next. I open the paper to check the weather, and instead I see my receptionist splashed across the third page."

I nearly closed my eyes and gave up. But, just in time, I remembered the real reason for my visit. "I tend to favour the society columns myself," I said quickly. This was as far from the truth as I could get while still maintaining a straight face. "I noticed that your wife was off to another charity ball last Tuesday."

"Was she?" he said vaguely. "Oh, yes. That ball. What's it called? Violet or something. Everyone wears the same colour, and they all match the table napkins.

She likes those things. I don't. But she's been going to them since she was sixteen, so I guess they're second nature to her now. Well, I think that should do it. I'll go and make up your prescription. You can have it filled across the hall in 2F. They've got quite a nice selection of frames there. I'm sure you can find something you like."

"Thank you, Dr. Cunderlik," I said. "I hope to see you downtown again soon. And I hope you get your Milne."

"What? Oh, thank you, Edna. Thank you very much."

He went into the back room, and I headed for the front desk to wait for my prescription. This time as I passed I took a quick peek into the cupboard behind the desk. It was divided into two sections. Cardboard name tags had been slipped into brass holders above the coat hooks. One said Marion, the other Anna. There was a pair of red rubber boots on Anna's side. For some reason, their presence seemed even sadder than the thought of Anna's picture being run in the blood-and-gore section of the paper.

"Tell me something," I said to Marion the receptionist. "Would you happen to know what Ms. Dellarosa was doing last Tuesday evening?"

She stared at me. "Now that's a funny thing for you to want to know."

"I'm sorry. You probably think I'm crazy. But there's an Anna Dellarosa in my Tuesday night Bible study group, and I'm just wondering if it might be the same one."

"Oh," she said, looking satisfied. "Well, I honestly couldn't tell you. I didn't know her well enough. Is yours short and blonde?"

"Tall and dark."

"Can't be the same one, then."

"Thank goodness," I said. "I spent my whole appointment worrying for nothing."

"He seems kind of distraught, doesn't he?" she whispered with a sideways glance and a toss of her lacquered head.

Not by my reckoning. But maybe Marion was a more sensitive soul than I. Dr. Cunderlik had seemed more concerned about the possible loss of the Milne than about the actual loss of his receptionist. But I said, shaking my head, "He probably shouldn't be working today."

"Just what I think," Marion replied.

At that point Dr. Cunderlik reappeared with my prescription, and I thanked him once again before heading over to 2F to get the pair of glasses I hadn't even realized I needed.

"So, how did it go?" Michael asked when he phoned at noon.

"Wonderfully well," I answered. "It cost me two hundred and thirty-two dollars plus tax, and I found out that I'm lucky to be able to get around without knocking myself unconscious. How's your day shaping up?"

"Great. We just got a new contract for a housing development north of the city. How did you spend two hundred and thirty-two dollars? I thought eye exams were covered."

"They are. But glasses aren't."

"Glasses?" I couldn't tell if he was amused or horrified.

"Uh-oh," I said. "Does this spell doom for us?"

"Of course not," he said genially. "I can't wait to see how you look wearing only your glasses. And just think what you might have been missing of me. I may look completely different to you now. Do these glasses make things look bigger?"

"That's the last thing you need," I said warmly. "Tell me something."

"Yes, I do."

"Do what?"

"Want to see you tonight."

"I'm seeing your mother tonight"

"So? See me after. I'll meet you."

"Okay. But that's not what I wanted to know. I was wondering if you think it's possible to kill yourself with a bus without the driver noticing."

"What?" he exclaimed.

"Do you think it would be possible to dive under the back wheels as the bus was turning a corner?"

"Edna," he said calmly, "having to wear glasses is not the end of the world."

"You're funny," I said. "But it's not me. It's someone else. It's already done."

"Oh. Does this have something to do with Grobbelaar?"

"Maybe. I'm not sure."

"Well, I guess it's possible. Although I'd think the subway would be neater. More instantaneous, that's for sure."

"That's what I've been thinking, too. So chances are it wasn't suicide. Why bother trying to destroy your bike, too? Don't most people who kill themselves give away personal possessions like bikes before they do it?"

"What?"

"This woman was on her bicycle, apparently on her way home, when the accident happened."

"Oh! You mean that one in Scarborough? I saw it in the paper. Can you believe the shit people want to look at?"

111

"Do me a favour, Michael. Have you got the paper?"

"It's at home somewhere. It's Sunday's."

"Can you save it? I want to see it."

"Fine," he said agreeably. "Anything else I can do for you?"

"Nothing I can think of offhand."

"How about with hand?"

So I gave him a few suggestions, just to make his call worthwhile, and then we hung up after arranging to meet at Bloor and Bay at nine o'clock.

MRS. CIPOLLONE WAS WAITING for me inside the back door of the Grobbelaar building. She seemed happy to see me, but more than a little on edge.

"I no understand why you want to come beck here again," she said as she held the door open for me.

I didn't show her my camera. "It's the collection," I said vaguely. "This may be my last opportunity to see it."

She shook her head and then grinned. "Hey, you hev a nice time at de zoo yesterday?"

"The zoo?"

She narrowed her eyes. "You no go to de zoo yesterday afternoon?"

I thought fast, groping for a reasonable response. But not fast enough.

"Oh, my son," she said sorrowfully. "He very lies. He tell me he take you to de zoo yesterday. You no see him again, eh?"

"But I did," I said, trying not to giggle like a moron. "We went out for a coffee instead. I wasn't up to looking at animals yesterday." Just acting like one.

"Ah!" She beamed. "Very nice, very nice. Maybe you like him a leettle, no?"

I smiled. "He's not bad."

"You come to my house whenever you like. My

hosband tink you very nice girl. He say you hev strong hends. Okay, you go up for look around, and I clean dis place."

She gave me the key, and I bounded up the stairs, pulling on my evening gloves as I went.

This time I headed straight for the study. I flicked on the ceiling light and took the box of postcards out of the desk drawer. I leaned one of the cards against the box and turned on the flash.

I took the picture side first, and then the message side. Then I put it back in the box and did the next one. It took me about fifteen minutes to do the entire box of twenty-three. I used up the last few exposures of the second film on some of the pieces in Grobbelaar's collection.

When I went back downstairs, Mrs. Cipollone was wiping down the glass counter at the front of the store. I ducked in behind the condom partition and slid the Bruno's box to the back of the leg-parts shelf. I wondered fleetingly if I should take the time to search for a bottle of edible toenail polish, but I decided that my best move would be to get out of there as quickly as I could. I went back to the broom closet to wait for Mrs. Cipollone.

"Seems kind of strange that you have to clean, even though no one's been in here," I said when she returned. "Wouldn't you think you'd get a holiday or something?"

"Oh, it's okay," she said. "Maybe I no work here too much more, anyway. I hev very bad veins in my legs. I get tired too fest. Maybe I like to sit down more."

"You're going to retire?" I said. "How long have you cleaned here, anyway?"

"Oh, maybe four years. I tink it's too lung, now." She sat down on her chair. "When you gonna come beck to my house?"

"Maybe next weekend," I said. "Michael will tell you."

"Dat's nice." She smiled. "Okay. You go now. I finish for put my stoff away."

I went through the alley back to Hazelton Avenue and walked past Fineberg's. The lights were out. The painting that had once been displayed under lights in the front window at night had been taken down, and the chains that had supported it dangled uselessly.

There was a dim light behind the smoked-glass door of the Lillian Allford Gallery, and it lit up the giant LA that was her logo. I decided that after I was through with my appointment with Detective Owl the following morning I'd go in and speak with Lillian about the possibility of her giving me some new information for my Grobbelaar notebook. Then I might even ask her for a job.

Michael came by the Bay-Bloor intersection five minutes early. It was just as well, since I had been waiting ten already.

"You got what you wanted?" he asked.

"Exactly," I said, smiling. "Did you remember to bring the newspaper with you?"

"I would have remembered, but I haven't been home. You should have asked my mother to bring it. Did you eat already?"

"Michael, it's almost nine o'clock. I had dinner at six."

"Could you eat a sandwich? If you don't mind the drive, I'll take you to my favourite place."

They weren't sandwiches. They were monster buns with slabs of breaded veal and a load of oily roasted red peppers stuffed inside. Michael ordered them in Italian over the counter of a dark little bakery on Caledonia that could have been the headquarters for some Sicilian assassination squad. I was glad to get safely back to the car.

We ate the veal buns on the way to my apartment and left a trail of roasted pepper fumes from the car to my door, against which Michael pushed me with the force of a large, muscular man crazed with lust, as soon as my feet hit the bottom step.

"I've been waiting all day for this," he informed me, pressing his body against mine. "Do you know I had to keep the business section folded across my lap for my entire meeting this morning?"

"Aren't you going to let me open the door first?" I asked, trying to fish the key out of my purse. "Or are we going to do it right here in the hall?"

"Whatever you prefer," he said, putting most of my ear into his mouth and breathing gently.

It is not easy to insert a key into a doorknob when your back is flush with the door and there is a full-grown man flush with you, but at last I managed it. The door flew open, and we went with it.

"Would you like something to drink?" I asked from under the coffee table. "I have a bottle of wine in the cupboard."

"Maybe in an hour or so," said Michael, and he dragged me feet first into the bedroom, where he showed me something a lot better than a trip to the zoo.

nine

My PHONE RANG AT SEVEN-THIRTY the next morning.

"Edna?" Gerald whispered.

"Where were you?" I demanded.

"I can explain. But not now. Have you got it?"

"No, I haven't. I put it back. Did you kill Grobbelaar?"

"*No.* I told you that already. You put it back?"

"Exactly where I found it."

"I'm dead, Edna. I'm dead. Say goodbye. I'm going to my reward."

"Don't be ridiculous, Gerald. There are no rewards for your behaviour."

He hung up.

DETECTIVE OWL RANG MY BUZZER an hour later.

"Well, this is certainly a pleasant turn of events," I said as he held the patrol car door open for me. "I thought you might be planning to cage me in the back."

"Look, Edna," he said. "I'm sorry you feel you're getting short shrift out of this deal, but I think it'd be better for both of us if we tried to get along, okay?"

"Why is that?" I asked.

He cleared his throat and said, "I imagine you'll feel just as relieved as I do when we bring in the person who killed Grobbelaar. And the more you can help me, the sooner that will be."

"I see. What about your helping me?"

"You seem to be managing fine on your own," he said coolly.

"What's that supposed to mean?"

"I think you know what I'm talking about." He kept his eyes on the traffic.

"Detective Owl," I said. "Could you stop at that photo lab over there, please? I have some film to drop off."

"Can't you do it later?"

"I'd rather do it now, if you don't mind."

He sighed and pulled the car into the buses' and taxis' lane. I ran into the store and ordered one-hour service.

"Thanks a lot," I said when I got back into the car. "That was a real help." We drove for a few minutes before I brought up Anna Dellarosa.

"I knew this was coming," he groaned.

"Well? What do you expect me to ask you about? What you ate for breakfast? Don't you think it was kind of a coincidence?"

"That's all it was. A coincidence."

"Balls! She was probably pushed, and you know it."

"Pushed?" he snorted. "Don't you think that pushing a woman under a bus would be a pretty idiotic thing to do?"

"I didn't say it wasn't. But that doesn't mean someone didn't do it. Slashing a throat is pretty idiotic, too, if you ask me."

"The bus driver said she was alone. The street was empty. He thought she'd stopped, and she probably thought he'd given her the right of way. That's all there is to it. It was a sad accident."

"That's what it looked like," I said, raising my eyebrows. "Did you check her body for drugs?"

"Edna!"

"Stephen! You said we couldn't discuss the

Grobbelaar case. If this really was just an accident, then you should feel quite free to talk about it. What if someone knew that she was going to be on her bike and purposely drugged her?"

"Hoping that a bus would conveniently drive over her?" He smirked. "Face it, Edna. You're way off base. This is typical of what I've been warning you about. Your inexperience is leading you to all kinds of conclusions that a professional would never make."

"But was she impaired? That's all I want to know."

"No, she wasn't."

"So — " I smiled " — you checked."

"Of course we checked. It's routine."

"Okay. But that doesn't mean she was still seeing and thinking straight."

"What?"

"What if she'd been really upset about something?"

"Now you're suggesting suicide?"

"Not necessarily. In fact, I really doubt it. But what if she was feeling completely unbalanced because of something she'd recently done? Maybe she was emotionally overwrought, and not paying much attention to what else was going on around her. Did you ask any of her associates if she seemed distracted?"

"If you're about to tell me that Anna Dellarosa killed Heinz Grobbelaar, you might as well forget it. She had an alibi for last Tuesday evening with at least forty witnesses to back it up, some of whom we actually managed to track down."

"What was that? Oh, don't make a face! She's gone now, so you're not breaching any confidentiality rules."

He took a deep breath, as if he were about to lose his job over it, and said, "She was a singer in a bar band."

"Don't tell me!" I cried. "Country?"

He nodded.

"So that's why she talked like Loretta Lynn."

"You talked to her?" he snapped, frowning. "When?"

"Just over the phone."

"You called her?" His voice was really loud, almost shouting, and all of a sudden he seemed to be paying more attention to me than he was to the road. Maybe if he actually did have a photographic memory he could drive using the glance-and-blink method, like flashing a sudden bright light in a dark room and knowing exactly where everything was in a split second.

"I'm afraid that's privileged information," I said quietly, hoping that the tone would catch on.

"What did you say to her?" He looked as though he were about to burst into flames and explode or run a red light.

"Oh, calm down," I said. "I didn't even know it was her. I had to get my eyes checked, and she happened to be working the day I made my appointment. I didn't even mention Grobbelaar, if that's what you're worried about."

"I hope to hell you didn't."

"Why? Oh, dammit, will you lay off the garbage about confidentiality? You talk about trying to get along, but you seem to take great delight in watching me bash my head against the wall. Anyway, if I were you, I'd be more worried about Harold Cunderlik than Anna Dellarosa."

"You're bluffing. You have no idea what you're saying."

"I know what I'm feeling. And I feel that Cunderlik has something to hide."

"Well, you might as well cancel your appointment. I don't want you going near him."

"Too late. We're talking after the fact."

"Jesus Christ," he said. "And I suppose you told him everything you know."

I gave up on the gentle approach. "How stupid do

you think I am?" I yelled. "I think I know something about discretion, although I'm sure you'd never admit it."

"What did you say to him?" he asked, lowering his voice slightly.

"I was just checking his wife's alibi. So now I know that she didn't do it. As for Harold, I really don't know. He seems nervous about something, expecially when you mention Grobbelaar. He glosses over it, as if he doesn't really hear. And then he runs off at the mouth about something else entirely."

"And what did he say to you?"

"That I have an astigmatism and I'm short-sighted. I have to get glasses."

"I mean, what was he running off at the mouth about?"

"His collection. He has this psychological thing about buying paintings. Gerald always had quite a time with him. Cunderlik will look at a hundred paintings and not feel a thing. But then, all of a sudden, he'll see one that he can't live without, and he'll make himself sick worrying that someone else will grab it first. I've known him to call the gallery ten times in a day, just to make sure that the one he wants hasn't been stuck with someone else's red sticker."

"What's he waiting for?"

"Partly the money. He has to get Dottie to give him his allowance, although God knows why she puts up with him. The other thing, I think, is like delayed pleasure. He gets off on the thrill of knowing he might lose it. The stupid thing is that most of the time no one else is even remotely interested in the painting he wants. He just likes to create this fantasy that there are important people out there who feel he's big-time competition."

"That's crazy."

"I'll say. How he ever managed to hook someone like Dottie, I'll never know. She seems like such a responsible woman. Maybe her thing is having a husband who's genuinely cowed by her. Anyway, I'm of the opinion that Harold has done something that he doesn't want Dottie to know about, and he's scared silly that she's going to find out. I also think that Grobbelaar knew about it, and Harold was probably paying him to keep his mouth shut. And since I couldn't just come out and ask him what he was doing last Tuesday, I can't cross him off my list of suspects."

Detective Owl stared at me. "Well," he said, "that still puts you a pace or two behind us."

"You mean you know what he was doing last Tuesday?"

"I know what he says he was doing."

"But we have no witnesses."

"We did have one sure bet. But out of the other forty, we can't seem to find one who remembers. I'm afraid Dr. Cunderlik doesn't have a particularly memorable face."

I blinked. "You mean Harold Cunderlik is a country music fan?"

He turned up one side of his mouth and raised his eyebrows. "Now you know everything I know about Harold Cunderlik . . . except what he did to merit a blackmail attempt."

"Attempt? You mean he refused to pay?"

I could tell that Detective Owl was torn between telling me (and reaping the enjoyment of proving that he knew more than I did) and not telling me (and starting another argument). He decided in favour of looking smart. "Cunderlik says he never paid. I think he's telling the truth. Apparently Grobbelaar only approached him a few weeks ago, and Cunderlik managed to hold him off. I think he told him that he'd need some time to get the money together."

"He would have, too," I agreed. "He'd probably have had to sell a painting. He couldn't have asked Dottie for the money." I snickered. "That would have been ironic! All right. Tell me what he did. Was it illegal?"

"No."

"So he's not going to get dragged into court or anything."

Detective Owl shook his head. "You're getting carried away again."

"Well, I wouldn't have to, if you'd tell me what I want to know. Okay. Skip it. Who's the guy who says he owns Grobbelaar's stuff? I'm dying to see it, by the way."

"I'm sure I'll be able to tell you later," he said. "But you must realize that if I tell you now you may be biased in your assessment."

"But you've already told me it's fifteenth-century Italian. Isn't that going to bias me?"

"Let's just see what happens," he said quietly.

He parked in a no-parking zone with his Constable on Duty sign in the windshield. I felt rather self-conscious climbing the steps to The Chocolate Box with a police detective behind me, almost as if I'd been arrested and was being taken back to the scene of whatever crime I'd committed. Detective Owl unlocked the door and held it open for me.

"Quite a place, eh?" I said, as he closed the door behind us. "Do you know what all these things are for?"

He ignored me and walked to the back of the store, to the door I'd gone through the day I found the body. I felt a twist of apprehension in my gut. He opened the door and motioned me up the stairs.

"I hope this isn't too upsetting for you," he said.

"I think I can keep a grip on myself," I replied, trying to affect a dazed, troubled look that spoke of some recent trauma. It wasn't difficult to do. "Is everything cleaned up?"

"Oh, we move pretty quickly these days," he replied jauntily. "Forensic was out of here by Thursday afternoon." He unlocked the door at the top of the stairs.

I tried not to look immediately at the glass case. I tried to recreate the feeling of surprise and awe I had experienced the first time I'd entered the apartment. Detective Owl watched me expectantly.

"It's incredible!" I breathed, gazing slowly around the room. "You told me, but I never imagined . . . ! There must be several million dollars' worth of stuff up here. And that's just a preliminary estimate." I walked over to the display case and put my fingertips onto one of the doors, holding my face as close as I could without leaving a nose smudge on the glass. "May I handle them?"

He shrugged. "You're the expert. Do what you have to do."

"I notice that someone's already been here," I said with my back to him. "One piece seems to be missing. Did you already take it out?"

"It's evidence," he said ambiguously.

"All right," I said, turning around to face him again. "I think the best thing to do is make up a quick catalogue. Is there a table or a desk somewhere where I can sit down and write?"

"There's a study over there," he said, pointing.

"Oh, great. Maybe what I'll do is take out the things one at a time and make a few notes. Darn! Too bad I don't have a camera with me. I could have snapped a shot of each piece as we go."

"I can get you one," said Detective Owl. "Let me phone in to the station." He went to the kitchen and used the white Contempraphone by the fridge. I wondered if the rotten meat was still festering inside.

I watched him from the living room. He was staring into space unblinking, puzzling, perhaps, over some aspect of the Grobbelaar case that had escaped him. Tall foreheads suggest large brains; he must have had a doozer. He had a pleasant face, with a well-shaped mouth. He began to smile at someone at the other end, and I could see his teeth. They were perfectly even, except for rather elongated canines. I became quite absorbed in studying him.

"Edna?" he said. "Oh, I'm sorry. I didn't mean to startle you."

"That's all right." I smiled. "I was just wondering whether to start at the top or the bottom."

He smiled back. "An officer will be here to take the pictures in about forty-five minutes."

"Great. Let's get going."

I had brought a fresh notebook with me, and I used a page for each object, writing a brief description of each, noting any special characteristics that I felt were pertinent to my assessment. Detective Owl sat quietly in a chair beside me. I could feel him watching me.

"You don't have to stay, you know," I said after a while. "I'm not frightened of being here by myself."

"I have to stay," he replied. "You can't be here alone. Am I bothering you?"

"No," I said. "But you should be out looking for clues, shouldn't you?"

"That can wait." He gave me a smile that was almost warm, then added promptly, "But don't let me distract you from your work."

"No," I said. "Never."

The other officer arrived and spent ten minutes shooting close-ups of everything in the collection. I got the impression from the way he adjusted the positions of the artifacts that he was more used to dealing with bodies with tape marks around them than marble sculptures.

"So what does this bigwig do for a living?" I asked after the photographer had left.

"Who? The fellow who claims he owns these?"

I nodded.

"I can't tell you that," he said apologetically.

"Of course not," I said. "Well, I can tell you one thing. He's got to be pretty bold to come forward because I'd say that most of these pieces, if not all of them, have been stolen from churches. Are you sure he's not some con artist who wants to cash in on Grobbelaar's death?"

"I'd guess not," said Detective Owl. "What makes you so certain that they've been stolen from churches?"

"Churches don't sell this stuff," I said emphatically. "And they sure don't give it away. Did you know that there's almost as much money in stolen religious relics as there is in stolen paintings? That's why so many European churches look so empty now. They weren't always that way. They've been looted."

"Okay," he said. "Let's assume that you're right. Would you say that this might also belong to the collection?" He reached into his pocket and pulled out a small zip-lock bag, the kind that jewellers use to package cheap jewellery. Inside it was a round, amber-coloured stone, with a dark, pea-sized spot in the middle.

I had a feeling that I knew where it belonged. "Looks like a marble," I said, taking the bag from him and trying to be casual. "Or an eyeball. Where did you find it?"

"In the shop. Under a shelf just outside the door to the stairs."

"I don't know much about gems," I admitted. "But I

suppose it could belong to the collection." I took a deep breath. "Do you think it has anything to do with the murder?"

"Possibly. We only found Grobbelaar's prints on it."

"So it wasn't just dropped in the shop, then."

"No." He took the bag back and stuck it in his pocket. "Now, what I'd like to know is where you think this collection came from."

"You already know they're Italian."

"Yes. But I want an area. Italy wasn't even Italy in the fifteenth century. Are they Roman? Florentine? Venetian? What?"

I looked at the cabinet. "The difficulty with what you're asking me is that they may not have all come from the same place."

He shook his head. "This . . . gentleman seems to think they have."

I touched the face of a fourteen-inch-high marble Madonna. "She's beautiful, isn't she? She doesn't look as though she came from any of the well-noted schools. She's sort of simple looking. Take a look at the drapery. I'd almost say that she was the fifteenth-century equivalent of folk art. Probably carved by someone who did something else for a living. Maybe some peasant who had a special love for the church." I picked it up and looked at the bottom. "There's nothing written here. No date, or even initials. But that's good, isn't it? You'd think that if this were carved by a peasant, he wouldn't know how to sign his own name anyway."

I put the Madonna back on the shelf and concentrated on the pewter chalice next to the space where the goblet should have been. "I'll have to do some research before I can tell you for certain. But I'd say that they came from a church in a town, not a city. Even the small chapels in Rome and Florence had the same kinds of sculpture and tapestries as the larger ones."

"Better than this, you mean."

"No. Not better. More formal. More distinguished. I'd say that in their day these were probably considered to be poor imitations of what you could find in the city churches."

"But today?"

"They're the work of people who never made it to the big time. But that doesn't mean that they're not worth a heck of a lot of money."

"Where's the town?"

"Well, there's definitely more of a Roman influence than a Florentine one. I'd say middle or south. More likely middle."

"That's it?" said Detective Owl. "I was hoping you could get a little closer than that."

"How much time do I get to make my report?"

He looked at his watch. "How does a week sound?"

"Okay," I said with a nod. "In a week I'll try to give you the closest region. I don't think I can get more specific than that."

"That's fine," he said. "Now how about some lunch?"

ten

BEFORE DETECTIVE OWL PICKED me up that morning, I'd spent an hour going over Grobbelaar's dossier on the Allfords. It was useless trying to do any kind of translation with my *Let's Visit Germany* phrase book, but I'd noticed that the name Anna Dellarosa appeared several times in Allan's file. So did the word *Tochter*. I was hoping for a chance to check out my hunch.

Ellen was on the phone again when I went into the Lillian Allford gallery after lunch, but she hung up almost as soon as she saw me. We stood facing each other across the desk.

"Well?" I said softly, just in case there were any gallery-goers behind the partition. "Did you do it?"

"Yes," she said steadily. Her makeup was on straight, and she looked perfectly composed, as if she were not even distantly related to the wreck who had visited me at home on Friday. "I spoke to a very kind officer, the one leading the investigation. He told me that they had found the — " she lowered her voice " — materials during their search, and that they had confiscated them. He said that as long as I hadn't done anything against the law, I didn't need to worry about them getting out where anyone could see them." There was something else. Her forehead was wrinkled. "And," she whispered, "I also told Walter."

I looked down at her hand to see if she was still

wearing her wedding ring. She was. "So?" I asked. "Did he send you packing?"

"No," she replied quietly. "But he nearly hit the roof when I told him that I'd spent fifteen thousand dollars trying to keep it from him." She smiled slightly. "I think that if Grobbelaar hadn't already been killed, Walter would have gone over and done it himself."

"Well, good for you," I said. "You were right to tell him. He'll get over it eventually."

"Oh, I think he's already over it," Ellen said with a giggle. "Saturday he went out and bought me a merry widow and a roll of film."

I guffawed, which was exactly the worst thing to do at that moment, because from behind the partition, frowning behind her dark-rimmed glasses, came Lillian Allford.

"Good afternoon, Edna. How are you?" She had a slight accent. Hungarian. Ellen had once told me that Lillian was the child of some countess in exile, but it seemed to me that most Hungarians were anyway, so she might not have been as special as Ellen liked to think.

"I'm fine, thank you, Mrs. Allford," I said. "I was wondering if you could spare me a few minutes. I'd like some advice from you."

She inclined her head slightly to the left so that her dark hair with its expensive auburn highlights moved away from her ear to reveal a diamond stud the size of my baby fingernail. "Why don't you come into my office?"

I followed her to the back of the gallery. She sat in front of the Jack Bush, and I sat near the Kurelek.

"Now, how may I help you?" she asked. Her posture was fantastic. She held herself bolt upright and still managed to look as though it were the most comfortable position in the world.

"I seem to be in a bit of a quandary," I began. "As you know, I lost my job when the Fineberg Gallery went under."

She pursed her lips but said nothing.

"And now I find myself in the rather awkward position of having an empty bank account," I continued.

She frowned. "And you think that I can help you?"

I looked at the Bush. "I have a couple of drawings," I said confidingly, "and I was considering putting them up for sale to raise some money. I have a good idea how much I can get for them. That's not what I want to know. The problem is that I'd rather sell just one, not both, and I can't figure out which one to keep."

"Ah," she said with some relief. Obviously she'd imagined that I was there to beg for money. She placed her right hand on the desk, and her left one, with its ring to match her ear studs, over it. "Why don't you tell me about them?"

"One is a Tattersall," I said in my business voice. "Sanguine chalk on parchment. Nineteen eighty-two. The other is a 1974 carbon with ink washes by Giovanni Pasqualino. Now, the problem is that I'd like to hold on to the one that's likely to increase more in value."

"To be sure."

"But first I need to know whether the rumours I've been hearing are true."

"Rumours?" she asked, forgetting her posture and leaning forward slightly.

"My luck!" I said forlornly. "I've heard that both Pasqualino and Tattersall have been up to things that might affect their careers."

"Oh?" She raised her eyebrows so that they looked like two brown pigeons perched on the upper rims of her glasses. "How peculiar."

"You understand why I'm concerned?"

"I don't see why you think I would have any — "

"Please," I said. "This means a lot to me."

She tapped her fingers on her desk. "You really should be discussing this with their dealers. I've never even handled Tattersall's work, and the only Pasqualinos I've sold were on resale for exceptional clients."

"But that's exactly my point," I said. "Why would their dealers tell me anything . . . unfavourable about them?"

"Why should I?" She shrugged.

"Because I thought you might have heard the rumours."

"I hear rumours all the time. And they stop right here." She tapped her lips lightly with her index finger.

"Listen, Mrs. Allford," I said. "Whatever you say will be our secret." I smiled reassuringly.

"I despise gossip," she pronounced, and I realized that she was about to tell me anyway. "I hope you realize," she said in a low voice, "that if I do tell you what I have heard, I am only doing so because I trust your integrity. I have heard some very respectable things about you, Edna."

"Thank you."

"And if this ever got out, the career of one of Canada's finest painters could take a sudden turn."

"Believe me, Mrs. Allford, I have kept professional secrets before, and I can do so again."

"I am aware of that, Edna." And then she added acidly, "Working for Mr. Fineberg, you would have to have done so. All right. You may know that Gwen Tattersall has been the close companion of the writer Zylie Wedge for the past twenty-odd years."

"Yes." I nodded seriously.

"A good part of the mystique surrounding the Gwen Tattersall legend is based upon the fact that she has apparently eschewed all men, in any function. She won't work with men, she won't exhibit with men, and

on occasion she has even refused to speak to men."
Lillian Allford uncrossed her legs and recrossed them in
the opposite direction. "Zylie Wedge is of a similar
propensity. Much of her writing has been called stri-
dently anti-male, and although I do find some merit in
her work, I must say that at times I, personally, have
found it offensive."

She leaned even farther forward. It was coming.
"Now there has been a rumour, and I stress *rumour*, that
Gwen Tattersall has been keeping company with a
man."

Keeping company? That was a euphemism if I'd ever
heard one! "With one man," I gasped, "or several?"

"One," said Lillian. "One particular man. I don't
even know who he is. I don't think he's anybody, really.
But the point is that if it were true, it would turn
Tattersall's entire career into a farce. It's something that
she would never want the general public, the art-buying
public, to discover."

"How about Zylie Wedge? Does she know?"

"I have no idea. I suspect not. I can't tell you who
told me this, but it was someone whose judgement I
trust. This person seemed to think that she was the only
one who knew of this relationship." For someone who
despised gossip, she wasn't doing too badly.

"Isn't it curious," I said with an ironic smile, "that
this should come up right now? Right after Heinz
Grobbelaar's death, I mean." I thought I saw a flicker of
some half-concealed expression in her eyes, but I
couldn't be certain. I asked in a confidential tone,
"Weren't Tattersall and Wedge implicated in that illegal
anti-pornography raid on his store a couple of years
ago?"

"They were never arrested," she said. "But there was
some suggestion . . . I believe they received a warning."

"All right," I said, leaning back in my chair again.

"Now what about Giovanni Pasqualino? Is it true that he may have done something illegal, something that might hurt his career, too, if a lot of people knew about it?"

She smiled thinly. "Wherever do you come up with these ideas, Edna?"

"I have big ears," I said noncommittally. "I like to protect my investments." Great, I thought. Now I sound like a character out of *The Godfather*.

"Well, as far as Pasqualino is concerned, I can tell you honestly that I haven't heard a thing about him. Other than the usual talk about drinking binges and womanizing." Her lip seemed to curl as she said this.

"Fine," I said. "So if you were I, then you'd be more likely to part with the Tattersall?"

"If I were you, I'd hold on to both of them. Just because Gwen Tattersall wouldn't want her collectors to know about her relationship doesn't mean that she has gauged the situation correctly. For all I know, a revelation of this sort might throw her into just the sort of limelight she seems to be forever seeking."

"It's her relationship with Wedge that would suffer, I suppose."

"I would certainly think so. But that shouldn't affect the price of her work."

"Well, that sounds like reasonable advice," I said. "But it doesn't solve my financial woes."

"My advice where those are concerned," she replied, "is to find yourself a good-paying job with a reputable gallery that won't turn belly up before you're ready to retire."

I was amused to hear her use a word like "belly." I smiled. "Do you know any galleries like that?"

She returned the smile and waited for a few seconds before saying, "I am about to leave for Ottawa to spend a week with my husband, but if you'll come back on the seventeenth, I'm sure I'll be able to come up with one or two ideas for you."

"Well, that would be terrific," I said, standing up and holding out my hand. As she reached across her desk to shake it I said, "I suppose I'll be able to see things in a whole new light by then. I was in to see Dr. Cunderlik yesterday, and I found out that I need glasses. Imagine that! I never even realized it. But boy, he sure was down in the dumps. His receptionist, Anna Dellarosa, was killed on the weekend. You might have read about it in the paper. He was quite shaken up about it."

Lillian Allford's face turned grey. Her hand, which had been in the middle of a friendly shake, suddenly became rigid, and I pulled mine away. We both pretended not to notice the change in her demeanour.

"Thank you very much for seeing me," I said. "I hope that I haven't taken up too much of your time."

"Not at all, Edna," she said with renewed composure. "I look forward to seeing you again next week."

"Enjoy your trip to Ottawa." I opened her office door. "It's a beautiful city. Don't miss the National Gallery."

"I won't." She was sitting down again, twisting her diamond ring.

Ellen was in the midst of dealing with a customer who was standing in front of a still life in acrylic, trying to get Ellen to explain it to her. I grinned as I passed them and murmured, "See you next week."

I stopped at the phone booth around the corner and took out my notebook. I dialled the very first number.

"Allan Allford and Associates." It was a young man's voice.

"Allan Allford, please," I whispered.

"He's just getting ready to leave on a business trip, but I'll see if he can pick up his line. May I tell him who's calling?"

"That's entirely confidential."

There was a pause as he made his decision. Then, "All right. I'll buzz you through."

I waited for almost a minute. Allan Allford was probably reprimanding his underling for not pressing me harder for identification.

"Allford," he said at last.

"Mr. Allford," I whispered. "I have a message for you. It's about Anna Dellarosa."

He was silent for a moment. "Anna Dellarosa? Who is this?"

"A concerned citizen," I said, thinking, That ought to floor him. Political people were always worrying about concerned citizens with big mouths, even if they did speak in whispers.

"What do you want?" he asked. He had a smooth voice that sounded under control, even though I could tell that his breathing had quickened.

"I want to inform you that it's not over yet. Just because Grobbelaar and Dellarosa are out of the way doesn't mean your troubles are over."

"You're making this up," he said in an attempt to sound firm. "You have no idea what you're saying."

"Oh, but I do," I whispered softly. "And so will the public very shortly."

"How much do you want?" he said so quietly that I almost couldn't hear him.

I hung up the phone. That ought to scare the bejeebers out of him. If my hunch was correct, and I'd been using my German phrase book properly, then it wasn't only Harold Cunderlik who needed to worry about Anna Dellarosa's untimely accident. It was also Allan Allford, her father.

eleven

I HAD TO PICK UP MY GLASSES AND
the prints on my way home, so I didn't get there until
nearly six. Michael was supposed to come over as soon
as he finished work at six-thirty. I had only a short time
to try on my new glasses and acquire a severe headache
brought on by the failed attempt of my eyes to adjust
to seeing through plastic.

"They look great," Michael told me when he arrived.
"You look even brainier than you did before."

"But I feel wretched," I complained. "My head is
throbbing."

"So is mine," said Michael, grabbing my hand. "Just
feel it."

Afterwards we had order-out fish and chips with
white wine while we watched *Casablanca* on video.
When the movie was over he said, "So, how did it go
with Owl today?"

"All right," I said, rubbing the bridge of my nose. "I
took a lot of notes, and another cop took pictures of
everything. I'm supposed to get those tomorrow. Anyway, I have to go to the library to do a bit more research
in the morning so I can make up a report for the police."

"And for that they're paying you fifteen hundred
dollars? No wonder my taxes are so high!"

"And there was also a free lunch," I told him.

"He took you out for lunch?"

"It wasn't great," I said, ignoring his look. "I ordered

the most expensive thing on the menu, and it was the stingiest portion I've ever seen."

Michael grinned. "And did he try anything with you?"

"Who, Owl? Are you kidding? All he wanted to talk about was the collection. And what kind of a man Grobbelaar was. Just because you can't keep your hands off me doesn't mean everyone else feels the same way."

"As long as I have my hands on you, they'd better not," he said, rolling me onto the floor and kissing me. "Take off your clothes. I want to see you again."

"Michael," I said as I pulled my shirt over my head. "Did you remember to bring that newspaper article with you?"

"It's in my briefcase," he mumbled, licking my shoulder. "Over by the door. How come you're so interested in it, anyway?"

"She was my optometrist's receptionist."

He rubbed his chin against mine. "Did you know her?"

"No," I said, wriggling out of my shorts. "But I know her father's wife."

"Do you want it right now?" he murmured into my navel.

"I want it right now," I sighed, lying back and flinging my glasses onto the carpet.

"THERE'S ONE THING I'm curious about," I said to Detective Owl the next morning at eight o'clock. He had come to drop off the photographs and had accepted my offer of breakfast.

"What's that?" he asked, spreading a thin layer of my mother's homemade apple jelly on his toast.

"How the heck did Grobbelaar find out about all those people in the first place?"

Either he had given up fighting me on the proper-procedure issue or my mother had slipped a dose of sodium pentothal into the jelly.

"We deliberated over that for days," he said, setting his knife down on the plate. "It seemed impossible that a man who apparently kept to himself most of the time would know so much about such personal aspects of people's lives. In most cases even their spouses didn't know what Grobbelaar knew. And then we thought of the rental business."

"Don't tell me! He zipped himself inside an inflatable dolly and listened as they whispered their secrets into her ear."

"Good guess," he said, and drank his orange juice in one gulp. "But you're slightly off base."

"But I'll bet they'd all bought or rented something from his shop, right? Is that the connection?"

"Yes," he replied.

"Okay." I closed my eyes and rested my chin on my hand. "I know he must have had physical proof of what they'd been up to."

"Thinking like a pro," he said. I wondered if he was being sarcastic, but it was hard to tell because he was stuffing another piece of jellied toast into his mouth and looking through my kitchen window at the legs walking out to catch the bus.

"He had recordings," I said to the side of his face. "But that's ridiculous. Who records something they don't want anyone to know? Unless — " I paused and stared at him " — unless they didn't know they were being recorded."

"Good," said Detective Owl. He reached for the bread bag. "May I?"

"Go ahead."

He popped two more pieces of bread into the toaster.

"He bugged their phones," I said.

"What would make him decide to do that?"

"I don't know. He liked the way they talked?"

"Try again. You're getting warmer. You were warm before."

"What was I saying before? The inflatable dolly? Oh. So he must have bugged something they rented. Their videos. He bugged their videos? Hah!"

Detective Owl was looking right at me, chewing his toast faster than I would have thought humanly possible.

"He bugged their videos?" I said again. "How could that be? Is that it? How do you bug a video?"

"You don't bug a video. You bug a camera. You hide a voice-activated recorder in the carrying case."

"You're kidding," I said. "He did that?"

"That's it," said Detective Owl. "We found the recorders under false bottoms in several of the light and binoculars cases, too. All he had to do was wait for the tapes to come back." He bit into his fifth piece of toast, chewed it rapidly, and swallowed. "Our guess is that it started out as a purely voyeuristic exercise."

I shook my head. "What was he, some kind of electronics expert?"

"Some kind," he replied with a slight smile. He chomped down again on his toast. "I imagine he must have heard a lot of talk in his little shop, and eventually he started sending his funny cases home with people he knew were having trouble."

"And why are you telling me this?"

"What do you mean?" he asked through a full mouth.

"I mean, you've been saying all along that you wouldn't discuss this case until you had it all figured out. Does this mean you've done it?" I searched his face for signs of self-satisfaction, but I only saw a few toast crumbs on his chin.

"Well, we're pretty close," he replied. "I can't see any harm in letting you know now."

"Great," I said. "Who done it?"

"I can't tell you that." He finished his tea, wiped his mouth with the paper serviette, and burped quietly. "Excuse me," he said.

"You don't really know, then," I said. "Want more tea?"

"No. I've had enough. I do have a few good ideas."

"Well, so do I," I said. "But that doesn't mean I'm ready to make an arrest. Have you at least got it narrowed down?"

"We're getting there."

"You're evading me, you know."

"Not purposely. I gave you a reasonable answer to your question. I think you're getting a little carried away and you're trying to take advantage of my generosity."

"Generosity!" I scoffed. "You're probably about to hand out a press release saying everything you just told me."

"Edna," he said impatiently, "the papers know nothing about this. Absolutely nothing. And if they do find out, I'll know how."

"Not by me," I said. "I know when to keep my mouth shut."

He shook his head and said, "Do you think so? Then why are you always arguing with me?"

"You're the one who starts it all the time. I've been getting the impression that you like to argue with me."

He stuck the last bite of his toast into his mouth and pushed his chair away from the table. "I really should go now. Thank you for the breakfast."

"Not at all," I said as we walked towards the door. "My toast is your toast."

He smiled. "Well, goodbye, Edna. I'll see you when your report is done."

"Goodbye, Stephen," I said. I closed the door and went to the kitchen window. As soon as his car was gone I raced out to the phone booth.

MY CALL WAS ANSWERED by the same woman I had spoken to on Friday. "Haylew?" she said.

"Hello, Mrs. Birch," I whispered. "Is Arthur still at home?"

"Oh," she said. "It's you again. Yes, just a minute. I'll call him." She placed her hand over the mouthpiece, but she must have left gaps between her fingers because I could hear every word clearly. "Arthur! Honey! Get the phone! It's for you."

He came on cheerfully a second later. "Yo!"

"Arthur Birch?" I whispered. "Is that you?"

"Yes," he replied. "Doris, hang up the phone, darling. I've got it." I heard a click. "Yes?" he repeated. "What can I do you for?" He was certainly feeling chipper. No portentous moment of fear for him.

"Are you familiar with the name Heinz Grobbelaar?" I rasped.

"Who is this?" he demanded. "Is this some kind of sick joke?"

"It's no joke. I want you to tell me where you were last Tuesday evening."

"Last Tuesday? That was the night he was . . . Listen, buster, whoever you are. The cops have already asked me that. If this is some kind of prank, you might as well forget it. I can have this call traced. I won't play games."

"This is no game," I said as hoarsely and vilely as I could. "I know what you've been up to, and soon the rest of the world will, too." I hung up, feeling somewhat discouraged.

It sounded as though Arthur Birch was a pretty dauntless character. If he was the killer, he certainly hadn't come close to breaking down and confessing to me.

I realized that I had to force myself to come to a conclusion of some kind. I knew I'd feel more than slightly put out if I didn't figure it out by the time the cops did, and I would have preferred to do it before then. Especially after all the time I had invested in the affair. But the time aspect was nothing compared to the thought of Detective Stephen Owl patting me on the shoulder and saying, You see, my dear, that's what happens to amateurs. For all their self-aggrandizing talk, they never get anywhere. Actually, he probably wouldn't say "my dear." He'd say, "Ms. Heathcott" or "Edna," as he'd been doing lately, with that complacent smirk that drove me wild.

I opened my notebook and stared at a blank page. I had to admit that I hadn't done a very thorough investigation. Detective Owl probably had everything from credit card slips to immunization records to help him. All I had was my telephone and a list of names. And a set of photographs of postcards. I knew, I just knew, they were significant. Why would a man who had no relatives and probably no friends have saved a box of tacky scenics unless they meant something important?

I had to find out what they said. I had struggled unsuccessfully with my phrase book over Grobbelaar's files, but I was feeling particularly hungry for a challenge after my breakfast with Detective Owl, and I got it out again. I also got out my set of prints.

The first card had been sent from Halifax, in November three years earlier. There was a picture of a harbour with some kind of fishing boat in the foreground. The printer had overdosed the sky and water with cyanine, and the boat looked as though it were floating on an ocean of blue tooth gel. The handwriting on the reverse was clear, almost stiffly written.

My phrase book was arranged in two sections: English to German and German to English, both in alphabetical order. I flipped through the book until I found the closest thing to *"Habe ich dich nicht schon einmal gesehen?"* The translation read, "Haven't I seen you somewhere before?" I looked at the picture side. I didn't think the sender was referring to the fishing boat.

The second card had been sent two months later from Paris. It was a night shot of the city featuring the Eiffel Tower. *"Ich vergesse nie ein Gesicht."* This time the translation was "I never forget a face." I wrote this under my translation of the first card in my notebook.

The third card was from Uruguay. *"Ich hoffe es geht Ihnen gut. Ich denke oft an Sie."* "I hope you are well. I am thinking about you." There were several more along this line from various European cities, and then one from Sault Ste. Marie that read, *"Sie haben ein sehr schönes Haus."* "What a fine home you have."

I knew that it was broad daylight. I knew that I was in one of the safest areas of the city. And I knew that these cards, on the face of it, seemed pleasant enough. But I was suddenly struck with that eye-watering, throat-tightening feeling that I usually got only when I watched a really good suspense film. I couldn't help thinking that these cards were really threats, messages that only Grobbelaar himself might have understood, and that even the German-speaking fingerprint officer hadn't cottoned on to it in his mad rush to sweep the place clean.

The next card was from Chicago. *"Wir müssen uns mal treffen."* "We must get together sometime." The thing that suddenly struck me as being particularly odd was that many of the messages were similar to the phrases in my book. From Toronto: *"Ich freue mich, Sie wieder zu sehen."* "I look forward to seeing you again." From Calgary: *"Ich werde die Zeit nie vergessen, die wir zusammen verbracht haben."* "I will never forget the time we spent together." From Melbourne: *"Ich hoffe Sie bald wieder zu sehen."* "I hope to see you again soon."

Of course I could have been wrong about my prickly feelings. Maybe Fat Heinz had had a lady friend who liked to travel. Or a secret admirer too shy to sign her name. Stranger things had happened. Dottie had fallen for Harold. Ellen had married Walter. But it seemed more likely to me that the cards had been written by the murderer. But by someone on the blackmail list? It was possible. Just because they were written in German didn't mean that the writer was German or even spoke German. Why would most of the cards have been composed of stock phrases out of a German-English travel aid?

But if the killer had written the cards, Grobbelaar's blackmailing of him or her had to have started at least three years ago, when the cards first began to arrive. That probably eliminated several of the people on Grobelaar's list. It let Harold Cunderlik off the hook, because Detective Owl had told me that Grobbelaar had approached him only a few weeks before the killing. I felt somewhat disappointed. Harold would have made a good killer, with his latex hands and abraded palm.

Another factor I had to consider was that the cards had been sent from around the world. That meant that the sender must have been someone with a lot of money. Or an artist who received a lot of travel grants.

I decided to put the card photos away for the time being and take a look at the newspaper that Michael had brought over. I had been putting it off, thinking that in the past week my curiosity had been bordering on macabre, but I realized that if I seriously meant to find out everything I could about Anna Dellarosa, I had to see the article.

Dr. Cunderlik had been right. "Splashed" was exactly the word to describe the way the photographs had been laid out. There was a half-page colour picture of the accident site, with a black-and-white inset of Anna in a graduation cap and gown, her head tilted at that unnatural angle that all photographers seem to favour for their subjects. She had been a beautiful girl. The article included a description of the accident according to the bus driver, a quote from a police investigator who said that no charges would be laid, and a brief profile of Anna, who was described as a promising young talent on the country music scene. There were a number of touching words from her closest friends, but Anna's mother, Mary, was said to be unable to speak to the media. A disgruntled tone underlined this point. No father was mentioned.

The next step in my investigation was now clear to me, but in the interest of decency I decided to wait a few more days before I took it. I folded up the paper and tucked it under the couch.

By then the morning was almost gone. Detective Owl had put the photographs of Grobbelaar's collection into plastic sleeves in a binder. I put the notes I had taken on each object beside their corresponding photos and stuck the whole bundle in my purse. Then I set out for the reference library.

I decided to take the subway to St. George and do a little gallery tour first. I came out of the Bedford exit and walked north. To my complete amazement, as I turned onto Prince Arthur, I saw Dottie and Harold Cunderlik coming out of a house near one of the galleries. It was one of those sandblasted renovations that had been converted to a lawyer's office. Dottie looked like a tall glass of iced tea in her rust-coloured silk suit and light, foamy hairdo, but Harold was a wreck. Even from a distance, I could see that his tie seemed to have been pulled an inch too tight and his face was shining. He put his hands in his pockets, took them out again, and then looked around dazedly, as if he didn't know where he was. Dottie wasn't looking at him, and I couldn't help thinking that her expression looked set, as though she had said to her coiffeur, "Do my face, too, while you're at it," and he had erred badly on the side of grimness.

I stooped and pretended to tie up my shoe, partly in order to hide my face, and partly in the hope that I would catch some of their conversation as they passed on the other side of the street.

But all I heard was a disconnected "I don't know why I ever — No — I can't — I'll never understand — " from Dottie in her low, important voice, and a sort of high-pitched, hysterical sob from Harold.

I stayed close to the ground until I heard a car door slam and saw Harold stumbling off towards the other end of the street. Then I stood up, rested my notebook on the hood of a parked car, and wrote down everything that I had just seen and heard.

AT FOUR O'CLOCK I opened my apartment door. I don't remember the exact moment I realized that the curtains had been pulled back. If I hadn't been so busy thinking about Harold and Dottie, I probably would have noticed even before I unlocked the outside door of the building, because the kitchen window was wide open, too. I think it only registered after I had taken several steps inside: there was too much light and fresh air. I couldn't smell last night's fish and chips any more.

I stood stock-still in the middle of the living room and listened. All I could hear was the sound of the traffic outside and the faint whisper of the kitchen curtain grazing the sill. I wondered, in the same instant, whether running back outside would take longer than grabbing the rolling pin that was hanging above the stove. I went for the rolling pin.

In the next two minutes I looked under the bed, behind the doors, and in every closet. I even stood in the bathroom, poised and ready with my wooden weapon, and yanked open the shower curtain. There was nobody there. Still feeling alarmed, I reclosed all the curtains and performed a second check to make sure that nothing was missing.

In the bedroom the quilt had been disturbed, and a book that had been lying on the bedside table was now on the floor. Boxes and cans in the kitchen cupboards had been shifted. It had all been neatly done. I might not even have noticed if it hadn't been for the open curtains.

Or for the package on the kitchen table. It was a plain cardboard box, about the same size as the ones used to gift-wrap neckties. I knew that I shouldn't touch it. It could have been a bomb. But when I listened carefully, I couldn't hear any ticking. I put on my oven mitts, thinking that at least I wouldn't erase any of the sender's fingerprints, and opened it.

Inside, nestled on a bed of crinkled pink tissue paper, was a small, cream-centred, white chocolate penis, definitely a Grobbelaar specialty. It had been broken in two, and the filling was oozing out onto the paper lining. On the underside of the box lid, in black crayon, were scrawled six words: *"Next time this will be Fineberg's."*

twelve

I DROPPED THE BOX. IT LANDED UP-side down on the floor with the edge of the pink paper poking out one side. I was still staring at it, horrified, when the phone rang.

"Edna, this is Detective Owl again."

"Yes?" I whispered.

"I just wanted to let you know that you won't have to worry about this Fineberg business any more. We picked him up this morning."

I leaned against the counter. "Oh," I murmured. "Well."

"He's in the Toronto General. We located him this morning."

"The Toronto General! Is he all right?" A thousand gruesome images leaped to mind.

"He'll live."

"Is he — " I paused and closed my eyes " — intact?"

"Intact? What do you mean?"

"What's wrong with him?"

"Cardiac arrest."

"He had a *heart attack?*"

"Too much excitement," said Detective Owl. "He's not cut out for this kind of hide-and-seek. Oh. And he doesn't have to worry about the murder charge, either. His alibi for Tuesday night checks out. He's just going to have a nice long rest in the hospital. So I wanted to let you know that you don't have to worry about him any more. And after you get that report finished for me, you won't even have to worry about the police."

"Great," I said. "That's great. I'm glad Gerald's all right."

"Incidentally," he added, "you might be interested to hear that The Chocolate Box was broken into last night. Looks as if someone's been after something of Grobbelaar's."

"In the apartment?" I asked in a low voice.

"No. In the shop itself. Someone trashed the place. It looks like an aftermath scene from *Caligula*."

I said nothing. I was staring at the box on my floor.

"Edna? Are you all right?"

"Of course, Detective. I'm just overwhelmed with relief about Gerald, I guess. Absolutely overwhelmed."

"Glad to hear it," he said cheerfully. "Well, I'd better let you go. Call me if you have any questions about that report. And leave this Grobbelaar business alone. You're out of it now. Do you understand?"

"Yessir."

"All right. Goodbye, Edna."

I hung up the phone and picked up the box. I cleaned the goo off the linoleum tiles and threw it into the garbage. Then I phoned the Toronto General Hospital and asked for Gerald Fineberg.

JOHN HENDERSON had a desk in the *Art in Canada* office on the Esplanade, not because he did his writing there, but because it was a convenient place to dump the hundred or so press releases he received every week. He showed up on Thursdays to collect the mail, chat with the editor and art director, and take interviewees to lunch on his magazine charge card. I knew because I had called on Tuesday to make an appointment to see him about some research I was doing on a collection of European antiques.

He would be able to see me between ten o'clock and ten-fifteen, the secretary had told me. So what time should I arrive? I'd asked her. She'd told me that she meant I would have fifteen minutes with him, starting at ten o'clock.

It was a typical magazine office, one large room divided into a noisy labyrinth of cubbyholes by blue-cloth-clad partitions, most of which were treated as bulletin boards by the staff and covered with layouts, photographs, calendars, and tear sheets. The anorexic receptionist offered me a back issue to read while I waited for The Critic to arrive. I held it on my lap, but I preferred to listen to her trying to put off a caller who was obviously an artist seeking a review.

John Henderson appeared just as she was saying, "I don't care if the Queen of England owns ten of your paintings. You'll have to send a press release, just like everyone else."

"Miss Heathcott?" he said. He didn't hold out his hand to be shaken. He had a bored look on his face. At least he did on the lower half of it. His eyes were too distorted behind his thick glasses for me to discern their expression.

"Thank you for seeing me, Dr. Henderson," I said to his back. He was already retreating through the blue maze towards his desk. I followed close behind.

There was a door installed in his cubbyhole, unlike most of the others we had passed, and he closed it behind us. He pointed a finger at the chair that faced his desk, and I sat in it.

"Now, what is it that you want?" he asked impatiently.

For the first time I was grateful to be wearing glasses. If the glare of the fluorescent lights was making his eyes, even as enlarged as they were, difficult to see, then they were doing the same for mine. I looked straight at him and said, "I have some photographs I'd like to show you."

I thought he shifted slightly in his chair, but he said nothing.

"I am doing some research for a private client," I continued. "This work consists of tracing the origins of some fifteenth-century religious relics. I have my own theories, of course, but I feel that in order to be fully confident in the report I present to my client, I should have the corroboration of an expert such as yourself." I smiled slightly, lips closed.

"May I see the photographs?" he said. This time when he spoke he put a little expression into his words.

I took five of the photographs in their plastic sleeves out of my handbag and placed them on top of the pile of letters on his desk. Then I adjusted the position of my glasses and leaned back in my chair again.

"Private collection, eh?" he said. "Lucky guy." He laid the photographs out side by side and bent over them. His tweed jacket was hanging on the back of his chair. He had his sleeves rolled up to his elbows, and I noticed that he had no hair on his arms. He was wearing a Timex watch. "Definitely fifteenth century," he pronounced. "Early fifteenth century. These are excellent photographs. Very clear." He looked up. "Professional, I assume."

"Yes," I said. If you could count police file photos as professional.

"They're Italian," he said, picking up the photo of the marble Madonna. "There's a Roman influence in this one. But I couldn't say with any measure of certainty that they are actually Roman. I really should see the actual pieces."

I could see the face of his Timex. It read ten minutes after ten. If I were going to bring up the subject of Grobbelaar, I'd have to do it pretty soon.

"You may have seen me before," I said chattily, feeling like an idiot. "I used to work for Gerald Fineberg. Right next door to — "

But before I could finish, his phone rang. He actually raised his palm to signal me to shut my trap before he picked it up, as if he thought I was going to run on indefinitely.

"Yes?" he said, still examining the photographs. "She is? Well, tell her to — no, don't. I'll be out in a second. I'm standing up now. Tell her to hang on." He slammed down the receiver, threw open the door, and ran out without even looking at me.

"Shit," I said to the Jack Chambers poster on the wall behind his desk. I picked up a magazine from his bookshelf and began to read a Henderson article entitled "How New Age Thinking Is Affecting Hyperrealism." I got as far as "The abbreviated superimposition of presumptive misapprehension over the inherent semblance of ratiocination leaves the viewer feeling, if nothing else, perplexed," when the receptionist interrupted me.

"I'm sorry, Ms. Heathcott, but Dr. Henderson has been called away suddenly. He asked me to tell you that he will be free to see you next Thursday between nine-thirty and nine-forty-five, if you'd like to come back."

"No, thank you," I said, standing up and replacing the magazine on the shelf. "I'll be busy that day."

She scooped up my photographs and said, "Are these all yours?"

"They certainly are." I reached across the desk and she handed me the pile.

"I'm sorry about your interview," she said as we walked back to the front desk.

"So am I. Dr. Henderson is such a charming gentleman. You must feel very lucky to work with him."

She stared at me for a second and then let out a shriek of laughter that probably would have got her fired in a regular office. In that place it was likely accepted as just another eccentricity of one of the artsy personnel.

GERALD WAS LYING behind a closed curtain in a semi-private room. There was no one in the other bed. He looked green. He opened his eyes halfway when I said his name. He tried to say Edna! What a surprise to see you. But it came out more like "Edna! What a hurprie to hee you."

"I didn't know you wore dentures," I said.

"I'm palling apart," he moaned. "They can't pind my teeth."

"Are you sure you didn't kill Grobbelaar?" I asked.

"Yeah. I'm hure."

I put my face down close to his and whispered, "Then what were you doing with his goblet?"

He stared back at me mutely. His eyes were opened wide. Ellen was right. They were a yellowish colour.

"If you don't answer me," I said sternly, "I'm going to tell the police that you stole it."

"No," he said. "All right. I went in to talk to Grobbelaar that morning about the rent. He wah dead, and the goblet wah lying at the bottom ob the tair."

"At the bottom of the stairs?"

"That the honet-to-God truth, Edna. I did go uptair to get the computer dik, but the goblet wah already down there. I didn't tut anything in the cabinet."

He started suddenly, and his eyes shifted to the left. I turned to look. A large nurse had entered the room holding something shiny and pink in her outstretched hand.

"Oh, Mr. Fineberg," she said cheerily. "Look what we have here! Open up, now. That's right. I'll just pop them in . . . there! How's that?"

"Great," grumbled Gerald. "Now can you get me a new heart?"

The nurse winked at me. As soon as she had gone I leaned closer to Gerald again.

"Why in God's name did you leave the goblet in the shop?"

"I wasn't going to. I was all set to take it with me, but when I got to the front door I could see someone across the street in a car, waiting for me. One of the sharks. I couldn't just walk out of there with it. I figured I'd get an opportunity to go back later. But I didn't."

"What about the stone?"

"What stone?"

"The round piece of amber that belongs in the goblet. The police found it in the shop."

"I don't know what you're talking about. I never saw a stone."

I thought about that for a moment before I said, "Well, your friends are still after you. They sent me a present yesterday. They broke into The Chocolate Box all right, but now they're looking for you."

"That's impossible! I told them where to find it. Are you sure you put it back exactly where you found it?"

"I'm positive. I can't believe you're so unscrupulous that you'd let a loan shark take a priceless antique. He's probably just going to melt it down. How much money do you owe them anyway?"

Gerald closed his eyes. "Three hundred."

"Three hundred thousand?"

"Plus interest." He opened his eyes again. "Forty per cent. But Edna, if they're still looking for me, it means they couldn't have found the goblet."

"Well, I can't imagine anyone else finding it there."

"The police? Maybe the police found it."

"Well, if they did, I can't say I'm sorry. But I'm not involved any more. This is your problem now. So I'd appreciate it if you'd tell your friends to leave me alone. Now, I think I'd better go." I turned away from him, but he reached out and grabbed my skirt.

"Edna! You have to help me. You can't leave me here to die."

"You're not dying, Gerald. You're in serious but stable condition." I patted his hand. "Now, I'm sorry, but I really have to go."

"Oh, Edna, please! I've just thought of something you can do. Just one, simple thing. It's not even illegal."

I looked at him and frowned. There were tears in the corners of his eyes. I sighed. "Are you sure?" I asked.

I HAD A LUNCH DATE with Michael. I met him near the St. Clair West station at one. He unlocked the passenger door and held it open so I could get in. But instead of closing it after me, he flipped a catch so that my seat reclined suddenly against the one behind it and threw himself on top of me.

"Michael," I gasped. "I can't breathe."

"Then don't," he said, pulling the door shut. "I'll breathe for both of us." After a few minutes he whispered, "Edna, I have something for you."

"I know," I replied with some effort. "I can feel it."

"No," he whispered.

"No?" I opened my eyes.

"Look to your left. It's on the back seat."

I turned my head. It was a corrugated cardboard box. "A box," I said. "What's in it?"

He pulled away and manoeuvred himself over the stick shift into the driver's seat. "Open it."

"It's heavy. I can't lift it."

"So leave it there and open it."

I leaned over the back of my seat and struggled to pull the wide band of packing tape away from the box flaps, a challenge made even more insurmountable by the fact that Michael had his right hand under my skirt and was in the process of supplementing his activity by bringing in the left to join it. I did, however, meet with eventual success, and got the top of the box open.

"It's an aquarium," I said.

"It's a terrarium," said Michael. "I'll be bringing over the plants and the turtles later."

"Turtles?" I yelped.

"It's kind of a hobby," he replied. "I have a large tank at my office, and some of them are getting too big."

"So you're giving them to me."

"No. I'm giving you two of the smaller ones. I'm sort of attached to the older ones. I've had them since I was fourteen. But I'd like you to have the two little guys."

"Turtles," I said. "Well."

"I'll be arranging the tank for you. All you have to do is water them and feed them and sit back and enjoy them."

"Amazing," I said, gazing at the tank.

"What is?"

"Do you realize that we've known each other for less than a week and already you're giving me your most prized possessions?"

"No, I'm not," he said. "I only lend you my most prized possession." He turned the key in the ignition. "Come on. Flip your seat back up and we'll go over to your place and get to know each other better."

I WAS SITTING at my kitchen table in the early afternoon, looking through a pile of books on early Renaissance tapestries, when my phone rang. I slid my chair across the floor and grabbed the receiver off the wall.

"Hello?" I said, filling my voice with as much desire as it would hold, just in case it was Michael on the other end, calling back to thank me for lunch.

It wasn't.

"Miss Heathcott?" he snapped.

"Yes?"

"Where have you been? I've been trying to reach you for hours."

"Who is this?" I demanded, although I had a fairly good idea.

"This is John Henderson." His voice was loud, crisp, and irritating.

"Oh, Dr. Henderson!" I cried. "You've called to apologize for running out on me this morning." Apologetic was exactly the opposite of how he actually sounded. About to burst a blood vessel was more like it.

"No, Miss Heathcott," he said nastily. "I am calling to get my letters back."

"Letters?" I said. "What letters? I don't have any of your letters."

"There were some letters on my desk when you came to see me this morning. When I came back from my emergency meeting they were no longer there. Having ascertained that my secretary does not have them in her possession, I can only deduce that you absconded with them, for what insalubrious purpose I can't presume to imagine."

"Well, you deduced wrongly," I said. "I never took any of your letters. I didn't touch anything on your desk, so you might as well — oh." I stopped.

"Oh?" he said. "To what does that vacuous vocable refer?"

"To the fact that your secretary bundled up my photographs for me, and she may have inadvertently included some of the correspondence on your desk. To be perfectly honest, I haven't looked at my things since I got back."

"Miss Heathcott," he said wearily, "may I suggest that you do so immediately?"

"By all means, Dr. Henderson. Please hold the line."

I put the phone down on the counter and went to get my bag from where I had left it beside the door. I pulled out the binder in which I had stuffed the photographs on my way out of the *Art in Canada* office. There were the photographs, and there were four sheets of paper stuck in between them that were definitely not mine.

"Dr. Henderson?" I said into the phone. "They're here."

"I'm not at all surprised," he replied. "I suppose that you've read every word of them, too."

"I'm not a speed reader," I told him. "Do you think I'm capable of reading four letters in ten seconds?"

He ignored me. "I'd like you to put the letters into an envelope. I'm going to send a taxi immediately. I want them back this afternoon. And I beg you to use discretion. Behave like the mature adult you seem to be."

I had no idea what the heck he was talking about, but I promised to return the letters to him, and he hung up.

I probably could have been a discreet, mature adult if I wasn't after anything more than his opinion of Grobbelaar's collection. But I was, and the fact that I might have something on John Henderson that required extending my behaviour beyond its already uncomfortably distended capacity for tact and diplomacy was an opportunity I couldn't pass up.

I spread the letters across my table.

The first was a dull memo from his editor regarding an upcoming deadline, the second, a form letter inviting him to take advantage of discounted subscription rates from a magazine clearing house, and the third, a note from someone named Betsy Blume thanking him for speaking at a colloquium on military symbolism in the work of some European sculptor I'd never heard of. But the fourth letter was the one he must have been worried about, and as I read it I could understand why. "My darling," it read,

> I write to you as the world, which once held so much joy, collapses around me. I am racked with anguish, and only you can release me from this prison into which Fate has cast me. I beseech you, Johnny, don't play with my heart. I can't stand it. I have nowhere else to turn if not to you. I awaken in the middle of the night filled with terror, wondering what grievous ills will befall me, will befall us, next. If you have done this thing that I begged you not to do, for God's sake tell me, and let us put an end to this agony. I must be with you. My wife wants me out, and I have nowhere to go. Please rescue me. Whatever you have done, I forgive you.

And it was signed — of course, because even through the purple prose I recognized the handwriting from my glasses prescription — "Harold."

Harold Cunderlik was having an affair with John Henderson? It was almost too bizarre to imagine. I'd always had a difficult time with the idea of a bright, high-class, chairwoman-of-the-board type like Dottie going after a smarmy bore like Harold, but the thought of the highbrow Dr. Henderson cuddling the wretched Dr. Cunderlik in his hairless arms was almost too much to handle. All I could picture was Harold gazing at John across his lens machine and saying coyly, "Actually, I don't have to touch your eyes at all."

I giggled. I laughed. I screamed. And then I crossed John Henderson off my list. If his relationship with Harold Cunderlik was the thing that was getting him blackmailed, then he was no more likely to have committed the murder than Harold was, providing my postcard theory was correct.

The sad thing was that apparently poor Harold believed that John *had* done it and had worked himself into a snivelling mess over the thought. I almost picked up the phone and called him. Now I understood what had been going on between Dottie and Harold when I caught them coming out of the lawyer's office on Wednesday.

I folded up the letters and put them into an envelope, which I addressed to Dr. John Henderson, care of *Art in Canada* at the address of the magazine. Inside the envelope flap I wrote, "Dear John, If it makes you feel any better, I know you didn't kill him." Then I sealed it and wrote SWAK on the outside.

The taxi arrived twenty minutes later. I handed the envelope to the driver and sent him on his way.

Then I sat on my couch with a glass of milk in my hand, stared at my original Spencer, and went back four and a half centuries to a small church somewhere near Rome.

thirteen

I HAD ASKED MICHAEL TO SET UP THE terrarium on the dresser in my bedroom so that the first sight I saw upon waking would be Guido and Maria Teresa, the painted turtles, ambling over the moss under the azalea bonsai. That was exactly what happened on Friday morning, except that when my clock radio came on at seven-thirty I was too distracted by the news to give my new pets the attention they deserved.

"Police say that Arthur Birch, a Toronto high school principal, has been missing since Wednesday morning, and there are fears that he may have been kidnapped. Ronald Holmes has this report."

Ronald Holmes came on the air, and I sat up in bed and turned up the volume.

"Arthur Birch is the principal at Robert R. Dunsmuir Collegiate. He is respected by teachers and well liked by students. Wednesday morning he left his home at eight thirty-five and did not show up for work. Police say it is unlikely that he met with an accident, since his home is only three blocks away from the school, and no one in the vicinity reported any unusual occurrences. They have suggested that he may be experiencing what psychologists refer to as 'fugue,' a sudden loss of memory brought on by an emotionally traumatic incident. But his wife, Doris, says that no such events have occurred recently in his life. She has her own theory about what has happened to her husband. Doris Birch."

Doris's voice was higher pitched than I remembered it. Between sentences she breathed deeply and loudly.

"He got these calls over the phone. Two of them. The first one was Friday when he wasn't here. The second one was Wednesday morning, right before he left. Right before the last time I saw him."

Her voice broke for a second, but she regained enough control to say in a regulated crescendo:

"Whoever it was spoke in a whisper, and I'm sure it was to disguise their voice. I think my husband was being threatened by some terrorist, and all I can say is, whoever you are, however sick or depraved you may be, please let Arthur go. I need my husband back."

She then broke down completely, and the reporter came back on the air.

"Police say that their investigation will be limited to the Metro area unless new evidence surfaces. Ronald Holmes, Toronto."

I sat frozen to the edge of my bed. I wondered whether I should call Detective Owl and tell him not to bother following up on the mysterious-caller lead, but I immediately realized that that would have been an even bigger mistake than actually having called Arthur Birch in the first place. What if he was the murderer and he had somehow figured out who had phoned him? What if he really had traced my call? Maybe he had gone into hiding and was just waiting for the right opportunity to leap out at me with a sharpened weapon from some shadowy *cul-de-sac*, like the guest parking lot for my apartment building.

I didn't have much of an appetite for breakfast, but I boiled an egg anyway and drank a glass of juice. In case I was going to be pursued by a reckless lunatic with a knife, I'd need my strength.

I also needed strength for the call I was about to make. I found the number in the phone book.

"Hello?" said a woman. I could tell that she was smoking. I heard the little "pfftt" as she inhaled.

"Hello. Is this Mary Dellarosa?"

"That's me," she said and coughed once. "Who's this?"

"You don't know me," I said slowly. "My name is Edna Heathcott. I was wondering if I could talk to you about Anna."

She said nothing for a moment. I could hear a voice in the background singing, "Yoo-hoo-oo down't love me he-he-enny mo-ho-hore." Then she asked, "Are you from that paper or something?"

"No. I just wanted to offer my condolences."

"Well, it's very sympathetic of you to call. Were you a friend of Anna's? How are you, dear?" *Dear*? I took the word as a clear signal to proceed.

"I'm fine," I replied. "How are you?"

"About as good as you can be a week after your only living relative gets taken from you."

I wasn't certain how proper etiquette would have me respond, so I murmured something about a senseless tragedy and then plunged in head-first. "I was wondering if you felt up to having company today." I tried to make it sound as though the proposed visit would be a mere social call and nothing imperative that couldn't wait.

"Well, I dunno," she said and fell silent again. "I suppose so. Everyone says I should keep myself busy. Sure. Come on over. D'you know where I live?" She told me. "Maybe we can talk about all the good things we remember about Anna."

"That sounds like an excellent idea," I said, wondering how I would ever manage to do that. But I arranged to arrive at her house at ten.

Mary Dellarosa lived in a small black-and-red-brick bungalow in Leaside. The front door and shutters were enamelled a stunning shade of chartreuse, which must have had the grey-and-white neighbours considering the possibility of forming a spray-can vigilante squad. But the small lawn was neatly trimmed, and the shrub roses beside the front steps were cared for lovingly. I rang the doorbell, which played the first four bars of "Edelweiss," and a woman opened the door.

After hearing her voice over the telephone I had been expecting to see a tough-looking woman, well into middle age, with smoker's pucker lines around her mouth, which I was certain would be painted a brilliant shade of vermilion. At first I thought that I must have the wrong house. But then she spoke.

"Hi. You must be Edna."

She couldn't have been more than a decade older than I, and there were no lines around her mouth, or anywhere else on her face, for that matter. She had huge blue eyes that were only slightly pink from crying, and her makeup job was what *Chatelaine* would have called understated. She was dressed in a short jersey knit dress that clung to her trim figure. It wasn't an expensive garment, and on most women it might have looked cheap. On Mary Dellarosa, however, it looked almost elegant.

I held out my hand to her and said, "Mrs. Dellarosa. I can't tell you how sorry I am."

She looked at me and held out her hand. I noted the size of the almost realistic emerald on her right ring finger. "Thank you. I appreciate that. Come on in. You're not planning on standing out there all day, I hope."

The hallway was covered in an ornamental turquoise wallpaper with baskets of irises embossed in gold foil. We bypassed the tiny living room, most of which was taken up by a huge, dark TV cabinet and two La-Z-Boys, and went through to the kitchen where there was a copper kettle boiling on the gas range and an AM radio wailing some kind of cowboy music.

"Have a seat," she said, and I squeezed by the counter into a velour-covered kitchen chair at a table made of wood-grained Formica. There was a butter dish with a dozen cigarette butts in it and a set of matching salt and pepper shakers in the centre of the table. A few stray grains of salt had been swept under the rim of the butter dish.

Mary sat down beside me and took out a cigarette. "So," she said, lighting it with a match from a tiny silver box, "I don't remember Anna ever mentioning your name. How long did you know her?"

I wondered for a moment whether I should lie or pretend not to understand the question. But then I decided on a simple "I didn't, actually," and waited for her to howl at me to get out of her house.

But she said only, "Oh. Then you were a fan of hers," and took a drag from her cigarette.

"I guess you could say that," I replied quietly.

"She was my only child," said Mary. Her lip was trembling, and I reached over and took the hand that wasn't holding the cigarette. "Thank you," she said.

"Now, Mrs. Dellarosa," I began.

"Call me Mary."

"Mary," I said. "I don't know if you feel like talking about this right now, but I have some questions I'd like to ask you about Anna."

"Oh, but I want to talk about her," she said. "You ask me what you want. Whatever. Do you know, all's I ever hoped for was someday somebody coming to me and saying, 'Tell me about Anna from the days before she got famous, before she got her big recording contract with that big record company.' That was just what I thought was really going to happen. And I was going to act just the same as I always did, untouched by the fame of it all. Would you like a coffee?" She stood up and took the kettle off the stove.

"Yes, thank you."

When she sat down again I said, "Now, Mary, what I'm going to ask you may seem really off the wall. And you don't have to answer if you'd prefer not to."

"As long as you don't ask me if this is my natural colour," she said, patting her hair and winking at me. "That's the only question I ever refuse to answer."

"All right." I smiled. "But feel free to boot me out if you think I'm out of line."

"I'm sure I won't have to do that."

"Okay," I said and took a deep breath. "Does the name Heinz Grobbelaar mean anything to you?"

She sipped her coffee. "No. Should it? Is he some kind of talent scout or something?"

"No," I said. "He's dead."

"Oh, no," she sighed. "That's a shame."

"I don't know if it is or not. He was a blackmailer."

"So why should I know him?"

"Because," I said slowly, "he was blackmailing Allan Allford."

She set her coffee mug down on the table and stubbed out her cigarette. "Yeah?" she said. "Who's he?"

"Mary — " I spoke quietly and confidentially " — I know that you know who he is. Please believe that I'm not telling you this to cause you any pain. And I certainly don't want to make what's happened any more difficult for you. But it's very important that I find out all I can about Allan Allford."

She looked at me for a minute while she lit a fresh cigarette, inhaling the smoke, sizing me up. And then she asked finally, "Why?"

"Because he may have killed Heinz Grobbelaar," I said.

She responded immediately by breaking into wild,

almost frightening laughter. All I could do was stare at her until she finished. "I hope," she said at last, "that they get him for it." She shook her head. "The sad thing is that the sorry bastard isn't man enough to kill anybody. He couldn't of done it. How did you find out about me? Who else knows?"

"I happened to come across something Grobbelaar had written. Apparently he put some kind of recording device into some electronics equipment that the Allfords rented from his store, and he was able to listen to their private conversations. As far as I know, no one else knows . . . except a few extremely discreet police officers."

"Well, I never!" she said, and studied me for a long time. "Okay. What do you want to know?"

"Do you feel you can tell me everything? I know there's no reason on earth why you should, but you have my word that it won't go beyond this table."

She smiled ironically and tapped her cigarette against the rim of the butter dish. "I guess I don't care who knows about it now. D'you know I'm thirty-nine years old, and I've spent more than half my life keeping quiet for that son of a bitch? And now look at me! I have no family. A few good friends, mind you. But I could of found a decent guy, got married, had a whole family. But not if Mr. Asshole Assfart — that's what I call him — had his way."

I sat back in my chair.

"Okay," she said again. "I'm fifteen, right? But I look older, maybe over twenty. Anyways, I can pass for age of majority, and I can get into bars. I don't drink too much because I don't want nobody throwing me out or asking for ID or nothing.

"Anyways, I meet this guy, about thirty or so. I can see he's married by the ring and all, so I don't want to get involved. But he says, 'Come on, it's all right, my wife don't care, I'm the one with all the money, she'll never leave me.' And he looks like he's got a lot of money, too, so I figure, what the hell? Maybe he'll buy me a fur coat or something. So I go with him to a hotel. Big mistake. Afterwards, after he has sex with me, he says, 'Okay, when can we do this again?' So I says, 'Tomorrow, I guess. That would be a good time.' He asks me how old I am, and I tell him the truth. I figure we've already done it once, he's not going to stop now. And he doesn't.

"So anyways, we keep meeting at this fancy hotel downtown, and getting this room, and then one day I tell him I'm pregnant, and he breaks my nose. Just like that. Bang! Right across the face. So I go to pieces, naturally, and tell him I'm going to go and see his wife and tell her, and all of a sudden he gets real nervous and tells me no, not to, because his reputation will be sullied. I remember that word 'sullied' because it was the name of my ex-boyfriend before Mr. Asshole Assfart. Sully.

"So he says, 'Wait. Don't do nothing yet.' All's I have to do is wait, and he'll see what he can do. 'First,' I says, 'fix my nose.' So he says, 'Maybe we can fix the rest of you, too.' And I says, 'No, I'm Catholic. I can't.'

"So I wait for a week, and I'm scared, really scared, because I don't hear nothing from him, and I'm going to have to tell my mother how I really got my nose broke. Remember, I'm only fifteen. I don't really want to get the law after him, because, after all, I still kind of like him. Up till then, anyways. After a week, though, he meets me at the hotel with this legal document that him and his father made up, and I have to sign it, right?"

She stopped talking to drink some coffee. I watched her without saying anything.

"Okay," she continued, "so I sign it. I guess you want to know what it says. It says I'm going to get fifty thousand dollars plus a house to live in if I promise never to tell anyone about what happened."

"Fifty thousand dollars?" I said. "And a house?"

"Don't think the house was such a big deal," she said. "You should of seen the mess this place was in when I moved in."

"Nevertheless," I said. "A house."

"Yeah. So I sign it, like I said. And I get my nose fixed, and I'm almost glad he broke it because it's much prettier now. Anyways, I had Anna, and she was the best thing that ever happened to me. I gave her everything. And then I used up all the money, and he had to give me more."

"He did?"

"Don't forget, the guy's loaded."

"Yes, I realize. But still — "

"By then he was getting real famous as a lawyer, you see. He told me, before I got pregnant, that someday he's going to be the prime minister. I guess I was supposed to feel important or something because I was his mistress. That's what he called me. So he pays me the money. He makes up this fund, and the money that comes out of it is for Anna, until she goes out on her own. Which she just did, last year. He got her this job at this eye doctor's. This doctor knew his wife."

"Did Anna know about this?"

She suddenly looked older. Her face seemed to collapse, and her cigarette hand shook. "I never told her," she whispered, "until a couple a weeks ago. All along I told her that her father was this French guy who went back to France and never saw her. Then she got this idea that she's been working for a year, and she should take a holiday and go to France and find him. So then I had to tell her. And she decided she wanted to see Mr. Asshole Assfart for herself. That was — " She choked and began to weep.

"Saturday," I finished for her.

"Saturdee," she sobbed. "That bastard. He told her to get out of his sight."

"I'm sorry," I said, putting my arms around her. "I'm so sorry."

I DECIDED TO CALL Detective Owl.

"Yes, Edna," he said. "Have you got that report finished?"

"No," I said. "My week's not up. But I have to talk to you about something."

"Fine. Can we discuss it over the phone?"

"I suppose so," I said. "I may need some serving and protecting."

"Oh, great," he muttered. "What have you done now?"

"Maybe this should wait."

"Maybe it had better not."

"All right," I said agreeably. "But before I get into the real reason for my call, I have to ask you something. Did the police find any significant clues in the Grobbelaar murder while they were investigating the break-in the other night?"

He paused. I knew that he was trying to figure out why I was asking. "Like what?" he asked finally.

"Oh, I don't know. Anything of Grobbelaar's? Anything he might have left in his shop that was of personal value?"

I could practically hear the wheels turning in his head.

"No, Edna," he said. "There was nothing of Grobbelaar's in the shop. Nothing more than the merchandise. But even if there were, it's none of your business. Now what is the *real* reason for your call?"

"I don't want you screaming at me," I warned him. "I'll hang up if you do."

"I don't scream," he said. "I raise my voice when necessary. I'm hoping to hell that this won't be one of those times."

"So am I," I said with feeling. "Arthur Birch."

"What about him?"

"Is he dangerous?"

"What the hell is that supposed to mean?"

"I mean, is he a psychopath who will stop at nothing to protect himself?"

I heard stifled laughter. "Do you even know what you're saying?"

"If you mean, do I know what a psychopath is, yes I do. I wouldn't use a term like that loosely."

"All right," he said more seriously. "Do you have reason to believe that you have somehow incurred the wrath of Arthur Birch?"

"I have no idea if I have or not. He told me he could trace my call. Is that true, or was he bluffing?"

"You called him?" he yelled.

"Sounds awfully close to screaming," I told him.

"You called him?" he said quietly. "Why?"

"Why not? I felt like talking to him. I wanted to hear the sound of his voice, to find out if it was murderous or not."

Detective Owl was saying, "Oh, Jesus, oh, Jesus," over and over again.

"Stephen," I said. "Are you still there?"

"What did you say?"

"Stephen, are you still there?"

"No!" he roared. "To Arthur Birch!"

"Oh," I said. "The possible psychopath. I asked him what he was doing last Tuesday between seven and nine."

"Jesus H. Christ," said Detective Owl.

"But he wouldn't tell me. He said he'd already told the police and that he wouldn't play games. And then he told me that he could have the call traced. At the time I thought he was bluffing, but in light of the fact that he is now on the loose, I am wondering if there is any possibility that he may try to come after me."

"Do you realize," said Detective Owl so slowly that light could have shone between his words, "what a mess you are making of my investigation?"

I didn't answer. I did have a good idea, of course, but I wasn't going to admit it to him.

"I suppose it was you who called him on Wednesday morning."

"I never told him I was a terrorist," I answered.

"Jesus Christ," he said again.

"Look," I said. "All I want to know is whether he's dangerous. Should I be walking around with a leather stud collar on?"

There was a moment of silence.

And then he said, "I'm not going to tell you."

"Oh, come on, Detective. This isn't a game."

"You're damn right it's not!" he exploded. "So I wish you'd stop acting as if it were."

"Listen," I said. "If I promise not to bother you any more about this case, will you at least tell me whether I can go to sleep at night without worrying about whether I'll see the next day?"

He sighed. "I can't believe I ever thought you were like all the other busybodies I've dealt with. You're not."

"I'm not?"

"No! You're a thousand times worse! Never, in all of my days on the force, have I ever met anyone as interfering and destructive as you."

"Well," I said. "What can I say? I'm certainly not flattered."

"As far as we can determine," said Detective Owl, "Arthur Birch did not kill Heinz Grobbelaar, and it seems unlikely to me that he would be interested in killing you. Although I might."

"Thank you," I said with dignity. "That's all I wanted to know. I'm sorry to trouble you. I'll speak to you next week when my report is finished. And that will be the end of it."

"Good," he said.

"Bye," I said and hung up.

fourteen

MY LIST OF SUSPECTS WAS shrinking fast. I felt that the only people who were really likely to have killed Heinz Grobbelaar were Gwen Tattersall and Giovanni Pasqualino. After my conversation with Mary Dellarosa, I was convinced that Allan Allford couldn't have done it. It wasn't in his character, however terrific his motive might be. He would rather have set up Heinz Grobbelaar in a mansion in Forest Hill with seventeen servants than cut his throat.

Now Lillian, on the other hand, was probably quite capable of killing someone. But throat-slashing wasn't her style. She was no Lady Macbeth. She would rather have poisoned him, neatly, quietly, and effectively.

No, it had to be Pasqualino or Tattersall. Either one of them could have sent the postcards, too. Pasqualino seemed to be on an eternal quest for inspiration at the expense of the Canada Council, and Tattersall might have accompanied Zylie Wedge on some of her lecture tours. And the idea that she might have had a secondary motive — that of ridding the city of one of its pornography outlets — was particularly appealing.

I lay in bed on Saturday morning, watching Maria Teresa clambering onto the back of Guido, who was still sleeping inside his shell, and tried to look at the problem of tracing a killer from as many new angles as I could. Then I showered and ate and went out to the phone booth to dial Gwen Tattersall's number.

It was obvious that I had woken her. "Hello?" she tried to say. Her voice was more than just gravelly. "Rocky" might be more apt.

"Hello. May I speak to Ms. Tattersall, please?"

"Speaking."

"Hello, Ms. Tattersall. My name is Betty James, and I'm a freelance journalist. I'm doing a piece on interregional cultural ties and the travel imperative, and I was wondering if you might have a few moments to answer some questions."

"Well," she said, "I don't really know. What magazine will be publishing this article?"

"I can't really tell you for certain. *Saturday Night* has expressed an interest, but they want to see the finished piece."

"I understand. Well, I suppose I've got a minute. What is it you want to know?"

"Thank you. I appreciate your generosity. Now, my thesis is that human beings have an innate need to move around, something that goes beyond the search for food and shelter. What I'm talking about is a yearning for new sensory input, simply to replenish the exhausted creative processes."

"How fascinating," Gwen Tattersall murmured.

"But I also believe," I continued, "that there is a pattern to this movement, that there are actually some locales more conducive to this renewal process than others. Now, I'm wondering whether you could tell me, on a scale of one to ten, how the following places have refreshed your creative drive. Let's say that one represents an absolute failure to inspire, and ten represents the ultimate in inspirational value. If you've never travelled to one of the locales that I mention, please just say zero. All right?"

"All right," said Gwen. "Fire away!"

"Calgary."

"Umm . . . five. Neutral."

"Sault Ste. Marie."

"Seven."

"Halifax."

"Am I allowed to use half points?"

"Just the closest number up," I said.

"Okay. Eight."

"Paris?"

"Four. Too stifling."

"Belgium?"

"Zero. Never been there."

"Hmm,"I said. "All right. How about Australia?"

"Zero to that one, too. Although I do hope to go someday."

"I see," I said. "Okay. Britain?"

"Nine."

"Venezuela?"

"Zero."

"Well," I said. "This has certainly been a great help to me. I thank you very much for your time."

"That's it?" she asked.

"Unless you have any comments to add."

"Actually," she said, "I would like to point out that I have always found travel to be one of the most exhilarating activities I can think of, and I do think that your theory is correct. Very interesting."

"Thank you," I said modestly.

"Well, good luck with your article. I'll be keeping an eye out for it. Betty James, you said?"

"Yes. Thank you again."

"You're very welcome. Come to my next show. I'd like to meet you."

I was beginning to wonder if Heinz Grobbelaar might have slit his own throat. It certainly didn't seem likely that Gwen Tattersall had done it, anyway.

I dialled Giovanni Pasqualino's number.

"Yeah?" he said.

"Oh, Mr. Pasqualino, I'm so glad I caught you at home."

"Who is this?" he asked.

"My name is Betty James," I said and recited the same spiel I had given to Gwen Tattersall. But when I came to the part about rating locales according to their power to inspire, Giovanni Pasqualino let out a howl of exasperation.

"First of all," he said loudly, "*that* is a crock of horse shit. I don't know where the hell you people get your ideas, but I'm sick and tired of pandering to the media. Why don't you give up trying to make a buck off the really talented people and get yourself a job in an office where you belong?"

"I don't think you — " I began.

"Secondly," he said, mowing over my words like a tank out of control, "I've been to every country on the face of this earth, including Outer Mongolia, and there is no way in hell that I'm going to tell you on a scale of one to ten how they influenced my work. They *all* influenced my work. How could they not? Now, go back to your desk and put that in your article, and if you ever come up with a sane, intelligent question about my paintings, I'll be more than willing to help you. Goodbye." He slammed down the receiver.

Gotcha, I thought. It had to be him. Hostile, defensive, and peripatetic. The perfect murderer.

"Wow, do you look great," Michael said, putting his arms around me and kissing my neck.

"Thank you," I said. "I'm feeling pretty great."

"I'll say you are," he whispered, letting his hands roam freely across my backside. "How are Guido and Maria Teresa enjoying the top of your dresser?"

"Fine, as far as I can tell," I whispered back. "They

don't seem to pay much attention to me, though. They're not the most exciting creatures I've met."

"A turtle's mind is a mysterious thing. If I lived in a glass case in your bedroom I wouldn't take my eyes off you."

"If you lived in a glass case in my bedroom it wouldn't be your eyes I'd be worried about. What time does your mother want us?"

"Five. I thought you might like to go to a movie later, so we're eating early again. Now, where should I put my toothbrush?"

"Your toothbrush?" I asked. "Is there some bizarre thing we still haven't tried yet?"

"You mean you've never tried the toothbrush trick before?" he gasped, throwing me down on the couch and baring his teeth. "You get a toothbrush, and you very . . . carefully . . . insert it . . ."

"Get off me, you sicko!" I laughed, pushing at his shoulders.

" . . . into the toothbrush holder until morning," he finished.

"You want to stay here overnight?"

"I thought it might be fun."

"I agree. As long as you don't mind the fact that I have to go out tomorrow morning at eight o'clock."

"Why so early?"

"I have to catch a worm." I smiled at him.

He looked at me out of the corner of his eye and said, "All right. But you'll have to get up at four o'clock, then, because I have plans for something that's going to take at least three hours."

"My God, Michael. I have to be able to walk tomorrow."

"Don't worry about that. By the time I'm finished with you, you'll just float away."

"EDINA!" CRIED MRS. CIPOLLONE as we came in the front door. "Havar you?"

"Great. How are you?"

"Oh, it's okay," she said and smiled broadly. "Dis time you no so nervose, eh?"

"Nervous? Who said I was ever nervous?"

She winked at me and led me into the kitchen. Mr. Cipollone was sitting at the table trimming his fingernails with a paring knife that had been sharpened so many times that the blade was actually concave. The television on the refrigerator was on, and he was listening to an Italian soap opera as he worked.

"Hey! Salvato!" Mrs. Cipollone said.

He looked up and said, "Edina! You come for eat again, eh?"

Mrs. Cipollone said something to him in stern Italian, and he brushed the nail trimmings off the tablecloth into his hand.

"How are you, Mr. Cipollone?" I asked.

"No too bad, no too bad. You get a job yet?"

Michael snickered behind me.

"Actually," I replied, stepping firmly on his toes, "I'm doing some freelance work right now."

Mr. Cipollone stared blankly at me.

"Oh," I said. "I'm doing a report for the police on an art collection." I decided not to mention whose collection it was. "They're paying me to tell them where this collection originated. They think it may be stolen."

"Ah!" he said. "Very good! For how long you do dis?"

"I'll be giving them my report on Tuesday. Then I'll have to go out and look for something permanent."

"Why don't we sit down?" Michael suggested.

I offered to help his mother with the dinner, but she told me to relax. Mr. Cipollone went back to his nails and his soap opera, and Michael tried to see how far he could get his hand up the leg of my shorts without anyone noticing.

We ate another huge meal, during which I submitted not only to an astounding array of meats and vegetables but also to a rather intense series of questions regarding my upbringing in Elegance and what my parents did for a living. By the time we got to cake and espresso, I figured that it was my turn to do some questioning.

"What part of Italy are you from?" I asked Mr. Cipollone.

"Me?" He set his espresso cup down. "I come from a little village about halfaway between Pescara and L'Aquila. You know where dat is?"

"No," I said. "But I know where the major cities are. Where's it close to?"

"If you look at the map," said Michael, cutting himself another piece of cake, "it's pretty well exactly halfway down the boot, maybe slightly to the right. East of Rome. Maybe a two-and-a-half-hour drive by car."

"It's called Orazio," said Mr. Cipollone. "Maybe I go back dere somatime for visit." He nodded and opened the Centerba bottle for the second time. Mrs. Cipollone poured more espresso into his cup.

"Do you have relatives there?"

"Oh, ya. Lotsa lots. I hev a seester, Giannetta. She marry a man wid a ristorant. Make lotsa money."

"What's it like there?"

"Very nice," said Mrs. Cipollone. "Montains, fresh air. De sommer no too nice. Lotsa flies, too hot. Ma, it's okay."

"Are you from the same place?"

"Oh, no." She shook her head. "I am from Villa Santa Chiara. Is too far from Orazio. Maybe twenty-five meenoots by car. You want more cake?"

"No, thank you," I said. "But twenty-five minutes doesn't sound too far."

"Oh, ya." She nodded. "Maybe twenty-five meenoots now. Maybe tree days when I live dere."

"They put new highways in," Michael explained. "Cut right through the mountains. Tunnels, reinforced mountainside roads, the whole thing. The Americans did a lot of it after the war as part of their rebuilding program. Where my mother once travelled on a mule for several days you can now pass through in under an hour."

"So how did you ever meet?" I asked.

"When I hev to get married," said Mr. Cipollone, "I ask around. Maybe somabody know where I find a good wife."

"I live wid his cosin when I am younger," said Mrs. Cipollone. "She introduce us."

"And it was love at first sight," said Michael with a grin. He refilled both our espresso cups and passed me the sugar bowl.

"Oh, no," Mrs. Cipollone said seriously. "I no like him too much. *Ma*, maybe after a few weeks I like him more better."

"After I tell her I want to come in Canada," Mr. Cipollone said, laughing. "She no is too stupid, my wife."

"And do you still have family in Villa Santa Chiara?"

"Oh, no," she said sadly. "I lose my family in de war. I no hev nobody close. Jiust Salvatore and my children. And grenddaughters. Everybody here in Canada." She smiled. "Maybe somaday my son get married and I hev tree more."

"Well," said Michael rather loudly. He set his espresso cup down with a clatter. "I guess we should get a move on if we're going to catch that film." He stood up.

"Thank you for the wonderful dinner," I said to his mother. "It was very nice of you to have me."

"Oh, it's notting," she said as I got up from my chair. "You come whenever you like."

"I certainly will," I said, turning around to glare at Michael who had just goosed me.

"Come on," he said. "Bogie's waiting."

"You have a great family," I said in the car. "Your mother's very kind."

"She has her moments," said Michael, looking over his shoulder to back out of the driveway. "She used to beat me with a broom when I was a kid."

"She didn't! Wait until you meet my mother if you want moments."

"What do you mean?"

"Prepare to be strung up and grilled."

"Oh, come on! She can't be that bad. Is she bigger than me?"

"No. But her nose is four times as long. And she believes in the small-town stereotypes about certain ethnic groups."

"She doesn't like Italians?"

"Her idea of Italians is spaghetti, Puccini, and Chianti. Oh, and men with hairy arms in undershirts doing road work."

"Does that mean she likes them or she doesn't?"

"I think my mother will probably think it's very romantic that I have an Italian lover," I said, grabbing him in a place not recommended by most road safety manuals.

"Lover?" said Michael, raising his eyebrows. He didn't make a comment about where my hand was. Possibly he was used to being grabbed there.

"What would you call yourself, then? Please don't say 'boyfriend.' The word makes me retch."

"How about 'fellow turtle fancier'?" he suggested. "Now, Edna, I have a favour to ask you."

"What?"

"Make sure that when we get out of the car you stand directly in front of me, as close as you can, the whole way into the theatre."

AFTER I THREW MY HUSBAND OUT of our small but charming one-and-a-half-storey, turn-of-the-century buff brick home, I had a lot of time to think. My parents, of course, wanted me back with them, to start fresh, to pretend that the whole thing had never happened.

"What will we say to the neighbours?" was my mother's biggest worry.

My father was more concerned about whether I'd be able to pay back the money we had borrowed from him to buy the house, the value of which had increased, with the help of a floor sander and a heat gun, from twenty-four nine to thirty-two five in two years. Part of the separation agreement was that my husband got the car and half of the furniture, and I got the house, the rest of the furniture, and all the bills. So I sold the house, paid back the fifteen thousand I owed my father, and quit my job at the bank. Then I applied to the Ontario College of Art and was accepted on the merit of three dozen botanical studies in water-colour that I had done for my Grade 13 biology course. Although I imagine the look of desperation in my eyes must also have played a part in my admission.

I studied there for two years, then transferred into a B.A. program in art history at the University of Toronto and graduated when I was twenty-six. By then my mother had stopped being worried about what the neighbours would think and switched to feeling frantic about what kind of job I'd be able to get. Much to the surprise of everyone in my family, Gerald Fineberg hired me. I figured that it must have been because I had discovered by then how to talk to city people. There was a certain tone of voice I had learned, one that suggested urgency and the possibility of lost opportunities, one that no one in Elegance ever used unless they were about two hours late for a private appointment with the Queen. I took the job because he gave me time off during the first two summers to complete my master's degree.

What plagued me throughout the better part of *The Maltese Falcon* was the thought of walking into the Lillian Allford Gallery the following week and asking for a job. No matter how much I loved selling paintings, I couldn't see myself working for a woman who had the morals required to stay married to Allan Allford. I knew that she knew everything about the Mary Dellarosa payoff. I even went as far as to assume that she'd probably been in on it herself, if not at the start, then at least later on. And she knew that I knew something about it.

But she also must have realized that I was no slouch when it came to getting things done. I was certain, despite her beating about the bush, that I'd be hired if I wanted the job. At the moment, however, I felt as though I'd rather be helping Dr. Harold Cunderlik into his latex gloves every morning than helping someone like Lillian Allford to increase her profit margin.

"Hey." Michael nudged me. "Where are you? I've been holding this Sprite under your nose for the past five minutes. Or have you been sucking it in through your nostrils?"

"Sorry," I whispered. "I'm back on Hazelton Avenue."

"Well, come back here," he said, putting his arm around me. "I do want you for more than your body."

Which may have been true. However, he later demonstrated, to my complete satisfaction, that my body wasn't just going along for the ride.

fifteen

"GOOD MORNING," SAID MICHAEL for the second time.

"What time is it?" I croaked.

"Quarter past seven. Time to get up. Your worm is waiting."

"Oh, God," I muttered. "It feels more like quarter after five."

"No," he whispered, rubbing his stubbly face against mine. "That was the first time I woke you up."

I crawled to the shower and was back on the edge of the bed, towel-drying my hair, when the news came on. Nothing about the Grobbelaar investigation.

"Good," I said. "What would you like for breakfast?"

"Coffee," Michael said from beneath the quilt.

"And what else?"

"Nothing. Just coffee."

"No juice? Cereal? Toast and jam?"

"*Mangiacake* food," he said. "Got any cold pizza?"

"Pizza?" I shrieked. I pulled the quilt away from his face and squinted at him suspiciously. "And what the heck's a *mangiacake?*"

"A cake-eater," he said, laughing. "You know. All you WASPs ever eat is cake." He turned the quilt down farther. "Get under here. I'll eat you for breakfast."

"I'll make the coffee," I said, and leaped off the bed.

We stood at the door as I was leaving. "You're sure

you won't be bored?" I asked. "What are you going to do here all day?"

"I'll take out your underwear and imagine you in it."

"Okay," I said casually. "But if you're gone when I get back I won't panic."

"I won't be," he promised, putting his arms around me. "Now kiss me goodbye."

THE LYTTON TENNIS COURTS were empty. Lying on the crushed brick surface was a thin puddle of water that reflected the clear sky like a calm, deep lake. I sat down on the bench facing it for only a minute, just long enough to drop two keys through a gap between the boards that made up the seat. Then I stood up again and climbed the hill to Alexandra. I didn't look back. I wasn't interested in seeing what happened next.

I checked my watch. It was quarter to nine. I decided that the best thing for me would be to take a nice long walk, just to keep myself calm. I went as far north as Lawrence and then walked across to Bathurst where I rested for a few minutes in a bakery, eating a bagel with cream cheese. It was about ten o'clock when I got to Coldstream and headed east towards Gerald's house.

I only went as close as I had to in order to see the large U-Haul van parked in the driveway. The front door of the house was open. After a while two men came out carrying what were clearly paintings wrapped in blankets. They slid these onto the truck, and then headed back up the front steps with more blankets in their arms. One of them lingered on the porch to light a cigarette. I thought I saw his hand, but I wasn't certain. I moved a little closer, standing behind the thick trunk of a maple.

The second time they came out of the house I had a clear view of the smoker. His right thumb was gone.

Trying to ignore the clenching in my abdomen, I stood and watched for a moment, memorizing his face, guessing his height and weight. In broad daylight he looked like someone I would have passed in the street without giving a second glance. If it hadn't been for the missing thumb, I was sure I would never have known him. Then he spoke to the other man, and although I couldn't make out individual words, I recognized his cool, sullen tone.

I wished that I had brought my camera with me. I could have given Detective Owl a photograph of the man who had attacked me.

Then I got a better idea. I waited until the two had gone back into the house, then I walked briskly back to Bathurst, and went into the nearest telephone booth. I picked up the receiver and dialled 911.

"Ten-forty-six. Emergency."

I took a deep breath, raised the pitch of my voice about an octave, and shrieked, "Oh, thank God! I don't know what to do! My neighbour's away in the hospital, and his house is being broken into. Imagine the nerve of those people! In broad daylight, even! You've got to send someone right away."

"May I have your name and the address, please?" Her voice was so calm that I almost forgot to sound hysterical.

Almost. But not quite. "Oh! It's Pat Wilson on Coldstream Avenue." I gave her Gerald's house number.

"Thank you, ma'am. A car will be there in the next few minutes."

"Oh, please hurry. I can see them now. Shall I give you a description? There are two of them, with a big truck."

"Thank you for calling, ma'am. Please hang up now. This line must be kept open for emergencies."

"All right," I said with a luxurious smile. "Goodbye."

"YOU WHAT?" SHOUTED GERALD. He was sitting up in his hospital bed looking more red than green.

"It makes sense, Gerald. You didn't really want to give away all your paintings to a loan shark, anyway. Your Riopelle alone would have more than covered the principal. And the Bush would have made up the interest. And not only that, but why should I let that creep just walk away? He could have killed me."

"But the *police*? These guys have the police on their payroll! Now I'm really dead."

"Oh, come on, Gerald. This isn't New York. They're probably being locked up as we speak. And just think how thrilled the Payco Loans Company is going to be to hear that someone else is trying to beat them to the loot." That thought gave me almost as much pleasure as imagining the look on the face of the thumbless thug as the police took him into custody.

"But the big guy," said Gerald. "What about him? I'm lying here helpless, and he's probably sending out another pair with machine guns. You might as well kiss me goodbye now."

"Oh, Gerald," I said. Then I realized that he was leaning over the side of the bed. I wondered if he was ill. "Are you all right?" I asked, standing up quickly. I reached for the little kidney tray on the bedside table.

But he looked up at me, smiling. He had a brown paper package in his hand.

"What is that?" I asked suspiciously.

"My insurance. I had a feeling you were going to mess up my plans, Edna."

"Mess up?" I said loudly. "I never — "

He put his finger up to his lips. "Sshh," he said. "I don't want the nurse coming in here. Just take a look at this." He began to unwrap the package. "It's a little something I kept in my safe-deposit box. Belonged to a Mrs. Taylor. Lovely lady. She didn't have a clue, of course. Can you believe it? Five hundred dollars. Cash. Took it in a flash. Thought it was some mess her husband had forgotten to throw in the trash."

I stared at the little painting, vivid with bold strokes of ochre and cadmium and swirling with viridian and manganese blue.

"But that's a —" I began.

Gerald shushed me again. "Our secret," he said. "The finance companies mustn't find out. Do you understand?"

"I'm leaving, you lout," I said. "Goodbye."

"All right," he replied calmly. "Just don't go blabbing this all over the place. Remember, discretion is the mark of the sublime art dealer. And you do have the potential, Edna. Oh, and by the way," he added, lowering his voice, "that's not a Riopelle."

"But I saw it through your back window — "

"It's a Fineberg."

"What?"

"A squirt of paint here, a scrape of the knife there. Always impressed the hell out of the neighbours to see it there. That's why I thought the shark would take it. I figured he might have his own neighbours to impress."

"Gerald, are you telling me — "

"Yeah, they're all fakes. I never could understand why anyone would pay half a mil for a bunch of streaks and squiggles. In a way, I guess it'll be a relief to be out of the business. Maybe I'll get into real estate for a change."

"You hypocrite!"

"This is just between you and me, of course," he said, settling back against the pillows.

"You're also a liar."

"Who isn't?" He smiled lazily. "Now, run along,

Edna. Thanks for your help. I owe you one. Don't forget that. Call me sometime."

I SPENT THE AFTERNOON AT THE UNIVERSITY library, looking through the files on early Renaissance churches. I didn't get home until after six o'clock. When I unlocked my door there were no lights on, and there wasn't any sign of Michael. But it smelled as though he'd been cooking something great before he left.

I dropped my purse by the door and went into the bathroom. I had drunk six ounces of tea more than my bladder could comfortably hold during a forty-five-minute subway and bus ride, and I was lost in the pleasure of relieving myself when there was a sudden, thunderous roar from the living room that vibrated the toothbrushes in their holder. Brushes. Plural.

I sprang up from my perch, thinking that Kegel would have been proud, and hastily put myself back together. My first thought was that the sharks had been released, and they had planted a bomb under my couch. My second thought was to open the door and yell.

"What the hell is that?"

"*Tosca!*" Michael shouted back, adjusting the volume to a more comfortable level. "This is the Puccini part."

"The Puccini part of what?"

"The rest of the night," he replied.

"Where were you hiding?"

"Behind your bed. I was hoping you'd come in and get undressed. What are you doing with a rolling pin in there anyway?"

"Wouldn't you like to know! What have you been cooking?"

"Just you wait."

I followed him into the darkened kitchen, and he lit a match.

"Candles?" I said. "What is this?"

"I thought you might be hungry," he said. "This is the spaghetti and Chianti part."

We were halfway through our food and a third of the way through the bottle of wine when Michael said, "Your mother called."

"When?"

"While I was making supper."

"You talked to her?"

"Only for about ten minutes. Someone was in the background yelling, 'Keep it short! Think of the phone bill!'"

"My father," I said.

"I guess so."

"You talked to my mother for ten minutes? About what?"

"You, mostly. I told her what you'd been doing for the past two weeks. You should call her more often, you know."

"She said that?"

"No. She said that she's been anxious about you since the murder, but she didn't want to annoy you by phoning because she knows you think she's a worrywort."

"That's what she said?"

"You haven't called her since you found Grobbelaar?"

"No," I said. "And don't try to make me feel guilty, either. You don't know her. What else did she say?"

"She asked me who I was."

"And?"

"I told her I was the terrarium maintenance man."

"You didn't!"

"And she laughed."

"She laughed? She didn't threaten to call the police?"

"No. She said, 'I guess you must be Edna's boyfriend. She never tells us about her love life.'"

I stared at him. "Yes, I do. When I have one." Which was why she never heard from me.

"Well, you don't have to tell her anything now. I gave her all the details. All the polite ones, anyway."

"What did you say?"

"I told her that we've been hanging around together. I told her what I did for a living, how much money I make, what kind of car I drive, all the things I thought she'd like to know. She seemed satisfied. Then she said, 'Cipollone. That's Eyetalian, isn't it?' And I said, 'Yes, Mrs. Heathcott,' and she said, 'Oh, please call me Hettie.' And then she asked me what Cipollone meant, and I told her."

"And?" I said.

"And?"

"What does it mean?"

He smiled.

"Come on," I said. "I can always look it up in a dictionary. You might as well say it."

"Big onion."

"*Big onion?* Michael Big Onion?" I nearly fell off my chair laughing. "And to think I ever thought Edna was bad."

"Hey," he said. "Your mother didn't seem to think it was funny. She said, 'Oh, isn't that fascinating. I believe there's a Garlic on my husband's side.'"

"There is?" I wiped my eyes.

"That's what she said. She sounded sincere."

"Well," I said. "Well."

"She wasn't half as bad as you made her sound."

"Does she want me to call her now?"

"Nope. She said, 'Tell her to save her quarter. She can call me when she feels like chatting.' I told her I'd drive you up for a visit next weekend."

"You did?"

"Yeah. She said she wanted to meet me, anyway. To see if I'm really as perfect as I sound over the phone."

"Good Lord! You've charmed her!"

"I'm a charming guy."

"You certainly are," I said, taking a sip of wine. "Come on, Big Onion. Finish up. I want to see what you made me for dessert."

IN SPITE OF WHAT she had told Michael, my mother called me at five to eight the following morning.

"I hope I didn't wake you up," she said.

"No. I've been up for an hour. I'm working on a report for the police, and I have to get it finished today. I suppose Michael mentioned it to you."

"He said something about some stolen articles they had recovered," she said vaguely. "It has something to do with that sex-shop man?"

"Yes," I said. "Things that they found in his apartment."

My mother put her hand over the receiver. I could hear her saying, "All right, Bob. I'll tell her. Let me talk to her." Then she said to me, "He seems very nice."

"Who, Grobbelaar?" I said perversely.

"I thought his name was Cipollone."

"Oh, him. Yes. He's very nice."

"Is he serious, do you think?"

"Actually, he has quite a sense of humour. I thought you might have noticed that."

"Edna," she sighed. "You know what I mean."

"Mother, I've known him for less than two weeks. How serious can it be?"

"Well, he gave you that terrarium, didn't he?"

"He told you that?"

"Your father looked up the price in the Canadian Tire catalogue. Those things aren't cheap, you know."

"Mother!"

"The only thing I'm concerned about," she went on, "is salmonella. I thought that turtles spread salmonella."

"Don't worry. I won't be putting them in my mouth."

"No, but the germs. You handle the turtles, and the germs can spread. You'd be surprised, Edna. I hope you always wash your hands right afterwards."

"Every time, Mom."

"Well, good. I wouldn't want to hear that you've been rushed to the hospital with stomach cramps. Now your father is here, breathing down my neck. He wants me to tell you that when he was downtown yesterday he saw a sign in the chartered accountant's office. You know, a Help Wanted sign. The only thing is, you'd have to be able to type sixty words a minute, and I couldn't remember whether you ever got past fifty-two."

I considered the possibility of screaming, but the thought lasted for only a second when I realized that my mother would probably imagine that some lecher had just climbed in my bedroom window and was about to have his way with me. I said calmly, "Mother, I believe we've discussed this at some length before."

"Yes, we have, dear."

"And I don't intend to move back."

"So it *is* serious, then."

"Mom, this has nothing to do with Michael. This has to do with my career."

"Well, from what I can see, you haven't got much of one these days."

"How comforting," I said. "Did your mother call you up when you were nearly thirty years old and tell you that you'd ruined your life?"

"No," she said. "But she didn't need to. By the time I was your age, I was happily married with three children." I detected an almost imperceptible stress on the word "happily."

"All right," I said. "I have to go now."

"But you're coming up on Saturday?"

"I guess so. Michael wants to see where I grew up. God knows why."

"Because he's serious about you," my mother said. "He probably wants to make sure you come from good stock. That's very important to them, isn't it?"

"To whom, Mother?"

"Eyetalian people. Don't they place a great emphasis on the family?"

"I'll see you on the weekend," I said.

"What time?"

"I'll call you before we leave."

"All right, dear. Well, I'd better go now. Your father's blood pressure is rising a full point with each minute we talk. And I even called before eight."

"Say hi to him for me," I said.

"I will. Goodbye, Edna."

"Bye, Mom."

I went back to the kitchen table where I was adding the last few touches to my report on the Grobbelaar collection. I had two maps to refer to: one that showed how Italy looked during the fifteenth century, the other how it looked today. Out of curiosity I looked for Orazio and Villa Santa Chiara, but I couldn't find either. I assumed that villages didn't count for much with cartographers.

I had, with a fair degree of certainty, been able to place Grobbelaar's collection somewhere in the region of either Abruzzi or Molise. I was also certain that the tapestries had been woven by monks, because they shared a number of similarities with a well-known collection that now lay under glass in a French museum, but that had originally come from an Italian monastery flattened by an earthquake early in the nineteenth century. Whether that meant the church where Grobbelaar's collection had originated was attached to a monastery, I couldn't tell. But I made a note suggesting that it might be worthwhile finding out if the person attempting to claim the collection was able to demonstrate an awareness of the monasterial connection.

I was all set to roll my last sheet of paper into the typewriter when the phone rang again. I looked at the clock on the stove. It was ten-fifteen.

"Hello?"

"Edna?" It was Ellen, sounding even more breathless than usual.

"Hi, Ellen. So, what's new? I hope you're not calling with another scandalous problem for me to solve." I laughed lightly.

She didn't. "I guess you haven't heard."

"Heard what?"

"About Dr. Cunderlik," she said softly.

"If you mean about his receptionist, yes, I heard. In fact, I even went to see her mother."

"No," she whispered. Her voice had nearly dropped out of hearing range. "This is about Dr. Cunderlik himself."

"What? What happened?"

"Dr. Cunderlik," she said quietly, "died."

"He died?" I felt my legs go numb. I pulled my chair over and sat on it. "How?" My first thought was that Dottie had finally lost her cool head and backed over him with the Mercedes, or that perhaps John Henderson had gone berserk over the pathetic letter and strangled him.

But Ellen cleared her throat and said, "He jumped. Out a window."

"He killed himself?" I said, aghast. "When?"

"Yesterday. Lillian is away, so the answering machine at the gallery had my home number on it. His lawyer called me first thing this morning to find out whether we were selling any pieces from his collection, because Dottie wants them all back. That's when I found out. Oh, Edna! I can't believe it! I'm just shaking. Do you know I saw him only two weeks ago, when he brought in an Avery for resale?"

"Where was the window?" I asked.

"It was at his office."

"He jumped two storeys and killed himself?"

"Broke his neck," she whispered. "Can you believe this has happened? I've already talked to a number of collectors, close friends of the Cunderliks, and no one has any idea why he would have killed himself. He always seemed such a happy man. And he adored his wife. I can't believe he'd do this to her."

"Ellen," I said, "I don't think I can talk any more now. Do you know when the funeral will be?"

"Thursday. First thing in the morning. Call me back when you can."

"I will, Ellen. Thank you."

I didn't tell her what was on my mind. I didn't know whether I could have told anyone.

I should have called him, I thought. I should have told him that John Henderson hadn't killed Grobbelaar.

sixteen

GIOVANNI PASQUALINO LIVED IN what had once been a three-bedroom house overlooking Riverdale Park. In the early seventies he had bought it from an aging couple who were unable to maintain it any longer. Then he parked a dumpster on the front lawn and tore every room out of the second floor. What he was left with was a main floor kitchen, bath and living area, with a one-and-a-half-storey skylit studio above.

I recognized the house from an article I had read in a decorating magazine a few years back. "The Artist at Home," or something like that. Pasqualino had replaced his front lawn with a patch of vinca minor, and he had mounted one of his own bronzes in the centre on a rough slab of granite. A covered porch ran across the front of the house. A withered plant hung in a pot from the railing.

My plan was to leave my photos of the postcards at his door, ring the bell, and run like hell. Then I would phone him and see what kind of reaction I got.

I climbed the steps and took a quick look through the window to make sure that he wasn't hovering around, waiting for his mail to arrive. I knew he was in because I had phoned from a booth down the street and hung up when he answered. I decided to lay ten of the postcard photographs in two lines across the doormat. I arranged them neatly, picture-message-picture-message, so that none of the edges overlapped. I balanced for an instant on the threshold with my back to the door, just to make sure that they would be clearly visible when he came out. They were. Then I turned around to press the doorbell.

And he was looking at me through the window in the door.

I don't remember losing my balance. All I remember is that I was suddenly on my behind, staring up at the craziest-looking man I had seen in my life. And he was staring back.

"Who are you and what are you doing?" he asked in a surprisingly even voice.

I waited five seconds before I even opened my mouth, just to review the alternatives. I considered, Oops! Sorry! Wrong house! in which case I'd never get the answer I wanted. Or I could have burst into song to try to convince him that I was a singing chain letter. Or I could simply have taken advantage of my downward momentum, rolled off the steps, and run.

I chose the irrational approach.

"What am I doing?" I said, as if in astonishment, which wasn't difficult. "This is performance art. You surprise me, Mr. Pasqualino. You, of all people."

"Get up," he said. "Now."

I stood up. He looked me up and down twice.

Then he said, "I want to hear you say, 'Let us suppose that ten represents the ultimate in inspirational value.'"

"No," I said.

"It is you, isn't it? I never forget a voice."

"Shouldn't that be *face*?" I asked, taking a fast look downwards to see if the *Ich vergesse nie ein Gesicht* card was among the ones I had positioned so strategically.

Giovanni Pasqualino looked down, too. "I meant

voice," he said. "I never forget a voice. Now what is all this crap?"

"Actually," I said, "this isn't really performance art."

"No kidding."

"It's a study in innate creative sensitivity." I held out my hand. "How do you do? I'm Ann Smith. I'm sorry if I deceived you over the telephone the other day, but I'm sure you can understand what would happen if I failed to follow scientific procedure. Without the double-blind test it wouldn't be a valid study." I smiled self-effacingly as I grasped desperately for as many scientific terms as I could remember.

He stared at my hand for a moment and said, "I don't know what your problem is, lady, but if you don't get that garbage off my steps this instant I'm going to call the cops."

Great, I thought. Just what I need. I smiled again and said, "No, you won't."

"Who the hell do you think you are? Pick it up. Now."

"You wouldn't dare call the police, would you?" I went on, thinking joyfully that at last I was getting somewhere. I said, "Because you know that the police know about you."

"What?" he yelled.

I lowered my voice and raised my eyes. "You know that they know what Grobbelaar knew. And that means trouble, doesn't it?"

He stepped off the threshold and advanced a step. I took a split second to glance over my shoulder, just to make sure that there were witnesses out in the street in case I had to make a citizen's arrest. I noticed a single greyish man with dehydrated-looking skin crossing over to the park.

Giovanni Pasqualino glanced, too. Then he grabbed my arm and yanked me into the house.

"Let me go!" I intended to roar, but it came out more like one of Ellen's squeaks.

"Shut up," he said, and locked the door. "Sit down."

"Here?" I inquired, looking down at the black rubber-boot butler.

"In there," he said, pointing to what I imagined was intended to be the living room. It looked nothing like the "Artist at Home" article I had read. He must have hired a whole team of dial-a-maids to come in before the photoshoot. There were open books lying everywhere, dirty plates and glasses tucked into dusty crevices, and art supply catalogues, paint-stained clothes, and about twenty issues of *TV Guide* piled in layers like lasagne on the couch. The only place to sit was on top of these, and I knew that I'd only end up sliding onto the floor, which was so filthy that even my mother would sooner have kissed Guido and Maria Teresa on the lips than sit on it.

"I believe I'll stand, if you don't mind."

I don't think he heard me. He was looking wildly about, as if hoping to find something blunt to hit me with. Then, from somewhere out of the mess, he pulled a pack of cigarettes, lit one, and coughed.

"Okay," he said. "Now I want you to tell me everything you know."

"Starting from when?" I asked. I considered adding, Before or after the last Ice Age? but changed my mind when I noticed that his face had broken into a lustrous sweat, and there were wet patches under his arms that hadn't been there when he'd first opened the door.

"Starting from what you know about me."

If I hadn't been stupid enough to mention Grobbelaar already, I could have said, I know that you're an incredibly attractive man, and I've been waiting to meet you for most of my life. Then he might have been less inclined to dig a hole in his basement and bury me in it. "Well," I said, "I know that Grobbelaar was blackmailing you. And I know that he's dead."

"Go on," he said, grabbing my forearm and squeezing it like a tube of titanium oxide.

"Do I have to?"

"I want to hear you say that you know I committed murder."

I swallowed. "Do I have to?"

"Do you believe I could have committed murder?" His sweaty face was about an inch away from mine. I could see a tiny blue blood vessel pulsing under his right eye. He had a smudge of Hooker's green light on his cheekbone. His breath stank.

"That depends," I said, "on whether this is one of your good days or one of your bad days."

"You bitch!" he yelled. He threw his cigarette down and squashed it with his foot. Then he put his hands around my neck. "I could kill you," he said. He was probably right. It was all I could do to keep my eyes open and focused on his. He wasn't squeezing yet. He was just letting me know that he could. And then he let go.

"So, how did you find out?" he asked, suddenly quiet, turning towards the living room and lighting another cigarette.

I thought, So this is how I'm going to spend my final minutes: telling this homicidal lunatic how I know he killed a depraved pervert.

There was an unglazed terracotta pot filled with carbon sticks at the foot of the stairs. In one swift, quiet movement, before he had a chance to turn around again, I picked it up and threw it at him.

It didn't smash when it hit his head. It smashed when it hit the floor. Then *he* hit the floor face down, making a sound like "oomph." I checked to make sure that he was still breathing and that his cigarette, which had landed on the couch, was stubbed out.

Then I opened the front door, grabbed my photographs, and ran like hell.

THAT IS THE MOST idiotically dangerous thing that you have ever done, I kept thinking the whole way home. As soon as I got inside and locked my door, I went to the telephone. I did remember that I had promised not to mention the Grobbelaar investigation to Detective Owl again, but when I considered the fact that Giovanni Pasqualino had practically confessed to me — along with trying to knock me off in the process — I felt that I was entitled to break my word. I knew that once Detective Owl had calmed down enough to listen to the voice of reason, he would grudgingly admit that I had done him a heck of a big favour.

"Detective Owl, please," I said confidently to the person who answered.

"I'm sorry," she said. "He's not in today. May I help you?"

"But he'll be in tomorrow," I said hopefully.

"No, he's off for four days now. If there's something I can help you with, please let me know. I'm a detective, too," she added.

Talk about a let-down! My moment of triumph had been whipped out from under my feet in a few cold seconds.

"I was hoping to speak directly to Detective Owl." I tried to set my tone halfway between bold determination and dire urgency, but she didn't seem particularly sensitive to nuance. Her voice became tinged with annoyance.

"I've just told you that he's not here."

"Then could I have his home number, please?"

"I'm afraid that's absolutely out of the question. I just can't go giving out an officer's private number to anyone who asks. Who's calling?"

"My name is Edna Heathcott. I'm working on an extremely important document for Stephen, something of vital significance in the Grobbelaar case, and it is crucial that I speak with him immediately."

"I see," she said, clearly unmoved. "Well, I do have a message on my desk saying that if a Ms. E. Heathcott calls in with her report finished, I am to call him and let him know. Is your report complete?"

"Not quite," I said. "Almost."

"But you had a question you wanted to ask him."

"No, I had a statement I wanted to tell him."

She sighed. "Well, why don't you tell me, and I'll pass the message along?"

I took a deep breath. "Okay," I said. "Tell him that Giovanni Pasqualino should be arrested for murder."

There was a moment of silence, as if she were trying to decide how to interpret my piece of news. Then she said, "Ms. Heathcott, those of us who have been directly involved in the Grobbelaar investigation are fully aware of what Mr. Pasqualino has done. Now, I'd like to suggest that you leave the timing of his arrest up to us."

"The timing of his arrest? The man is a dangerous criminal. What are you waiting for?"

"Ms. Heathcott — Edna — I don't mind telling you that Detective Owl and I have discussed the cost-benefit factors surrounding your involvement in this case at some length. I also don't mind saying that I'm in favour of seeking a court injunction prohibiting you from harassing Detective Owl."

"Harassing?" I shrieked. "I give him pertinent evidence regarding a murder investigation and you're telling me that I'm harassing him? Since when did the police arrest witnesses for harassment?"

"Witnesses?" she sniffed. "Are you telling me now that you actually saw this murder take place?"

"No. But I saw one almost take place an hour ago."

"Oh, really? Then perhaps I should transfer you to the desk sergeant so you can discuss it with him. Now, I'm terribly busy at the moment, Ms. Heathcott, and I'm afraid I can't spend any more time chatting with you. I'm going to have to say goodbye."

"Goodbye," I said furiously.

I couldn't believe it. I had always considered the police to be concerned, rational human beings whose sole intent was to keep the world safe for honest citizens like me. It made my head spin to think that they could be aware that Giovanni Pasqualino was a murderer and yet seem not even faintly interested in doing anything about it.

Perhaps Giovanni Pasqualino had somehow managed to bribe the police into letting him off — although where a Canadian artist, even a reasonably successful one, would get that kind of money was beyond me.

I got out the phone book and looked for Owl Stephen. There was no listing. I dialled 411 and asked for the number. I heard the operator typing the information into her computer, and then a recorded message came on. "At the customer's request, the number is non-published. It is not listed in our records. I repeat — "

"Damn!" I yelled, slamming down the receiver. It occurred to me that Detective Owl and his injunction-seeking partner might possibly be breaking the law by failing to arrest Giovanni Pasqualino. Why had they been so anxious to keep me from knowing about the investigation, anyway? Maybe I had been on the verge of cracking open some ugly police scandal, the nature of which I couldn't even begin to imagine.

I considered calling the attorney-general's office, but I realized helplessly that I would only sound exactly like the misinformed busybody that Detective Owl was always accusing me of being.

I felt depressed or sick or something that wasn't

normal, and I was still sitting at the kitchen table, staring out the window, when Michael arrived at five-thirty.

"What's wrong?" he asked, taking me in his arms.

"Oh," I said. "Maybe everything. For one thing, my parents think I'm a failure. For another, my optometrist killed himself. For another, I was nearly killed myself. And for another, I finally figured out who killed Grobbelaar, and the police refuse to arrest the guy."

"You were nearly killed?" he said, backing away and staring at me. "How?"

I took a step towards him. "This man, Pasqualino, the one who I realized killed Grobbelaar, tried to strangle me." I frowned. "Don't look at me like that!"

"Goddamn it, Edna! What were you doing near him in the first place?"

"Please don't yell at me," I said quietly. "I've had a very difficult day."

"I'm sorry," he said and put his arms around me again. "I just can't believe you were nearly killed." He lifted my chin and looked at my neck. "Where are the marks?"

"I don't have any marks. I threw a pot at his head and knocked him out."

Michael stared at me again. Then he said, "Edna, I think we should go into the living room and sit down. I want you to tell me everything." It seemed to me that he was now on the verge of breaking into laughter, but it was hard to be certain because he kept his face turned slightly away as we walked over to the couch.

"You don't believe me, do you?" I asked.

"Of course I believe you, Edna. It's just incredible to think that the same man who murdered Heinz Grobbelaar just happened to try killing you, too."

"He didn't just *happen* to try it," I said hotly. "He got

upset when I told him I knew, and he pulled me into his house and — "

"You were at his house?"

"How else was I supposed to get to him?"

"Edna!" he shouted. "You aren't supposed to get to him at all. Getting to him is up to the police."

"But you don't understand," I said. "The police know he did it and they don't care."

Michael put his arm around my shoulder. "Does this guy know where you live?"

"No. He doesn't even know who I am."

"Good. Then I don't think you have to worry about him coming after you. Maybe the police don't have enough evidence to make a case yet."

"Evidence? What kind of evidence do they want? The guy threatened to kill me when I told him I knew. Doesn't an admission count for anything?"

"Did he actually say, 'I killed Grobbelaar'?"

"Well, no. But he told me he wanted *me* to say it.

Michael snorted. "I know you don't mean it to be," he said, "but you have to admit that it does sound kind of funny. You're sure you didn't kill him?"

"He was still breathing when I left. Right now he's probably sitting on a pile of dirty books with an icepack on the back of his head."

He shook his head. "Well, you could always charge him with assault," he said. "If he doesn't charge you first. Was there blood?"

"Not a whole lot."

"Shit!" said Michael. "I'm never going to pick a fight with you. Edna, I think you'd better just give the police a few more days and see what happens. I don't know too much about the law, but I think that he actually has to come out and say that he killed someone before it counts for anything."

"Okay," I said, snuggling up to him. "So, how was your day?"

"Fine," he said. "But you didn't finish telling me about everything else. Your optometrist killed himself?"

I told him about Ellen's call and then about the conversation with my mother that morning. He listened carefully, keeping his arm tightly around me, and then he said, "Well, I'd say that I'm pretty serious about you. Your father's right about the cost of terrariums." He pushed me back against the side of the couch. "And I don't just sleep with every woman who asks me, you know."

"That's not what your mother told me," I whispered. "By the way, speaking of her, I almost forgot to ask you."

"What?" he murmured, nuzzling my clavicle.

"I finished my report for Owl today, and I had the map of Italy out. I tried to find your parents' villages, but they weren't marked."

"No, they wouldn't be," he replied against my shoulder. "They're practically deserted now. After the war there wasn't any decent work, so most of the people emigrated."

"And now they all live near St. Clair and Dufferin."

"No," he said with a smile. "Well, some of them do. But most of them went to different places all over the world. You should see what it costs to send out Easter cards to all the people my mother grew up with. The ones who are left, anyway. A lot of them were killed in the war, of course. She doesn't talk about that very often."

"I guess not," I said seriously.

"Hey," said Michael. "All this talk about death and violence isn't doing you any good. And it's certainly not making me feel like dancing for joy. Let's have some fun and games and get your mind off your troubles."

"Okay," I said. "Here's a fun game for you. Last one undressed has to wash the dishes tonight."

seventeen

On Tuesday morning I stapled my final report together and put it into a manila envelope. I would have liked to keep the photographs of the collection for my own files, but I didn't know whether the police would take kindly to that idea. If Detective Owl's female counterpart had anything to do with it, I'd probably be undergoing electroconvulsive therapy to wipe out any memory I might have retained about my work over the past week.

I wasn't looking forward to meeting the woman of my phone call, even if it did only mean passing the envelope across her desk. I somehow envisaged her as a cloud of noxious vapour with sharp fingernails and a wide mouth. And a gun. So naturally I was taking my time getting ready to go out.

At quarter to eleven the phone rang.

"Hello?"

"Edna, this is Detective Owl."

"Detective Owl! How nice to hear from you! How are you?"

He ignored my little stab at etiquette and said, "It's Tuesday."

"So it is. Thank you for calling to tell me."

He ignored that, too. "How is your assessment report coming?"

"Done," I said. "I just sealed it into its envelope, and I was going to put your name on it, but I knew that you wouldn't be there. What is the name of that very pleasant woman you work with?"

"I heard that you called yesterday," he said. "Mary Beth told me."

"*That* was Mary Beth Bone? Police spokesperson to the media?"

"Who did you think it was?"

"I don't know. She never told me. Now, don't worry. I'm just on my way out. The report will be on her desk in less than an hour."

"I'm not worried," said Detective Owl. "I was going to suggest that I come over and pick it up now, anyway. That way I can read it over and we can discuss any questions I may have."

Good, I thought. Once I had him cornered in my apartment I could nail him on the Pasqualino issue. "Good," I said. "That will save me a little time," as if I were in a mad rush to get on with other more important things.

"Okay," he replied. "I'll leave in a couple of minutes. I should be there by ten after."

"I'll have the teabags steeping."

He arrived wearing jeans and a T-shirt that read 100% Untarnished Copper. We sat at the kitchen table with tea and cookies, and I handed him the envelope. He opened it and pulled out the report.

"It's long," he said.

"I wanted to cover every possibility," I explained. "I've footnoted as much as I could, so you can double-check the sources if your claimant kicks up a fuss."

"Good idea." He glanced over the first page.

"I suppose you've got that one memorized now," I said.

He made a sound like a grunt and flipped over to the second page. Then he drank some tea and put the report on the table. "By the way," he said, "I thought you might like to know that two men were arrested breaking into Gerald Fineberg's house on the weekend."

I set my teacup down gently on its saucer. "Were they?" I said. "Imagine that!"

"They tried to convince the arresting officers that Fineberg had given them the key."

"Imagine! Why would Gerald have done that?"

He gave me the squint-eyed look. "They did have the keys. I guess Mr. Fineberg must have foolishly left them under his doormat. Funny coincidence, though. They both have long records of B and Es, with MOs that match the one used in The Chocolate Box break-in last week." He paused and added slowly, "And, uh, one of them is missing his right thumb."

"Wonders never cease," I said softly. I looked straight at him and smiled daintily. I didn't quite bat my eyelashes.

He went back to the report.

I finished my cup of tea and munched on a chocolate chip cookie. I didn't say anything until he had finished. He picked up the report and held it upright in both hands.

"You've done an excellent job."

"Thank you. Well, now I suppose you'll have to tell me."

"Tell you what?"

"About Giovanni Pasqualino."

He let go of the report. It went "blat" against the table. Then he slapped his hand on top of it. "Damn it, Edna! Didn't Detective Bone make it perfectly clear that we'll arrest him when we're good and ready?"

"Don't damn it me," I said. "People have been damning me left, right, and centre in the past few days. I want to know why, if you know the guy committed a murder, you haven't got him locked up where he can't kill anyone else."

He shook his head. "You're obviously as unfamiliar with the law as you are with police procedure. We can't just arrest someone until we have enough evidence to convince a judge that he should be tried. Right now we haven't even established cause of death."

"Cause of death?" I shouted. "Cause of death? Whatever happened to opened jugular? Don't forget that I saw the body. If this is some kind of police cover-up you won't be able to keep me quiet. I'll go to the newspapers and tell them everything I know."

Detective Owl started to laugh. "Police cover-up?" he snorted. "What the hell are you talking about? And when did you ever see the body? That woman has been a skeleton for the past three years."

I blinked. And then I said quietly, "What woman?"

"What woman? So you were bluffing!"

"What woman?" I said again. My heart seemed to have slowed to half pace.

"Sheila Ballantine," he said. "The woman Pasqualino killed three and a half years ago."

I felt sick. "You mean you're not talking about Heinz Grobbelaar?"

"No. I'm talking about Sheila Ballantine. She disappeared three and a half years ago. It was still an open case, and it wasn't until we got hold of Grobbelaar's dossiers that we were able to trace her whereabouts. She was buried right where the file said she was."

"Oh, my God," I said and closed my eyes to think. "But how do you know that Grobbelaar didn't do it himself?"

Detective Owl shrugged. "Pasqualino rented a camcorder from The Chocolate Box three years ago last January. Same time Sheila Ballantine disappeared. We found a copy of the rental receipt in Grobbelaar's records. Our guess is that he was trying to start his own little private film studio. You know. Porno films. Only that time it turned out to be a snuff film."

I looked out the kitchen window and said, "Strangulation."

"What?"

"Strangulation. That's how he killed her."

He shifted in his chair. "Now, what would make you say a thing like that?"

I turned to him. "Did Giovanni Pasqualino kill Heinz Grobbelaar?"

He paused. Then he said, "I'm afraid I — "

"Oh, come on, Stephen. What's the big deal? I'll tell you everything I know if you'll just tell me that one thing. Can you prove he killed Grobbelaar?"

"We don't think he did. He has a decent alibi. He was teaching a life-drawing class from six to eight. He says he hung around for a while after, cleaning up, and then he went home. We're still interviewing TTC drivers who might have had him on one of their routes. He says he was on the streetcar some time before eight-forty-five, but he can't remember the exact time."

"And then he went right home?"

"That's what he says."

"Great," I said. "Just great."

Detective Owl poured himself another cup of tea. "Now, you said you were going to tell me everything you know." He smiled. "Are you going to tell me you've cracked this case wide open?"

"Don't talk down to me."

"I wasn't talking down to you. I was being friendly."

"Oh, sure," I said. "All right. I'll tell you what I did yesterday, but only because I think it might be important for your case against Pasqualino. I don't want you yelling at me the way you did the last time. If you do, I'm going to stop right away, and you won't get another word out of me."

He was drinking his tea, but I could see that he was still smiling. "Go ahead," he said. "I'm listening."

I told him that I had gone to visit Pasqualino the day before, carefully omitting any reference to the post-cards. I watched the expression on his face change from mild amusement to restrained rage. But he didn't raise his voice. It was as if he had some kind of silencer in his throat to soften and elongate his words.

"What - the - hell - did - you - think - you - were - trying - to - prove?" he asked when I got to the part about Pasqualino dragging me inside and locking the door.

"I was trying to get him to admit that he had killed Grobbelaar. And he almost did, too."

"Except for the fact that he probably didn't do it," he said drily.

"But he must have thought I was talking about the murder he did commit, because he asked me how I had found out. And he was really nervous. I've never seen so much perspiration."

"So what happened?" Detective Owl asked. I was amazed that he still hadn't raised his voice.

I continued, "So he put his hands around my neck and told me that he could kill me. And that's why I think that he probably strangled Ballantine. He seemed to know exactly what he was doing."

He closed his eyes.

"Don't worry," I said. "I knocked him out."

"You *what*?"

"I hit him on the head with a pot full of carbon sticks."

"You *what?*" he said again. At last he was shouting. He even pounded the table, just once.

"I didn't hold it over his head, if that's what you think. I threw it at him. I was pretty lucky, too. I'm usually a lousy shot."

We stared at each other for a moment. Then he cleared his throat and picked up the report. "I think we'd better change the subject," he said softly.

"In that case," I said, beaming, "why don't you just tell me who killed Grobbelaar?"

He looked down at his hands. "You're not going to believe this."

"Try me."

He glanced up with an odd expression in his eyes.

"Figuratively speaking, of course," I added hastily.

He nodded seriously. "It seems that we may have been wasting our time with this blackmail thing."

"What?" I cried.

"We've gone over every single one of the victims' stories. They all have terrific alibis. We can't seem to find a connection with any of them."

"That doesn't make sense. How about any of their spouses? Ellen Mitchell-Spence told me that her husband was ready to kill Grobbelaar when he found out that she'd given him money."

"We've checked them all."

"So all this time, when you've been telling me you were getting some great leads, you were really just blowing out a lot of hot air?"

He frowned and said defensively, "This actually happens with astonishing frequency. Only sometimes it takes us months to discover that we've taken a wrong turn somewhere. At least this time it's only been days."

"Weeks."

"Only two."

"Fine," I said. "So you've missed something, then. Now, you're sure you've covered everything in his apartment? He didn't leave anything other than his disk that might be pertinent? Any . . . letters or anything of that nature?"

"We have all his files downtown. We're still going through them."

"And you're sure there's nothing else?"

"As sure as I can be. But then, I've been wrong before."

"But what other motive could there have been for killing Grobbelaar? Surely you don't think he was having an affair with some vengeful man's wife!"

"You never know," said Detective Owl. "Maybe some women would have found him attractive."

"The man weighed over three hundred pounds! It has to be something else. Burglary? Revenge? Jealousy? What about this person who says that Grobbelaar's collection belongs to him? Maybe he killed him."

"I think that's highly unlikely."

"Why?" I demanded.

"Because of who he is."

I waited. "Well? Who is he? You promised you'd tell me."

"Oh," said Detective Owl. "Well, I think, especially after reading your report, that this man probably does own the collection. At least, the people that he represents own it. He comes from the same area you describe. And the most telling factor of all, in my opinion, is that he's a monk."

"I knew it!" I cried. "From where?"

"A monastery, of course. In a small village in Abruzzi." He smiled. "Now I suppose you're going to want to know how Grobbelaar ever got hold of it."

"Right," I said. "How did he?"

"Apparently Grobbelaar was an officer in the German army during the war, and he was stationed in this village during the occupation."

"He stole it," I said in disgust.

He nodded.

"So how did this monk trace the collection?"

"Oh," said Detective Owl. "When we found the artifacts in Grobbelaar's apartment, we registered the collection with an international retrieval agency, thinking that it might have been stolen, or even connected to the murder. Even though it's turned out that there probably was no link, it did give this monk a chance to find it. Apparently that stone we found in the shop has tremendous mystical significance for the villagers."

"Incredible," I said.

"It is," he agreed. "I've talked to this guy for hours. He told me that the members of the local anti-Fascist resistance had hidden the church's treasures for safe-keeping. Grobbelaar somehow found out about the cache, and he and his men murdered several of the villagers who tried to protect it. This monk says it was the most vicious act he's ever witnessed. So I have to tell you, Edna, if we never do get the person who did Grobbelaar in, I probably won't lose much sleep over it."

I stared at him. "Stephen," I said. "What is the name of that village?"

"Oh," he said. "You won't have heard of it. It's so tiny it's not even on the map. I tried to look it up myself, and I couldn't find it. It's called Villa Santa Chiara."

eighteen

"**E**DINA!" CRIED MRS. CIPOLLONE, opening the door wide.

"What are you doing here?" said Michael. "I'm supposed to be at your place in an hour."

"I know," I said quietly. "There's been a change of plans."

He led me into the kitchen and pulled out a chair for me. "What's wrong? You look upset. I hope that guy hasn't been after you again."

"What guy?" asked Mrs. Cipollone.

"Giovanni Pasqualino," said Michael. "The man who killed Heinz Grobbelaar. He tried to kill Edna yesterday."

"What!" Mrs. Cipollone exclaimed. "Somabody try to keell you?"

"He didn't kill Grobbelaar," I said.

"Then why did he try to kill you?" asked Michael.

"Because he thought I knew about the person he did kill."

"You want a coffee?" asked Mrs. Cipollone.

"No, thank you."

"What person did he kill?" asked Michael.

"You sure?" said Mrs. Cipollone.

"Positive. Thank you. Sheila Ballantine. A woman who disappeared three and a half years ago."

"And Pasqualino killed her?" Michael said.

"That's what Heinz Grobbelaar found out. But that's not why he was killed."

Michael frowned. "What makes you think you know why he was killed? Was it in the paper? Did they get the guy?"

"No, they didn't get the guy. I think I'm the only one who knows. Unless you know. And I hope to God you don't, because if you do I think I'll throw up right now."

"What?" said Michael. "What the hell are you talking about?"

I opened my purse and took out my notebook and the photographs of the postcards. Mrs. Cipollone was filling the espresso maker. I waited until she had put it on the stove and turned on the burner before I said, "Mrs. Cipollone, could you please sit down?"

"What the hell are you talking about?" Michael said again.

"Miche," said Mrs. Cipollone. "*Aspett'.*" She pulled out a chair beside Michael and sat on it. "Edina, you talk now. I make my son be quiet."

"Does he know?" I asked.

"No," she replied firmly.

"Does your husband know?"

She shook her head.

"Who else knows?"

"Nobaddy."

"Nobody knows what?" Michael yelled, banging his fist on the table.

"Michael, please. I'm trying to tell you." I laid the photos on the table. "Do you see these?" I asked.

"Edna, what are you trying to prove?"

"Michael, *please,*" I said again. "If I can be this calm, then you certainly can."

He gaped at me. "No, I haven't seen them before."

"Now your mother," I said and looked at Mrs.

Cipollone. "I'm right about these, aren't I? These were threats, weren't they?"

"How should she know?" Michael said loudly. "Do you think my mother spent all her time snooping around Grobbelaar's apartment?"

"Miche," Mrs. Cipollone said softly. *"Stei zitt'!"* She turned to me. "I tink, maybe I make a mistake. Maybe my mind play tricks. I tink, if I am right, maybe he make soma kinda risponse. If he no is de man, he jiust put de cart in de garbige." She shrugged.

"But he kept them all," I said.

"Ya. He get a nice box and put it in his desk."

"So you knew."

"Ya. I know."

"And they were all in German."

She nodded. "I make a different writing, eh?"

"You copied it out of a phrase book."

She smiled and shrugged. "Maybe Heinz Grobbelaar get a better message if I write in German."

"You really sent those cards, Ma?" Michael said.

She nodded. The espresso maker began to spit. She stood up and took it off the burner.

"I'll tell you the rest," I said, opening my notebook.

"What makes you think you know?" he demanded.

"Michael, you aren't being very helpful. I've just found out something extremely distressing, and I could do with your support." I looked down at my notes. "Now, you know that I was supposed to take my report in to Detective Owl today."

"Yes," he said.

"Well, he came over to get it, and after he read it, I asked him if he could tell me who this person was who was claiming to be the real owner of the collection. And when he told me, I figured out who killed Heinz Grobbelaar."

"The guy who owns the collection?" said Michael.

I sighed. "Michael, haven't you been listening to what your mother's been saying? The man who really owns Grobbelaar's collection is a monk from Villa Santa Chiara. Grobbelaar was there during the war. He took the collection from the church there. He killed a lot of people and he stole it." I looked over to where Mrs. Cipollone was standing. She had her back to us, and she was holding the handle of the oven door. "And I think he killed your mother's family," I said quietly.

Michael stared at me. His hands fell into his lap. He shook his head. Then he turned around and started yelling at his mother. Long-sounding words in Italian. And he wasn't reciting from Dante.

Mrs. Cipollone kept her back to us but I could see that she was weeping. She bent her head and put her hands up to her face.

Michael pushed his chair away from the table and stood behind her. He hadn't stopped shouting, and it sounded as though he needed to take a good, deep breath.

"Michael," I said loudly. "Stop. Please."

It was as if I wasn't even there. Michael's hands had come suddenly to life, and they were moving around in front of him, beside him, describing great, angry arcs and short, fast jabs. Mrs. Cipollone stood like a piece of sculpted marble, immobile and silent.

I considered breaking the moment with something like, Boy, you Italians sure know how to express your-selves, but decided that he would probably turn and express himself to me. So I stood up and cried, "Michael! Leave her alone!" And then I wedged myself in between his wildly flailing arms and his mother's quivering back. "Stop it, Michael! Sit down and control yourself."

"She killed Grobbelaar," he said. "My mother."

"I know she killed Grobbelaar. Sit down."

"She's crazy," he muttered, and sat.

"She's not crazy." I frowned. I turned and put my

hand on her shoulder and said gently, "Mrs. Cipollone? Please come and sit down. I'll pour the coffee."

I found the cups and the spoons and the bowl of sugar and set them all carefully on the table. Mrs. Cipollone was looking out the window into the garden. Michael was looking at her.

"Sugar?" I offered.

"Tree," she whispered and bowed her head.

I put the sugar into her cup and stirred it.

"Michael?" I picked up the sugar spoon again. "Michael?"

"One," he grunted, not taking his eyes away from the top of his mother's head.

I put the cup in front of him, added sugar to mine, and sat down between them. "Now," I said, "we are going to drink our coffee before we say anything else."

Mrs. Cipollone's hand came up, and she took the tiny cup from its saucer. Some coffee spilled onto her other wrist, but she didn't wipe it away. Michael drank his in a single gulp.

"I'm finished," he said, slamming down the cup. "Now I want to know what the hell my mother is doing running around like a fucking hit man."

"Don't swear," I said. "She's your mother."

"She's a killer, for Christ's sake." He put his face in his hands.

"Don't you even want to hear her explanation?" I asked.

He looked up at me. "How come you're so calm about this?"

"I've had all day to think about it. You should have seen me this morning. Now, do you want to hear what your mother has to say or not?"

His face was white, but it was nothing like Mrs. Cipollone's when she finally looked up. "All right," he said slowly. "Let's hear it."

"Go ahead," I told her. "You'd better tell us everything."

When she spoke she was so quiet that it was as if the top half of her voice was missing. "I grow up in a leettle village in Abruzzi. I tell you dis already, no? Villa Santa Chiara. It's called dis becos we hev a very spaychal ting in our village. L'Occhio di Santa Chiara, de Eye of Santa Chiara. It is a spaychal stone, put into a cop in de chorch. When de monks drink out of dis cop, dey bring good luck to de village becos de eye of Santa Chiara watch over us.

"Ma, when I have twelve years, Italy make war. My fadder and madder make part of de resistenz, make a plan against de *fascisti*. Everybaddy heppy when Italy sign paper for peace. Den we hear de Germans are coming, and my fadder say he scared dey take everyting from our village. He hear bad stories about de Germans. Better hide de Eye of Santa Chiara for keep it safe.

"De man who command de Germans in Villa Santa Chiara is called Heinz Grobbelaar. He is a very bad man. First ting he do is send all de yong men for work in de nord in spaychal camps. I hev two broders, Mimo and Tino. Eighteen years and seventeen years. One day, dey hev to go, by trock, jiust like dat. Grobbelaar say when de war is finished dey come beck to us.

"Den Grobbelaar say we no can make de pasta or de bread no more. '*Ma*, what we gonna eat?' my fadder ask. 'Dat no is my problem,' say Grobbelaar. 'You give us all you flour and we make a bread for de German army, de men who really need for eat.' So we give enough flour for make it look good, and we take a turn to go down de mountain for make bread at night when everybaddy is sleep. We all very hongry, *ma* we still alive.

"Den Grobbelaar get greedy. He say, 'Why you no have notting in you chorch?' My fadder say we are a poor people, we no hev money for buy tings for our chorch. Grobbelaar laughs. He start to ask everybaddy, one by one. De people of Villa Santa Chiara are very scared, maybe somabody say somating, I dunno. *Ma*, he find out about where de people hide de tings and who hide dem, and he make all de resistenz people to go to de piazza. My madder is crying. She tell me to ron. So I ron. I ron fest, like a rabbit, maybe fester. I am so scared I wet my dress and I am sick, *ma* I ron.

"I hide for tree days. When I come beck, I look for my madder, and *comare* Elda say, 'Coma, you madder is dead.' And I ask for my fadder, and she say he is keelled, too. Grobbelaar shoot dem bote.

"I scream so loud *comare* Elda make me put a pillow over my face becos she scared de Germans hear me. Dey no like noise. Dey already keell seventeen people, and she no want us for be eighteen and nineteen. I say I wanna keell Grobbelaar, and she say no be crazy, maybe it's a better if I go some adder place. So I go. I stay wid de cosin of Salvatore. She can keep me, she say, until de war is over and Mimo and Tino come beck. For a year and a half I live wid *cugina* Alvana, and den de war is finished and I wait and wait, *ma* Mimo and Tino never come beck. Maybe dey die from starve, maybe dey keelled by guns. I no know. I never see dem again."

She stopped and looked out the window. Michael's eyes were closed.

"How did you find Grobbelaar?" I asked.

"When we come for live in Toronto, I work in a fattory, for fifteen years. Den my hosband say he tink I can finish work becos we hev enough money for live. So I stay at home, make a nice house, a nice garden, plant trees, flowers. Wintertime I make dresses for friends, read de jiornal. Den one day, maybe six years ago, I see a picture in de jiornal, a photograph of a man who hev a store in Yorkville. He hev to go in court becos he break de law. He let children into his sex store. I see him and tink, I know dis man. Dis is de man who keell my family. I go to his store and I look at him. I pretend I buy somating, and I talk to him. I am sure dis is de man. After a while I find out what time he go out, where he go. I follow, like a detective. Like Magnum P.I. I find de *agenzia* who clean his place, and I take a job. Pretty soon I make friends wid de lady who make de job list. I take a job at Grobbelaar's place. I go into his apartament and I nearly die. I see alla de tings from my chorch, all lined up on a wall. I no believe he keep everyting. But den I see de Eye of Santa Chiara. First I tink maybe I am crazy. Maybe I want for find dis man too much, I see tings dey no really dere. Even de Eye of Santa Chiara. So I send a cart to him. Jiust one. *Ma*, I send it by de cosin of my hosband in Halifax. She mail it for me. And, jiust like I tink he is gonna do, Grobbelaar keep it."

"And then you sent more."

"Ya. Twenty-four I send. I take lotsa time. I wanna make him nervose. I watch him. He sure is nervose. Maybe he no can eat notting except ice cream somatime. *Ma*, still he is fet. I tink he know for sure somabody is watching him.

"*Ma*, I no am sure what I do. Maybe I hev to tell de monks from Villa Santa Chiara I find de Eye of Santa Chiara. *Ma*, I tink, maybe it's better for show dem. So one night, a couple a weeks past, I decide to take de Eye. I bring a knife, becos I no wanna take de whole cop. I want jiust for take de stone, jiust for show. I tink I can turn de cop around and Grobbelaar is never gonna see it no is dere. So I make sure he's down in de store, I put on de robber gloves for cleaning becos I no wanna leave de mark of my hands, and I go up, very quiet, into de apartament. I open de copboard and take out de cop. Den I use de knife for try and push out de Eye. It no come too easy. I tink, maybe I no can do dis after all.

Maybe I should take de whole cop. *Ma*, I keep working. I am stubborn. I hev de hard head.

"*Ma*, before I can take out de Eye, I hear somabody on de stairs. I know it's Grobbelaar, and I am scared. I no know what to do. I tink, maybe I hide somewhere and he no see me. But I am too late, and Grobbelaar is putting de key in de door. So I tink, maybe I jiust smack him on de head wit de cop and ron around him, very fest. Den maybe he no see who is in his place. So I put in my pocket de knife, and I stend still, right next to de door, and when he push it open, I am ready.

"I give him a good whack, but he is too tall, and I no knock him out very nice. He make a yell, very loud, and try for grab me, for grab de cop. He try for push me down de stairs. What can I do? I am very scared. Good ting he is too fat or he get me for sure. But he is yelling very loud. He say he wanna keell me. I start for tink how he already keell my madder and fadder and my two broders, and I get mad. I tink, he no gonna keell me, too. So I let him hev de cop, and I get out de knife and say, 'You keell my family in Italy, Mr. Grobbelaar. Now I slit you troat like a pig.'

"Den hard and fest I make a slice across his neck. He try and scream, *ma*, jiust blood come out. I say, 'Now you jiust a dead pig,' and he fall down de stairs. De cop fall down, too. I am very scared. I walk beck down for get de Eye, but it no is dere. It fall out of de cop when it hit de floor. I look for it all over de place. I no can see it. I tink maybe it roll into de store, under de crack of de door. But I am too scared to go in dere. Maybe I hev some blood on me. I no want de poleetz for know who keell Grobbelaar. I make a big mistake, I tink. So I clean up lotsa lots, make sure I no hev blood on my shoes. I put my cleaning clodes over my dress, and I go home. I am very scared. I no sleep at all."

She looked at me. "You know all dis before?"

"I figured it went something like that." I looked at

Michael. His eyes were still closed. He could have been sleeping, except that he was sitting bolt upright and breathing fast.

"And that's what you were doing that evening when I caught you looking under that shelf of . . . chocolates."

"Ya. But I no find de Eye in de store. I no know where it is. Now I tink I lose it for good dis time."

"It's not lost," I said. "The police have it. But what about the goblet? Was that you who took it out of the shop after I put it back?"

"Ya. I see you take somating out, I see you put somating beck. I wanna see what it is, so I look, and for sure it is de cop. I put in a safe place." She shrugged. "So, now you gotta call de poleetz, eh?"

"I have to," I told her.

Michael opened his eyes. They were red. "Edna — " he began.

"Michael," I said, "you know what will happen if I don't. The police will eventually figure it out themselves. It's better if we get to them first."

"Why?"

"Because it is. Trust me. Please."

"I can't believe this," he said.

"I tell you, you are a very smart girl, no?" Mrs. Cipollone said.

"Why did you let me in there?" I asked her. "Didn't you know I'd see things? And why did you invite me for dinner?"

"Oh," she said, smiling. "I tink maybe my son tink you very smart, too. Maybe somaday de poleetz find out I kill Heinz Grobbelaar. Maybe Michael no find nobaddy nice den. Maybe it's a too late. I like you very much, Edina."

Michael said, "Oh, my God," and then something in Italian to which his mother responded quietly.

I listened for a few minutes, not understanding a

word. I was just beginning to gather up the photographs when Mr. Cipollone opened the front door. Michael and his mother stopped talking and looked at me.

"Edna," Michael said softly. "Please don't tell him. Not yet."

"I wouldn't. It's not up to me, anyway."

Mr. Cipollone came into the kitchen. "Edina!" He beamed. "You come for see me again, eh?"

"Hello, Mr. Cipollone. How are you?"

"Eh, no too bad. You get a job yet?"

"Not yet." I glanced at Michael. "I just finished my report for the police today. I'll start looking in the next few days."

"Good." He nodded. "You wanna eat, you gotta make a some money, no?"

"That's right," I agreed. "Well, I hate to leave so soon, but I really should be going."

"No," said Mrs. Cipollone.

"We'd like you to stay," said Michael. "If you want to."

"Stay for eat," said Mr. Cipollone. "My wife make *past' i fagiol'* tonight. You like very much."

I looked over at Michael's red eyes and then at his hands, which were hanging loosely at his sides. Behind his head, inside the sideboard, was the photograph of his three nieces. I looked for a while at the eldest, the one who was supposed to resemble Mrs. Cipollone at that age. Then I said, "All right," and put my purse down on the table. "What can I do to help?"

"Here," said Mr. Cipollone, opening the cutlery drawer and pulling out the knife with the concave blade. "You cut up tomatoes for *insalat'*."

nineteen

"**H**ELLO?" SAID MRS. OWL. ACTUally, it was more of a cracked gasp than an actual word. I knew that she had been asleep. I could hear snoring in the background.

"Is Detective Owl there, please?" I asked pleasantly.

"Just a minute." There was a rustling sound, as if sheets were being gathered or dispersed. Then I heard, "Stephen, honey. It's for you."

The snoring stopped.

"Who is it?" he whispered.

"I don't know. It's a woman."

"What time is it?"

"Quarter to six."

"Jesus Christ. Pass me the phone." More rustling. "Hello?"

"Detective Owl?" I said. "It's me."

"Ms. Heathcott." He was trying to sound sleepily indifferent, but I could tell that he was immediately alert. "Do you realize what time it is?"

"I have to talk to you," I said. "I'd like you to come over."

"Ms. Heathcott, I hope you realize that I'm not on duty until Friday."

"It's about what we were discussing yesterday."

"I see," he said. "Well, since it's an emergency. Where are you?"

"At home. In my kitchen. Eating breakfast."

"All right. But I'm only making this concession because I'm concerned about your safety."

"I appreciate that, Detective. I really do. When will you be here?"

"As soon as I can," he said with undue grimness. Possibly his wife was straining to overhear.

"Thank you, Stephen," I said. "I'll see you soon."

Fifteen minutes later he was on my doorstep. His hair was wet on the right side of his head, and dry and sticking up on the left, as if he had run straight out of the shower into the car, then driven off without rolling up the window.

"That was fast," I said.

"I have a special routine for emergencies. It's all a matter of knowing exactly where everything is at any given moment."

"Very convenient. Now, why don't you come in and sit down?" I led him to the couch and asked if he had eaten.

"No. I didn't have a chance."

"Would you like something now?"

"No, thank you. I'd like to find out what you think is important enough to get me out of bed at five-thirty."

"Five-forty-five," I said. "The sun was up." I sat down. "What's your wife's name?"

"Sandra." Sandra Owl.

"I'm sorry I woke her up," I told him. "I'm sorry I woke you up, too, but I figured that you'd probably be used to being called at all hours of the night."

"Don't apologize," he said, but his tone suggested that I'd better get to business or he was going to lie down on my couch and go back to sleep.

"Stephen," I said. "I'm afraid I have some news that will probably be gratifying to you but that, I have to tell you, is extremely troubling to me." I picked up the envelope containing the photographs of the postcards from the coffee table.

"What's that?"

"It's evidence, Stephen. In the Grobbelaar case."

That seemed to wake him up. He held out his hand and said, "Evidence? What have you got, Edna?"

"First," I said, holding the envelope tightly, "I want you to promise that I'm not going to be charged with anything."

"What — " he frowned " — have you done now?"

"Nothing now, exactly. I did it quite a while ago. And if you couldn't tell, then it doesn't matter."

"What did you do, Edna?" His voice was rising. So was he, out of the couch. I stuffed the envelope in behind my back just as he reached for it. He rolled his eyes and sank backwards again. "Sometimes," he said, "you're really infuriating."

"Do you promise?"

"All right!" he yelled. "I promise. Now give me the stuff."

"I hope you haven't got your fingers crossed or anything." I passed him the envelope.

He grabbed it out of my hand, opened the flap, and looked inside. "What's this?"

"Photographs," I said, "of postcards that the murderer sent to Grobbelaar."

He was spreading them over the coffee table. "I don't have to ask how you got these," he said without looking at me. "What makes you think the murderer sent them?"

"I don't think," I said. "I know. And I also know who it was."

He sighed. "Edna, I hate guessing games. Why don't you just get your mouth moving and tell me?" His stomach growled.

"Are you sure you don't want something to eat?"

"You're changing the subject."

"You're the one whose stomach is complaining."

"Ignore it. Talk to me."

"Okay," I said agreeably, and did. I told him almost everything. Then I reached under my chair and said, "And there's one more thing." I grabbed the gold goblet and held it up. In the morning light the hollow socket of the Eye of Santa Chiara seemed to be winking at us.

"Jesus Christ," he said softly. He stared at it without moving.

"I don't know if your language is inappropriate," I said, "or entirely appropriate. Stunning, isn't it? And look. I cleaned it for you. I didn't think you'd want all those messy fingerprints on it. All you have to do is snap the stone back in place, and it'll be as good as new."

He stood up. "I have to leave now."

"No, you don't."

"Edna, it should be clear to you that I'll have to talk to this woman."

"Sit down, Stephen. I want you to listen to me before you do anything you'll regret later."

"Regret later? You must be joking. This is a murder suspect we're taking about." He was standing between the couch and my chair, bent slightly at the waist, as if he were about to jump into the air and take flight.

"Please," I said. I stood up. I was about a step away from him, well past the established North American line of comfortable proximity. I could feel his breath on my face. I could hear his gastric juices rolling. "Stephen," I said carefully, "Mrs. Cipollone is Michael's mother."

"Of course," he said, backing up and sitting down again. "I knew you'd left out something important." He held the bridge of his nose and closed his eyes.

I sat down again, too, on the edge of my chair.

"Stephen — " I began.

"Be quiet," he snapped. "I want to know one thing." He looked me right in the eye. "Have you been stringing me along?"

"Stephen," I said, "if you're implying that I would intentionally lead you off track, then you're dead wrong."

"Just what am I supposed to think?" he asked loudly. "All I know is that you've been more than just casually interested in this case, and now all of a sudden you're telling me that the person who killed Grobbelaar is your boyfriend's mother."

"Yuck," I said.

"What?"

"I hate the word 'boyfriend.'"

"I'm sorry. Your lover."

"Almost as bad, but it'll do. Now, Stephen, let me clear up one thing. I had no idea that Michael's mother killed Heinz Grobbelaar until yesterday morning, when you told me the monk was from Villa Santa Chiara. You have to believe that. The only reason I didn't say anything then was that I felt I had to go and ask her first. She's a very nice woman in spite of how it looks."

"I don't believe I'm hearing this! Do you know how ridiculous that sounds? Do you know how ignorant *you* sound?"

"Nevertheless," I said, "I want you to pretend you never heard any of this."

He laughed. "Are you out of your mind?"

"Oh, come on, Stephen! Do you think she's a menace to society? Do you think that if she gets away with killing Grobbelaar she'll think she can sharpen her blade and do it again? Maybe next time she'll take out the fruit-and-vegetable man who sold her a rotten cantaloupe."

"That's nonsense," said Detective Owl.

"I know it is. That's my point. Besides, who's going to know? You don't have to say anything. You could just keep blundering off in the same direction you were already going in. I wouldn't tell anyone."

He looked annoyed. "I wasn't blundering. I was following a reasonable lead."

"I'm sorry. I shouldn't have put it that way. But why not? Do the police really care whether or not they find out who killed a war criminal?"

"Perhaps not," he said quietly. "We've been known to let the odd perpetrator off the hook."

"Please don't call her a perpetrator," I said. "It sounds so cold. She's an old woman with varicose veins. Her life was practically destroyed by that scum. As far as I'm concerned, she *should* have intended to kill him. He'd had it coming to him for a long time."

"Jesus Christ," said Detective Owl. "Will you listen to what you're saying?"

"Who knows," I went on cheerfully, "how many more lives he would have ruined if he'd gone on living? Harold Cunderlik probably wouldn't have been the last to take the fatal plunge. He might not even have been the first. Just imagine — "

"All right, Edna," he interrupted. "That's enough." He sat back on the couch and looked at me wearily.

I got up from my chair and sat down beside him. "I knew you'd go for it," I said, patting his shoulder. "You're actually a very right-minded man with a good working knowledge of practical ethics."

He snorted. "I don't know where the hell you come up with these ideas." But he smiled.

I stood up and walked towards the kitchen. "Now, what can I give you for breakfast?" I opened the refrigerator.

He said, "Got any cold pizza?"

I froze. "Pardon me?" I whispered, turning to look at him.

He was standing up, examining the Spencer drawing. There was no expression on his face. "Pizza," he said. "Cold. Got any?"

"You bastard," I said. I slammed the fridge door and went back into the living room. "Where is it?"

"Where is what?"

"You know what I'm talking about." I couldn't believe how calm my voice was, how even, how reasonable.

"Are you all right, Edna?"

"I'm fine. You're the sick one."

"Edna," he said, holding out his hands.

"Vicious pervert. As bad as Grobbelaar."

"Edna. Calm down."

"I am calm!" I screamed. "Where's the bug?"

"Edna — "

"You bugged my apartment, you slimy worm. Where is it?"

"Sit down, Edna. I want to talk to you."

"I'll stand, thank you. But I still want to hear you talk. Is someone listening to us now?"

"No," he said. "The bug's not here. I took it out."

"When?"

"Yesterday."

"I was here yesterday."

"No, you weren't. You went out at four-thirty."

"And you let yourself in."

"Yes."

"Why?" I demanded.

"To remove it."

"I mean, why did you bug me in the first place? Are you some kind of pervert?"

"I didn't bug you. The police did."

"Aren't you the police?"

"I mean, it was a police action, not mine personally."

"But you personally listened."

He closed his eyes. "Yes."

"And who else did?"

"Detective Bone."

"Detective Bone and who else?"

"One other officer. You don't know him."

"But he knows *me* pretty well."

He bowed his head and shook it. "No."

"Why?" I asked. "Why did you do it?"

"After I came to see you, Detective Bone felt that we had reasonable grounds to suspect that you and Fineberg might have been in on something together. I wasn't thoroughly convinced. I thought it was unlikely that you were a conspirator. But I was only one voice among many, and I've told you before that we always have to look at facts over feelings. A piece of Grobbelaar's collection seemed to be missing. And then we found out that you knew something about Renaissance artifacts, and everything seemed to click. We wanted to make sure that if you made contact with Fineberg we'd catch you."

"You think of everything," I said ironically. "How did you do it?"

"The day after I was first here, someone came in while you were out and put the bug in."

"Where?"

"On the phone."

"Which one?"

He looked away. "Both phones."

"And they picked up more than just phone conversations."

He nodded.

"I assume you had a warrant."

"Yes. Of course."

"You can go to hell," I said. "This is the most sickening thing that has ever happened to me. More sickening than finding Grobbelaar's body."

"I'm sorry, Edna."

"A little late for that, isn't it?"

"Edna, believe me, we never listened in on any of your . . . personal conversations."

"Oh, sure. You only knew what Michael wanted for breakfast."

He shook his head. "I only listened that morning to find out if you'd be going out because I wanted to take the bug out. I would have liked to get it out of here a week ago, but I never had a chance. As soon as we picked up Fineberg, you were off the hook. Anyway, by then we were off in another direction altogether. Edna, I promise you I never abused your right to privacy. I never would."

"Until Sunday," I said. "Why did you bring this up at all? Why couldn't you just let me go on not knowing?"

"I guess I had a guilty conscience. I wanted to apologize." He did look conscience-stricken. And, I thought, even a little terrified.

"This is unbelievable," I said. "I suppose you have everything recorded now for posterity."

"No," he said firmly. "I erased all the tapes."

"Well, that's a relief," I said sarcastically. "At least you can't sell them on the black market and retire."

"Edna, please." He was holding out both hands in a begging-for-mercy gesture. "You have to believe that I'd never do anything to hurt you."

"You're just another Heinz Grobbelaar."

"Oh, shit," he said.

We stared at each other for a moment, Detective Owl looking as earnestly repentant as he could, and I hoping to look as furious as I felt. His stomach grumbled again.

"I think I'd better leave," he murmured.

"I think you'd better," I replied in an even lower voice. "You can probably make it home for breakfast if you use your special emergency routine."

He turned towards the door. "If there's anything I can do to make it up to you . . ." he began.

"There is," I said to the back of his head. "I want you to promise me you'll keep Mrs. Cipollone's name out of your investigation. I want you to figure out a way to close this case so it's never opened again."

He opened the door. "I can't promise anything."

"But you'll give it a hell of a try," I said.

"Yeah," he replied without looking at me. "Goodbye, Edna."

I slammed the door behind him.

twenty

Lᴵᴸᴸɪᴀɴ Aᴸᴸꜰᴏʀᴅ ᴡᴀꜱ ᴅʀᴇꜱꜱᴇᴅ ɪɴ ᴀ long, plum-coloured suede skirt and a large, shoulder-padded angora sweater. Her hair was pulled back in an elegant chignon, a perfect dark foil for her diamond earrings.

"Come in, Edna," she said, moving towards her office. "Please sit down."

"Thank you, Mrs. Allford. How was Ottawa?"

"Delightful. A delightful city." She sat in front of the Jack Bush and moved her glasses from the bridge of her nose downward so that she could look over them at me. "Now, Edna," she said, folding her hands on top of her desk. "I'd like to make you a proposal. A business proposal."

I smiled.

She continued. "As you know, I have been in this business for nearly twenty years, and I have gained a reasonably good reputation during that time."

"More than reasonably good," I put in. "You're probably one of the most highly respected dealers in Toronto."

"Probably," she agreed. "I had always assumed that I would continue indefinitely in my position here, overseeing the organization and maintaining a hands-on approach with both artists and clientele." She pronounced it *clee-ahn-tell*, as if her trip to the Nation's

Capital had transformed her into an instant francophone.

"But now?" I murmured diffidently.

"But now I find that life has presented me with a host of new opportunities. You are aware, of course, that Ellen is now part owner of the gallery?"

"Yes," I responded.

"She is now ready, I believe, to take on the challenge of running the gallery in the capacity that I alone have fulfilled to this point. This, of course, means that I will be free to carry on with other pursuits, knowing that Ellen can stand in my stead. I will be free to evolve into a mere silent partner, as it were. Do you follow me?"

"Fully," I said.

Her lips twitched faintly, and she unfolded her hands and placed them in her lap. "Now you can well understand that in order to run a gallery of this size and . . . excellent calibre, it is necessary to have more than one individual on hand. We will need to employ a person whose knowledge and experience in the field are exemplary."

I adjusted my glasses and looked modestly at my lap. Not to mention, I thought, someone with a *cleeahntell* list of her own.

"Now, my proposition is this, Edna. If you will take on Ellen's position when she comes to take on mine, we are prepared to pay you nine hundred and fifty dollars a week, plus benefits, with the option to buy selected works of art at a twenty-per-cent discount."

So much for cool self-control. My jaw dropped, and my tongue probably would have started lolling, too, if I hadn't also felt an uncontrollable need to swallow. "Well," I gulped, "that certainly is a generous offer. That's almost fifty thousand a year."

Lillian Allford gave me a bland look. "Forty-nine

four," she said. "But we feel your presence here would be worth every dollar. We are fully aware of your talents."

I looked at the Jack Bush and pondered this. Then I said quietly, "Lillian, if you don't mind my asking, how much is Ellen making?"

If the question surprised her, she didn't show it. "Edna, Ellen is a partner. She takes a percentage of our profits. She doesn't receive a salary."

"No, of course not," I said. "What about before she became a partner?"

She looked through the glass wall of her office out to the gallery. "I don't see why that should be relevant."

"But wouldn't you like to know what Gerald Fineberg was paying me before you offer me forty-nine four?" I asked politely.

"That doesn't concern me, Edna. What concerns me is your potential to sell works of art in this gallery."

"Thirty-one thousand three hundred," I said anyway. "No benefits. Now, surely you can't expect me not to wonder why you are willing to hire me on at almost twenty thousand more than what I'm probably worth."

"I've told, you, Edna. I expect great things from you."

"That's extremely flattering," I said, not very loudly. I knew that Lillian appreciated subtlety. "But I'm afraid I won't be able to accept. I don't think I could possibly live up to your rather intimidating expectations of me."

"Of course you could," she said, and for the first time in my life, I thought I could hear a desperate note in Lillian Allford's voice.

I looked again at the Jack Bush and thought about Mary Dellarosa at her tiny kitchen table. I considered the possibility that Lillian thought forty-nine four was enough to keep me from telling the world about her husband. "I'm sorry, but you're far too generous, Mrs.

Allford. I couldn't possibly work here and not feel that I was taking advantage of you."

"I see," she said, pushing her glasses as far as they would go up her nose. "I'm very sorry to hear that, Edna." She took a deep breath that sounded like a sigh in reverse, and added, "I thought we had a sort of . . . mutual understanding that would make our business relationship a very satisfactory one." She frowned at a point somewhere above my head.

"I'm sorry, too," I said. "You're quite right about the understanding. But you would also be quite right to assume that nothing that I understand about you will be . . . *understood* by anyone else."

We looked at each other without speaking, and I watched her expression change slowly from confused, to concerned, to, at last, relieved. Then I stood up and held out my hand. She shook it. We said goodbye.

When I came out of the office, Ellen was on the phone again. She smiled and waved as I passed her, and I smiled and waved back. I felt somewhat relieved myself.

Next stop Fifty-two.

I WALKED STRAIGHT TO THE COUNTER and said, "Could I see Detective Owl, please?"

"May I tell him who's here?" asked the young officer.

"Edna," I said.

"Edna who?"

"He'll know," I smiled for about the fiftieth time that morning.

He picked up the phone and kept his eyes on me as he talked. "There's someone named Edna here to see you. What? Oh. About five-nine. Brunette. Glasses. What? Yes, she is." He laughed. "Yes, she is. All right." He put the phone down and said to me, "He'll be right out."

"Thank you," I said. "What am I?"

"I beg your pardon?"

"You said, 'About five-nine, brunette, glasses. What? Yes, she is,' chuckle, snort, guffaw, 'yes, she is.' What am I?"

"Smiling," he said. "You were smiling. He wanted to know if you were smiling."

"Oh," I said. There I'd been, imagining all sorts of lewd possibilities. I looked up as Detective Owl opened a frosted-glass door.

"Edna," he said.

"I'd like to talk to you," I told him. I tossed a quick glance at the other officer who was tossing several long ones back at us. "Do you have an office? A private office?"

"Yes," he said. "Come in."

I followed him down the hall, and we went into a tiny beige room containing a desk and a filing cabinet. There were four chairs pushed together against one wall, and another one behind the desk. Detective Owl moved one of the four so that it was facing the desk, and I sat on it.

"So, what are you doing here?" he asked, settling into his own chair. "You seem to be a little more cheerful than you were the last time I saw you."

"You knew," I said.

"What do you mean, I knew?"

"I mean," I said, "you knew already, before I even told you, that Mrs. Cipollone killed Heinz Grobbelaar. And that's why you let me know that I was being bugged. So that I'd realize you knew."

He looked up at the ceiling, then back at my face. Then he stood up. "Can I get you a coffee or anything?"

"All right. That would be nice."

"How do you take it?"

"Cream and sugar."

"I'll be back in a minute." He shut the door behind him.

I looked around the room for signs of Sandra. There wasn't even a picture. But maybe he didn't need one if he had a photographic memory. It was a pretty boring room. Even the window was frosted, so I couldn't see out.

He came back with two cups and put them on the desk.

"Yours is the one on the left," he said, sitting down again.

"I've thought about this a lot," I said. "There's no way you couldn't have realized that Michael was Mrs. Cipollone's son. You must have known that all along because you heard me talking to him over the phone. Isn't that right?"

He sipped his coffee. "That's right."

"Okay. But what I want to know is *when* you figured out the murder."

"All right," he said and cleared his throat. "I knew you'd been in Grobbelaar's apartment, because I followed you downtown after I heard the tape of you asking Mrs. Cipollone to let you in."

"You followed me?" I picked up my coffee.

He shrugged. "I thought you might be planning to steal the entire collection, you and Fineberg, and I thought maybe you were letting Mrs. Cipollone in on it."

"But we didn't. Steal it, I mean."

"Nope. But I decided to wait awhile and keep watching you. Well, actually, Mary Beth and I split the surveillance duties."

"Blue Fiat."

"How'd you know that?"

"Red hair and scarlet lipstick? And a severe frown? Didn't she tell you we exchanged glances at Avenue Road and Glengrove two Sundays ago?"

He shook his head. "No."

I decided to forego making a comment on Detective Bone's skills as a shadower of suspects. I said, "Okay, so what else did you find out?"

"Well, I heard Mrs. Cipollone's dinner invitation on the Saturday, and when her son showed up at your apartment the next day, I figured that something strange was going on."

"Sex, you mean?" I asked.

"That too." He smiled.

"So you barged in on us."

"I was concerned about you, Edna. I didn't want you getting yourself into a difficult situation."

"So you came to rescue me."

"I wouldn't say rescue, exactly."

"What would you say, then?"

"'Distract' might be a better word." He put his cup down on the desk. "I thought if I could get you into Grobbelaar's apartment and answering the questions I had about the collection, your own curiosity might be satisfied. I couldn't believe it when you went back again the next day, anyway."

"Did you know about the postcards?"

"I had them photographed."

"Great thinking," I said.

"After I realized that you'd taken one."

"What?"

"I went over the whole apartment, trying to figure out what you'd been doing up there. When I realized that one of the cards was missing I guessed that you thought there must have been some connection between them and the murder. So then I started thinking about them, too. But I couldn't understand why any of the blackmail victims would have been sending messages to Grobbelaar. If the postcards were significant, then it made sense that the blackmailing might have had nothing to do with his murder. So naturally I wondered if the artifacts collection might be the key. After you told me the objects had been stolen from a church I started running a more thorough check on Grobbelaar. Got into his war record, all that sort of stuff. I ended up talking to an official in Germany who had information on his time in Italy. He told me exactly when and where Grobbelaar had been stationed, and at that point I contacted a man in Villa Santa Chiara. A priest at the village church."

"So there was no monk," I said. "And there's no international registry for stolen art."

"Wrong," said Detective Owl. "About the monk, anyway. There is a monastery there. You were absolutely correct. But you're right about the registry. It doesn't exist."

"There's actually a monk who's been searching for the artifacts for forty-five years?"

"Not exactly. The monks believed that the collection had been broken up and spread all over Europe, if not the world. They never thought they'd get all the pieces back."

I smiled. "Nice surprise for them. So, how did you figure out that Mrs. Cipollone had killed Grobbelaar? You didn't overhear me talking about Villa Santa Chiara with Michael, did you? I'm sure he never mentioned the name of the village while he was in my apartment."

He picked up his cup again and swallowed a mouthful of coffee. "No, but once I'd heard the story from the priest about what had happened in the village during the war, I sat on it for a while, just thinking. I figured someone had a great motive for murder. Then when I saw your expression Tuesday morning after I told you where Grobbelaar had been stationed, something just sort of twigged. I got right back to the priest and asked for the parish records of births, marriages, and deaths from Villa Santa Chiara for the wartime period, and he had the town hall fax me a beautiful list of all one hundred and fifty-two families in the village. I just read through it."

"And found Mrs. Cipollone's name?"

"I found her maiden name. Giuseppina Uccello."

"I thought you weren't working Tuesday."

"I wasn't supposed to be."

"But — " I began.

He looked embarrassed. "I felt somewhat compelled to continue on my own time."

I grinned. "You mean you couldn't stand the competition."

He made a face.

"Did Detective Bone know?"

He shook his head.

"But you must have realized that I knew."

"I wasn't positive, but I figured that you probably only realized it Tuesday morning. You sure hustled me out of there fast enough, anyway."

"And I'll bet you thought Michael already knew. That's why you asked me the next day if I'd been stringing you along. You thought he'd been manipulating me."

"I had to consider that," he said slowly. "I'd spent most of Tuesday night worrying about what might happen to you if you confronted the Cipollones."

"You must have been thoroughly disappointed when you found out that I was still alive the next morning."

"Relieved is more like it."

"And you never intended to charge Mrs. Cipollone."

"I didn't say that." He frowned. "If you hadn't become so involved, Edna, I might not have had as much . . . insight concerning the case. I might have reacted a little differently than I did."

"I see," I said smugly. "So you're not quite as self-sufficient as you thought you were."

He squinted. "I guess that makes two of us," he replied.

I stared at the frosted windowpane.

"Edna," said Detective Owl. "I want you to know something. I never listened to you and Michael . . . you know . . . making love."

I looked at his face. I was certain I saw a twinkle in his eye.

"I couldn't do it," he went on. "Even though —"

"Stephen," I said, "that's enough of a confession from you now. I think we should forget that ever happened."

He nodded. "Fine. That's fine with me."

"Now, Stephen," I said. "What are you going to do about this case?"

"Well, I can't just close it," he said, scratching his head. "It's only been two and a half weeks."

"So, what then? Isn't Detective Bone going to figure it out for herself pretty soon?"

"Probably not," he said. "She's been assigned to an armed robbery investigation. That should keep her busy for a while."

"For how long?"

"Until something else turns up to occupy her."

"Oh," I murmured.

"But I did come up with something that you might be interested in." He shuffled through a stack of papers in the top drawer of his desk and pulled out a sheet, which he handed to me.

"What's this?" I asked. "A press release?"

"Read it."
I did.

Arthur Birch, aka Johnny Oakes, aka Henry Beech, aka Edward Forest, is wanted on fraud charges after he is alleged to have used phony teaching diplomas to secure a position with the Toronto Board of Education. Birch, 43, is described as short and slight of build with chestnut hair, blue eyes, and a moustache.

Police issued a warrant for his arrest after a photograph that his wife, Doris Birch, distributed when he was declared missing last Thursday, was recognized by a Dartmouth, Nova Scotia, woman who claims to be Birch's real wife. It is believed that Birch may have fled to the United States.

He is also wanted for questioning in connection with the murder earlier this month of Toronto store owner Heinz Grobbelaar.

I looked at Detective Owl and grinned. "Brilliant," I said. "He really *is* a psychopath, then." I handed the piece of paper back to him.

"But not likely a dangerous one," Detective Owl replied. "He's a runner. As far as we can tell, he's had at least four jobs with four different boards of education, including one in the States, and he probably had a wife in each place. Chances are, if no one's caught him yet, he won't be caught for a long time."

"Poor Doris," I said sadly. "When does this go out?"

"It went out this morning. It should be in the evening editions, if they care to run it."

"And what about Pasqualino?"

"The lab report comes back next week. We may be able to jump on him before that, though. I'm afraid that's all I can tell you."

"I understand. It's a confidential police matter."

"Right," he said.

I stood up. "Well, I guess I'd better go now. I'm supposed to meet Michael downtown for lunch. Thank you for finally being honest with me."

He stood up, too. "Edna," he said, walking towards me, "I'm sorry if I caused you any pain. I hope that you understand everything now."

"Stephen, I'm sorry I called you a slimy worm. I realize you were probably just doing the best you could."

"I've been called worse," he said, opening the door.

"I'll bet you have. I'll see you soon. Don't bother walking me out. I'm sure you're busy."

"Edna."

"What?"

"You never got your consulting fee."

I looked at him closely. "Stephen," I said, "tell me about your expense account."

"What?"

"Tell me with a straight face that you can authorize payment of fifteen hundred dollars for seven sheets of paper."

"Oh," he said. To my amazement, he seemed to be blushing right up to his high hairline. We looked at each other silently for a minute. Then he said, "But we still used your report. Do you think we're just going to hand over four and a half million dollars worth of art treasures to a bunch of monks without checking their story first?"

"How should I know?" I said. "I obviously have no idea how you operate. But you'd better forget about the fee. Keep it. Take Sandra on a holiday or something."

Detective Owl smiled. "I'll see you, Edna," he said.

"So, what do you think?" I asked Michael two hours later. "Is this how it's supposed to be?"

"What do you mean, is this how it's supposed to be?"

"Maybe it's just because it's empty," he said. "It seems kind of drafty. I think what it needs is a big tank of turtles."

"At least it has windows," I said. "Natural light is so much better than artificial for looking at paintings. I would have preferred north, but east will have to do."

"Do you have any idea how much this east light is going to cost?" he asked, pulling me towards him.

"That's your business," I said. "I'm only going to work here."

"All I can say is, if you don't double my money in five years, you're going to be out of a job." He kissed me.

"Is that going to be in the contract?"

"You betcha."

"Why are you unzipping my skirt?"

"I want to see how you look in east light."

"Can't you just imagine it instead? The agent may come back any second now, and I'd rather greet him fully dressed."

"Just think," he whispered against my neck. "All those people will be standing on this very floor at your first opening, spilling wine and dropping cheese and grapes onto it. Then your eyes will meet mine, and we'll both look down, just for a second. And do you know what we'll be thinking?"

"What?" I murmured, reaching around to rezip my skirt.

"Why didn't we do it while the floor was still clean?"

"You're sick," I told him.

"You love it." He grinned, throwing me down and landing on top of me.

I took off my glasses and closed my eyes.

about the author

Leslie Watts, who holds a degree in psychology, is an artist as well as a writer; she has previously published two books for children, one as writer and illustrator and the other as illustrator. The recipient of several grants and prizes for her work, she spent a year in Abruzzi, Italy, in 1984–85, writing and painting.

Ms. Watts and her husband, artist Tony Luciani, live in Harriston, Ontario, with their two small children.